THE STARS WAIT NOT

THE STAR REALM SAGA BOOK ONE

ANNE WHEELER

ILLUSTRATED BY MEAGHAN WARD

ISBN: 978-1-951910-11-2 [large print]

For Mom and Dad, who first read me fairy tales.

Once upon a time . . .

CHAPTER ONE

Ryllis jerked awake at the sound of footsteps in the corridor outside and put her hands over her eyes before the brightness of the lights above blinded her. The Vilarian Star Realm prison on Cereth, where she'd spent the past dozen lunar cycles, had advanced lighting that gave her an hour of replicated sunlight each day. It was enough to ward off any medical issues that they'd have to stop her interrogation to deal with—or so her captors thought. But as intense as the light was for that short time, it didn't have the warmth of the local sun, and it wasn't long enough to prevent her unending depression. She would never take that star—or unfettered access to the outdoors—for granted again.

Not that it was only the lack of sunlight that distressed her. The small cell, interrupted sleep, and cheap, tasteless food had worn on her from the first week of her new life, aggravated by the ceaseless questions and accusations of the Vilarian Imperial Fleet interrogators. The entire effect was intentional. They weren't torturing her—yet—but the effect was much the same. On her darkest nights, she thought of confessing to anything they wanted, as long as they let her go, let her stay on her home planet of Cereth, let her return to her beloved mountains and woods.

That, of course, was a fantasy.

The footsteps stopped before they reached her cell, and a low conversation took their place. Maybe they weren't coming for her after all— maybe it was another unlucky soul's time. She rolled on her back, closed her eyes, and breathed a sigh of relief. A five-minute reprieve was something to celebrate here, even if it was broken by the constant sound of door buzzers in the background. Too soon though, the voices became silent. The sound of boots outside resumed, and a scrape echoed through the cell as the steel door was pulled open.

"Amaryllis Camden."

Ryllis jerked to her feet at her name. Lieutenant Kresten Westermark stood there, tapping his stun stick on the frame and sounding irritated, as he did most of the time. It was a shared emotion—she would never tell him that his blue uniform with the silver edging made her stomach churn, or that the light galaxy on his chest pocket was an affront on a planet that had just wanted to be left alone.

"If you're not standing against that far wall in the next three seconds," Westermark said, banging the stick one more time for emphasis, "I'll have to come in there after you, and neither one of us wants that."

Ryllis glared at his impatience through the static field that remained across the open doorway—

it hadn't been more than five seconds since he'd opened the door. It was too early for this kind of rush, her body too stiff for any rapid movements, and her mind too muddled from sleep to force herself to move as quickly as Westermark wanted. She stretched her legs as she turned, making certain he couldn't see what she was doing—showing any kind of weakness was a mistake—but wasn't able to hide a yawn.

Westermark's gaze landed on her mouth, and he tapped the stick again. Despite his claim, she doubted he'd use that stun stick on her, but she'd heard the screams from elsewhere in the block, heard the swearing and orders and subsequent tears. Someone was certainly using them on prisoners, and she wouldn't press the issue. Satisfied she'd riled him enough for one morning, she did what he asked.

Slowly.

"Was that so difficult?" he asked. "Turn around and put your hands on your head."

Gritting her teeth, she turned and focused her stare on the far wall, then interlaced her fingers behind her head. There was a scrape along the pitted concrete, like someone had tried to claw their way out, and as always, she wondered what their story was. What had they done to end up here? And what had happened to them?

The static field dropped with a slight buzz, and even though she was expecting his touch, she jumped when Westermark's hands hit her shoulders. He chuckled at her reaction, and she hated him for it. She hated him for chuckling and for smelling like sandalwood instead of mildew like the rest of the prison and for waking her up and for interrupting her hour of sunlight and for touching her, respectful though he was.

"All right," he said, when he was finished searching her. Some of his irritation had disappeared, no doubt out of relief she hadn't resisted. Something was up. "Let's go."

Her fingers twitched, but Ryllis managed to keep her hands from his throat and let him guide her from the cell. Unlike some other guards, he didn't push her along the bright corridor hard enough to make her stumble, and his hands always behaved themselves. That was something, even though she loathed him for the consideration at the same time. It made it too hard to see him as the enemy, and they were all enemies here. She was constantly reminding herself that Westermark's kindness shouldn't earn him anything except the same slight gratitude she showed the people who brought her food and kept her from starving. He was still Vilarian, after all.

But worse than Westermark and the rest of the guards were the interrogators, alternately terrifying and frustrating. It had become a game of a sort—*will I be frightened or annoyed this time?* This time, as Westermark walked her inside the interview room and restrained her hands in the manacle bar bolted to the steel table that matched everything else in the wing, it appeared the questioning would be frustrating. It always was when the bespectacled fool sitting on the other side of the table, the one who spoke of her father with a certain respect he didn't deserve, was conducting it. He couldn't have been more than five solar cycles older than she—Vilarian solar tracking, of course, was all that was allowed on Cereth—but his mannerisms, those of a man three times his age and a thousand times his intellect, grated on her.

He'd been questioning her more and more lately, and he'd spent most of their sessions telling her the best she had to hope for was a transfer to a labor camp on Vilaria. Even if that was an exaggeration, one thing was certain: she was never going home. No one taken by the Fleet and accused of what they'd accused her of ever did. Sometimes she could maintain hope; this time, even if the fear had faded into apathy, it seemed there was nothing left to live for.

Westermark gave her a short pat on the shoulder and resumed his usual place by the door, like he and the fool were afraid she could fight her way out of the restraints and past the both of them. He'd neglected to push the metal chair under her all the way, so she perched on the very edge and waited. With any luck, there wouldn't be games today. Just questions. And questions she could ignore. Games, she was too tired to deal with.

The fool smiled and scratched at his face under his glasses. "Did you sleep well?"

"No." She tried to move the chair underneath her with her feet, but it was too heavy.

His smile slipped a bit at her frankness. "Oh. That's too bad. Last night they were talking about sending you away—though whether that will be better or worse for your sleep is anyone's guess."

Ryllis shifted as the sharp metal edge of the chair ground into her bottom. She wouldn't try to drag it back under her with her bare feet again, not with him looking at her like he was, but had he and Westermark made her this uncomfortable on purpose?

"You will kill me anyway," she said. In this concrete prison, she was as good as dead. "What do I care where you send me?"

"Maybe. Maybe not." The fool tapped his fingers on the metal table. "You cannot be freed, of course, but it is possible you will simply be removed from Cereth. The evidence against you is scant, and without a confession—well, as far as I'm concerned, you're guilty, but imperial law says we can't execute you without proof. Very likely, you'll be handed over to the Eradication Council on Vilaria. If so, they will determine your sentence."

Ryllis choked on a gasp she hoped neither of them had heard. The Eradication Council could sentence her to things the Fleet couldn't. Slavery. Torture, then execution. Reeducation camps. Even a lifetime in a civilian prison, not bound by the vague code of honor the Fleet seemed to be subject to, even if she scorned their methods most of the time.

"If you'd prefer to take your chances with the Fleet," he said, "I'm ready and willing to listen. Cleared out my schedule today, in fact."

"I've told you." They weren't listening to her. They never would. This entire thing was a sham. The tears threatened to break through, but before they could, the chair moved underneath her. She fell flat into the center of it, then looked up just in time to see Westermark move back against the wall. "I haven't done anything."

That wasn't true. Not in the least. But she hadn't done what they'd *accused* her of.

"A reliable source—a few, actually—say otherwise. We've been through this. I'm not going to go through it again with you. My schedule is cleared so I can listen to you talk. Not so I can repeat myself over and over."

"I haven't done anything."

Saying it again was the only thing she could do as the room began to spin. Was this it? Were they going to give up on her after this, move her somewhere worse? Something scurried in the corner of the room, and she glanced down just in time to see a rat disappear through a crack in the concrete.

I'm sorry, she swore she heard it say, but that was ridiculous. Animals didn't speak words to her, exactly, even if she felt their conversation. But even the rats had stopped talking to her here, as if they knew how doomed she was. She'd always disliked rodents, but in a prison, they were the only animals around. She missed their conversation.

"You have to believe me," she went on. "What else can I do to prove it?"

The fool just folded his hands on the table and smiled.

Kresten leaned against the cool wall, right over the deep gouge left over from some riot or another, and watched the woman fidget as Captain Sorenson droned on. He didn't blame her for not talking, but protesting her innocence wasn't going to get anywhere. Ryllis Camden's father and his new wife had been adamant about what they'd seen and heard, and there wasn't any reason to doubt a regional governor appointed by the emperor—Kresten's father—himself.

He frowned at her profile as her shoulders sagged. The accusations Captain Sorenson was making were all part of the strategy, but at the same time, he couldn't help wondering if the Fleet had arrested an innocent party. It didn't matter much, naturally—the Star Realm only gave casual consideration to such things—but it did mean the true offender was out there somewhere, and that bothered him, as it would bother anyone who cared even the least bit about justice.

But justice, thankfully, was not his problem. Officially, he wasn't in charge of detaining rebels or even investigating who they might be or what their plans were. Only questioning— and this mission didn't even involve that. His orders were only to rest, observe, and give advisory assistance, particularly if requested. The regular interrogators hadn't shown much interest in taking said advice, but that wasn't his problem either. The respite was his first priority. It was a way for Shadow Force to keep him useful while they waited to see if his post-telepathy blackouts would end.

Kresten crossed his arms over his tactical vest and suppressed a yawn as he watched her argue with Sorenson. Ryllis Camden was supposed to be an easy case, one who didn't require the telepathy which could exhaust even the most experienced interrogators. She'd even been just cooperative enough that they hadn't needed to resort to more drastic measures.

Yet.

I think she's working alone, her father had reported to the Fleet authorities on Cereth before he'd handed over a disk full of her alleged activities. *But that's up to the Fleet. You know I'll do whatever I can to support the Star Realm and His Imperial Majesty.*

It'd seemed like a good lead at the time, but nothing on the disk had panned out, security officials had said. Just a bunch of research on local plants and notes of the best places to find endangered ferns, and since Ryllis was a horticulturist by education, it was an apparent dead end. Even so, accusations like this, especially from one's close family, were never taken lightly. Governor Tavis Camden of all people knew how much he stood to lose if his daughter was found to be a traitor and he hadn't notified the Star Realm of his suspicions —or if he'd lied about her loyalties.

Yes, Ryllis Camden was almost certainly guilty of something.

If only he could read her mind. One or two small black circles on her forearm—more if she was unusually resistant—and he'd have access to all of her conscious thoughts, most of her unconscious ones, and a good deal of her memories. But the Fleet had forbidden him from so much as attempting telepathic interrogation for at least the next six lunar cycles, and he hadn't argued with the restriction. Finding out whatever nonsense some bitter Cerethian woman was up to wasn't worth waking up on the floor with his head thundering in protest. He'd have another chance later, and it would be with someone more important than Ryllis. Someone with information that would lead to a promotion and decorations.

Involuntarily, his fingers went to his chest, toward where his awards would be if he'd been wearing his formal uniform. They hit plain navy-blue fabric instead, and he clutched his hands at his sides in embarrassment.

It surprised his Fleet colleagues when they learned he craved job recognition like he did.

The last son of the emperor shouldn't want for anything, his superiors said in wonder whenever the subject came up, and Kresten was tired of explaining. No one outside the imperial family had ever been able to understand, as much as he'd tried to explain his dreams. Lieutenant Westermark was someone he'd built himself on his own merits. Prince Kresten was someone who'd had everything handed to him, and he wanted more than that. He wanted his own life.

Sorenson stood, and Kresten shook off his irrelevant thoughts, along with a heavy cloak of fatigue. It was only mental, he knew, the product of being treated like a telepathic invalid, but he was tired of it, too—and even more tired at the thought of debriefing with Sorenson later. The debriefing would go the same as the rest of them.

You could do this better, sir. Here's how.

Nah. She wasn't responding. It's a lost cause. We'll try it again tomorrow. Less sleep tonight. Start earlier in the morning. Wear her down. She's bound to start talking sooner or later. Perhaps the control chip would speed things up.

She wasn't responding because you did X, Y, and Z instead of Z, then waiting for her to mull over that, then trying Y and not bothering with X. The control chip would be excessive.

It always went the same way, and Sorenson was one of the worst for taking guidance. Kresten tried not to think about how frustrating his afternoon would be as he released Ryllis from the restraints and escorted her into the hallway outside, his right hand holding her wrist behind her back and his left on her opposite shoulder. The standard Fleet escort technique was overkill for someone like her—too slender to resemble the ancient warrior goddess on his home planet, and with dark pewter eyes, always touched with fear, the same color as her prison uniform.

It was the fear that made him wonder about her innocence more than her apparent delicateness, but policy was policy, and there was always the chance she had hand-to-hand training. Kresten stifled a laugh at the idea. She would have shown signs of that kind of thing before now. A covert warrior, she was not.

True to his suspicion, Ryllis didn't try to pull away as they approached her cell. She didn't speak to him, either. Not that he expected her to, but every so often, prisoners saw a guard as an ally. It'd happened before, occasionally to him. This morning, however, she didn't move her head, even to whisper at him, and as he walked her inside the stale room and stopped her against the far wall, she didn't protest, either.

Now.

Kresten glanced backward, and, seeing no one in the corridor outside, pulled a small piece of chocolate he'd unwrapped earlier out of his pocket. He pressed it into her right hand, palm out at the small of her back, then folded her fingers over it. Ryllis drew in a sharp breath but didn't move at his touch.

"Eat it now," he said under his breath. "Then put your hands behind your head as usual and wait for me to leave. There will be a sliver of soap under your mat after I do."

With no protest, her hand moved in front of her face, and he took a deep breath as her shoulders relaxed. Comforting her in such a manner was always a risk, but no one was outside—and if they were? They'd think he was disciplining her by making her stand against the wall with him breathing down her neck. It would frighten him if he were in her situation.

And if by some chance someone had seen what he'd done? Well, after a short explanation, no one would question him, either, for he wasn't really a guard—he could disregard all sorts of policies under the guise of manipulating her. Which, come to think of it, he could also convince himself of.

Less than ten seconds later, Ryllis put her hands behind her head and leaned her forehead against the concrete. Kresten backed toward the door, flipping over the mattress on the floor in a pretense of a search as he went by. It was how he usually left items for her, but right now he sensed she'd needed something more. Maybe it was the lifeless look in her eyes, maybe it was something he felt—his heightened empathy could be uncomfortable in a place like this—but whatever it was, it brought the last vestiges of the guilt he'd thought he'd disposed of to the surface. It was uncomfortable. Painful, almost like a strained muscle. He'd survive it, but he'd rather not.

He'd almost put the mattress back down when the flower laying on the concrete floor caught his eye. Kresten frowned at it as he pushed it around with his boot. It was crushed from Ryllis's weight, yes, but the color was saturated, a brilliant yellow that didn't fit in at all in this drab place. It should have been dead by now. Hadn't it been over a quarter lunar cycle since he'd plucked it from a bush outside officers' billeting and left it there for her? One thing was for certain—he'd been on Cereth too long if he was beginning to lose track of time like this.

Shaking his head at how trapped he was, he dropped the mattress and darted from the cell, then punched the button to raise the shielding field again. The camera came to life, and he slammed shut the heavy door before he could see the pain in her eyes. Security like this was overkill for her too, but this prison was designed for the dangerous ones, and there were no exceptions. He sighed as the panel turned green, marking the cell as secure, and went in search of Sorenson.

The captain was still in the interview room where Kresten had left him, his feet propped up on the table and his hands behind his head. Kresten froze in the doorway for a moment—he couldn't help comparing the visual to Ryllis in her cell.

"So?" Sorenson asked. "Let's hear it."

Kresten wanted to run away and never return.

"It's hard to tell," he said, sitting down in the chair where Ryllis had been. "On one hand, she looks so mystified by her circumstances that I have to wonder if she's telling the truth. On the other, she could be that well-trained. That blank look she's got most of the time—she's either scared to death and has checked out already or she's been taught how to mentally remove herself from the situation. Her insistence on her innocence—again, could go either way. I'm afraid I don't have new suggestions for you this time, sir." He hated calling the little pedant *sir*, but Sorenson would have his head if he didn't.

"Well," Sorenson said, stretching himself upright. "It won't matter anymore after this, I suppose."

Fear shot through him; Kresten gripped the edge of the metal table, letting it press into his skin. He hadn't known how he'd react when her fate was decided, and now . . . it was an unpleasant feeling, even worse than watching that blank look. For he hadn't been sure what would happen to her in the end, and with that uncertainty came hope. Unlike those taken specifically for enslavement, unlike the individuals who elected an indentured life on the empire's home world in exchange for some future favor, her ultimate fate as a political prisoner was as yet undecided. It happened that way for the ones unlucky enough to have challenged or were suspected of challenging imperial rule, like Ryllis. Execution, a life of captivity, or even the rest of her life in a dark prison somewhere—all were possibilities.

"Why won't matter anymore?" he asked.

"You didn't know?" Sorenson's boots hit the floor with a thunk; the front legs of his chair clanged on the concrete.

Kresten shook his head.

"She's being eradicated on Colonel Löfgren's order. You're to escort her to Vilaria and hand her over to the Eradication Council so they can decide her fate. Tomorrow."

CHAPTER TWO

*E*xile.

Ryllis repeated the word to herself as the small military starship burst from orbit, slamming her against her fake leather seat. The sudden increase in g-forces as they pulled away from Cereth should have been uncomfortable, but all she felt was relief.

They weren't going to kill her.

Until now, she hadn't been certain. First there had been her arrest, based on the thinnest of accusations—the source of which she was never told—the weeks of insisting that she had nothing to do with any resistance or terrorist attack, and then, finally, talk amongst the interrogators that she was to be released. She'd never thought that freedom would be so limited.

But how could she have ever imagined something like this? Cerethians had never used jump ships like the one on which she now sat— scorned them, in fact, as purveyors of destruction. The slow, sublight ships the Cereth system patrol had used before their integration into the Star Realm of Vilaria hundreds of years before seemed like toys compared to this ship that slipped through wormholes like the voles tunneled through the soil at home.

"It will be over soon, Amaryllis. Another thirty seconds of the worst, I would expect."

With effort, Ryllis turned her head slightly toward the voice next to her. Lieutenant Westermark was watching her from his own seat, seemingly unbothered by the shaking of the ship. Like the g-forces didn't affect him either, he put a hand to his mouth and yawned. She could barely breathe, so his comment and gesture had to be nothing more than braggery. Naturally, the ship didn't bother an officer of the Imperial Fleet. He'd probably been flying in space since before he was born—long before he'd ended up on Cereth as her jailer.

Oh, he hadn't been terrible, as jailers went. Much better than the rest of them. Beyond calling her Amaryllis, he'd been polite each time he'd taken her for another interrogation session, and every so often, just when she'd thought she couldn't stand the small cell one more moment, he'd leave a gift for her: a can of tea, a new bar of soap, a piece of candy. Except when he'd handed it off directly, she pretended she didn't know where they'd come from, and he'd never said a word about their little game. It had been something to look forward to, even when she'd been convinced her life was over.

The little flower had been more of a problem. She should have eaten it, but it had brought her so much joy even if it remained hidden most of the time—she hadn't been able to bring herself to destroy it like that. But as the days wore by and the petals refused to fade, it had become a danger to her. She'd stuck it under her mattress and hoped for the best.

Ryllis turned her head back to the small, round window, away from him, unwilling to admit she couldn't breathe—or that his intimate use of her full name bothered her so much. He had to know that was unacceptable on Cereth unless a couple was betrothed—she'd told the interrogators about the cultural quirk over and over as Westermark watched from his spot against the wall. At first, she'd thought he'd mastered how to sleep with his eyes open, but then once, as he escorted her to her thrice-a-lunar cycle shower, he'd muttered something under his breath.

You need to stop fighting this, Ryllis. Please.

It was the only time he'd called her by her shortened name, and when she'd looked back at him in shock, he'd looked away.

She had fought anyway. Harder, actually, buoyed by her hatred for the interrogators and

Westermark's unwelcome warning. What else was one supposed to do when their arrest made no sense and nothing they said was believed by anyone? Since she didn't know what they wanted, didn't know what she'd been arrested for, screaming her innocence was the only thing she knew to do. Even her father, the regional Cerethian governor, hadn't been able to win her freedom, and that meant she was in worse trouble than she'd ever imagined.

Not that it mattered. Innocent Cerethians were taken from their homes along with guilty ones all the time, never to return. The best she could hope for—well, was the best slavery on Vilaria or a quick death? During her whole time in the prison, she hadn't been able to decide.

But the Vilarians had won in the end, while she continued to debate the question, like she knew they would. Just as she'd been filing down a fork delivered with that morning's breakfast, they'd yanked her from her cell and brought her to this sterile, gray starship that would take her to her new life.

Trying to forget what was waiting for her on the other end, she gripped the harness tighter as they leapt toward another wormhole.

Kresten watched her struggle against the pressure of the accelerating ship. It was always like that during a first jump, whether one was a trained Fleet person or frightened prisoner just yanked from her home system. Most grew used to it after a few jumps; an unlucky few did not.

Ryllis—oh, yes, he might call her Amaryllis to her face, but only to watch her flush—wouldn't have to worry about that. Her trip was one-way, like the trips of all Cerethians the Vilarian chose to remove from their homeland. The decisions of the Eradication Council were irrevocable, and he would use that to his advantage. Sorenson, thank the Realm, had been wrong in that regard.

You're authorized to keep working on her if you'd like, Colonel Löfgren had written. *Whatever she knows isn't important anymore, but consider your post-mission leave an extension of your telepathic rehabilitation. If you'd like to keep her, just tell the Eradication Council, and she's yours. If not, let them deal with her. Your choice.*

It was an easy choice. The messages from his immediate commander had become more and more frequent of late and having a subject to practice on would make those messages go away, eventually. Yes, Major Dahl would expect it of him. That was the only reason he'd mentally agreed to Löfgren's offer. It had absolutely nothing to do with his fear for Ryllis's future.

His body became lighter as the jump ship slowed, and he twisted sideways to check on Ryllis. Her knuckles were white as they gripped her webbed harness, but she shot him a furtive look when—he assumed—she thought he wasn't looking. Kresten smiled at her, and she pressed her lips closed.

That's what you think.

"Six more hours," he said, unlatching himself. She would never risk it, but he needed a bit of freedom. "And another few jumps. Are you going to make it?"

Ryllis nodded. "It's not so bad anymore." Then, cautiously, as if she was desperate to know but didn't want to speak to him, she asked, "But it was horrible before. How many times have you done this?"

"Thousands," he replied.

"Then you are career Fleet."

"Yes. It was expected of me."

"You don't enjoy it."

"I've learned to. How else would I have been able to explore the galaxy?" There was another explanation for that, of course, but she didn't need to know that yet. "The ability to discover new lands is not an opportunity to be turned down."

That was a deliberate snub to her home world, brought into the empire by force after its leaders had insisted solitude and isolation was the way to peace. They'd only wanted to be left alone, numerous messages had said, but his ancestors hadn't cared. The seer had spoken, and two more systems had been taken before the solar cycle was out. Famine and utter ruin waited for Vilaria otherwise, the Light had told her. That kind of militaristic superstition was long since gone, naturally, but the empire remained. For who willingly gave up such power?

"I was happy not to explore," she said quietly. Her hands moved toward the harness latch, then stopped, almost as if she were afraid she would float away if she undid it. "How many planets will we visit before we reach our destination?"

Even through the heavy silence that surrounded him most of the time, he could tell the very idea distressed her, like it would most Cerethians.

"Straight there," he assured her. "I programed the nav system myself, and the software design won't let it deviate."

Ryllis glanced forward, toward the automated flight deck. "And then?" Her complexion grew pale.

Kresten scratched at his chin. "I have no idea," he answered.

That was a lie.

They jumped six more times before settling into orbit around a planet that was more blue than green. Freed from the pressure and nausea of the jumps—along with her harness—Ryllis stood with her nose against the aft viewing window and prayed she was mistaken, but the view looked exactly like the pictures in school.

"Vilaria," she said to herself. The imperial home world. The last place she'd ever wanted to see.

"Yes." Westermark edged next to her, and she jumped. "Did you expect something different?"

She didn't know why she answered. "A remote asteroid, perhaps. Or a space station." The large planet below looked too comfortable for someone who might as well be a hostage. Or a slave. "Is everyone eradicated from Cereth brought here?"

"You know I can't answer that."

It wasn't as though she would be allowed to associate with any of her own people, anyway. Association led to friends, and friends led to hope, and hope led to revolt. It was a pointless restriction in the first place, since not even the Cerethian elite knew how to operate a jump ship. There was no way home. There was only—

An even more horrifying near future occurred to her.

"How many are waiting for us down there?" she asked.

"You know I can't discuss security matters, either."

Ryllis fell silent at his misunderstanding.

Westermark narrowed his eyes as realization touched them. "You think we're going to parade you around once we land like a war trophy? We are not barbarians." His voice grew cold as he flicked a finger toward her head. "And it doesn't matter if we do or not. Everyone knows who you are and where you stand in this society, anyway."

It was the first time he'd ever said anything about her long hair, interwoven with the light amethyst ribbon of Therus, her district. They'd taken the ribbon during her  detention, and she'd re-plaited it as soon as the jump ship had leveled into cruise. The missing color had made her feel naked in a way the first contraband search at the prison never had.

"Then I am to be a slave."

"Likely."

"Permanently?"

"Yes."

She should have felt ill at his candor, but perhaps she'd already accepted her destiny, for she felt nothing but a tinge of dread as she stared at the planet below. "Where? With whom?"

He made a huffing sound. "That's up to the Eradication Council. They decide."

"Can I sway them in some way? Change my fate? Plead for better conditions?"

Westermark gave her a look. "You can do as I say when you go before them."

"You'll be there?" She frowned. "You must have more important matters to attend to now that you're home."

"What else is more important than ensuring a prisoner receives a fitting punishment?"

"I would think exile itself is punishment enough," she snapped at him. "Unless you mean to make an example of me."

"If exile was punishment enough," he said, "you would be deterred enough to not be here in the first place. And I would watch that tongue when you stand before them. Meek and compliant, if you can manage such a thing. Let's go."

He grabbed her arm, and Ryllis flung her elbow backward without thinking, catching him just under his solar plexus. Westermark grunted but recovered before she could spin around and strike him under the chin. His palm hit the back of her head, dislodging the ribbons, and she shifted to her left foot as he moved to push her to the ground. She needed to kick him—he'd discarded any semblance of armor when they'd boarded the shuttle, and his most sensitive parts were unprotected—but as soon as she moved one of her feet off the ground, he'd be waiting. She thrust her elbow back again instead, blindly and instinctively.

It didn't make contact with any part of him that time. Gasping, she tried to tilt her head for a better view, but her knees hit the ground, and the balance she'd clung to just seconds before disappeared. From her position on the deck, she could see there wasn't much point in fighting any longer. Not with the stun pistol in Westermark's hand.

"Bad decision." He flipped her to her stomach with one hand, pressing the gun against her head with the other. "Where did you think that would get you? That's exactly the kind of behavior that will earn you no favor on Vilaria."

Ryllis swore to herself as he jerked her up. She'd let her emotions and pride get the best of her, and now she'd lost her only ally. Westermark could have been a friend—had all but offered his assistance—and she'd thrown it away by attempting a senseless fight that hadn't had a chance of succeeding.

But on second thought, perhaps she hadn't fouled things up completely—for as he dragged her to the shuttle and barked a curt order at the pilot to take them to the surface, she realized she'd learned something valuable.

There were no allies on Vilaria.

She did not, as it turned out, have to appear in front of the Eradication Council, though whether that was standard procedure for prisoners or because she'd somehow managed to leave a bruise on Westermark's cheek was unclear. Instead, the Council came to her in a holding cell at the small garrison where she and Westermark had landed in the form of three dour men in tan uniforms, each wearing a stun pistol and carrying a tablet.

Ryllis stood silently in front of them, though she refused to lower her head as Westermark had instructed. It'd taken several of his threats to get her to stand at all, and he ought to have been grateful for any obedience she chose to show. She would never tell, but he would have been surprised to hear it was the tablets that frightened her more than their weapons—stuns pistols could only impart physical pain, and that was temporary. The tablets they carried had the power to destroy the rest of her life.

"Then let's hear it, Lieutenant," the oldest one said as another circled around her, scrutinizing, assessing. She wanted to kick at him. "You escorted her here personally, so you must have something important to say."

"I believe His Highness Prince Kresten has put in a request for an appropriate prisoner for his household," Westermark said tonelessly. "The next available, if possible. This one would be an acceptable choice."

The leader raised his eyebrows at Westermark. "Her hair is exceedingly dark, sir. I wouldn't want her to be a reminder of . . ." He trailed off. "And she stands accused of treason and sedition —hardly someone fit for a royal household. If the Fleet is through with her, perhaps an auction would be best. His Highness can choose from another group later, one more appropriate for imperial service."

Auction? Ryllis opened her mouth.

Westermark thrust an elbow in her ribs, not violently, but hard enough to distract her from what she meant to say.

"No," he said, an edge to his voice now. "That will not be necessary. This one will satisfy his needs."

Satisfy his needs? Her chest became tight, and it didn't have anything to do with how he'd just silenced her.

"Sir," the man said, with an odd look at Westermark, "I don't mean to squabble, but I was the under the impression that the prince does not—"

"He has decided to, and you question his change of heart at your own peril."

The man sighed. "My apologies. As long as you're certain. I only wished to ensure . . ." He paused, thinking. "Very well, Lieutenant. I trust you will make certain she is suitably marked per Eradication Council policy? Even His Highness"—there was a strange emphasis on the title—"cannot overrule that."

Westermark nodded, a glint in his eyes. "He is well aware of his responsibilities."

"Indeed he is. Then we have no further business here." He motioned to the other two, and they disappeared with short nods in Westermark's direction.

Ryllis looked helplessly at him as Westermark guided her out, in the opposite direction the men had headed. "How could you let them do that? You promised I wouldn't be a trophy!"

"No." Westermark held up a brief finger to stop her as they rounded the corner. "I promised you wouldn't be paraded around as a trophy. And you did ask if you could plead for a better placement. I just obtained you the best one of all."

She gritted her teeth. "How can I believe that? You may have promised it, but what about this prince? You don't know how he'll treat me."

Any bravery she'd been clinging to fled. Westermark had handed her over to a strange man like she was nothing more than property. To a man who was a prince of Vilaria. Cereth might be isolated, but she wasn't naïve. She didn't need to imagine the cruelty that awaited her—she knew. Westermark steadied her as she stumbled, images of abuse and torture taking the place of the memories at home.

"He won't harm you," he said. "I promise that, too."

"How can you be so certain?"

He blew out a deep breath, then lifted his hands out to his sides. "Because he's standing right here in front of you."

Standing . . .

The blood drained from her face. Westermark gripped her arm harder as she swayed, preventing her from falling to her knees like she planned. Unwanted and hated conqueror or not, she was standing on his planet, and . . . stars above, she couldn't remember half the things she'd said to him. Things she'd have never said if she'd known.

"Now you look down." He chuckled and lifted her chin with a light finger. "That's not necessary. I'm sorry for the deception. It's for my own security, you understand, and the kinds of courtesies you expect of us are limited to formal situations. The Eradication Council knows who I am, naturally, but they also know me as a Fleet officer, so there was no need to say anything else until you forced me into it. I needed to make sure you weren't going to . . ."

He shook his head, almost to himself.

"Of course you weren't going to attack me. I only knew it would be upsetting, and . . . I suppose I wasn't looking forward to subjecting you to the news. That was selfish of me, and I apologize."

Ryllis stared at him. Westermark was the name of the imperial family, of course, but it wasn't as though others didn't carry it. How would she have ever figured it out? The guards and interrogators had never treated him as anything but a security officer.

"You can speak, you know," he said. "You certainly didn't have a problem doing it before now."

"I—I hit you." It was the only thing that came to mind. What was the punishment for striking a prince?

"That you did. Rather hard, I might add." Westermark cracked a grin as he ran his hand over his cheek. "Don't do it again, and we won't have any issues."

Ryllis shook her head, not knowing why. "What am I supposed to call you?" Kneeling in front of him one time was one thing, but there was something distasteful about calling her captor by a royal title her entire planet tried to shun.

"Ah." He glanced sideways at her. "I've grown rather used to Lieutenant Westermark in recent years, I suppose. But His Highness is most appropriate for you."

Slivers of ice ran down her spine, like he'd just dunked her in cold water. It would be a constant reminder of his status—and hers. "And what did that man mean about being suitably marked?"

Westermark resumed his march. "We'll talk about that when we get home."

"Do not," she said, with an old courage she'd thought was gone, "refer to this planet as home."

Something odd sparked in his eyes as he skidded to a stop. "I don't think you fully understand your situation, Amaryllis, so let me be clear. You are now owned by the imperial family. You belong to me. You will die here on Vilaria, enslaved." He focused on her, and the full weight of his words settle into her soul. "That is the law. There is no other future for you. You can accept this and make the best of it, or you can fight it and be miserable. Best to forget Cereth ever existed—for you, it no longer does."

CHAPTER THREE

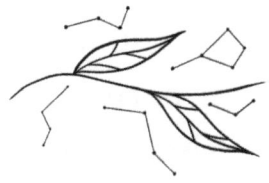

The shuttle landed on a lit pad, and Ryllis squinted outside into the dark. It was inky, almost thick, the darkness broken only by what looked like fog in the distance. The flight had been long, and Westermark had been silent for most of it, only asking her if she was thirsty and handing her a bottle of water before resuming his own distant stare out the window. His breath had changed every time she shifted on her hard seat and tried not to drift off to sleep, so he was paying attention to her actions, even if he'd pretended not to.

Dangerous, indeed. At least now she knew the secret he'd been hiding on the jump ship.

Ryllis leaned her head against the window. The gardens at Father's house would be coming into winter bloom shortly, and she should have been there to see them, this solar cycle and the next. Her life hadn't been perfect, but it'd been hers. She woke when she pleased, ate what she wanted, and filled her hours with whatever idle and not-so-idle work she desired. Now? The vagueness of her future was both terrifying and unfair.

A prince.

She hadn't been able to get the word out of her mind the entire flight. A prince of the Vilarian Star Realm, no less, one of the superstitious bastards who'd practically enslaved her own people centuries ago. The Cerethian planetary government—her father and the other sixteen regional governors—were no more than puppets because of this man. And now she was here on Vilaria because of him, eradicated from her home world for absolutely no reason. She was nothing anymore. She didn't exist, and no one would mourn her.

It was the reality that rolled around and around in her mind until it made her dizzy, and as it overcame the terror, she *knew*. Westermark's kindness, the compassion that had surprised her so when he'd left the first piece of candy under her mattress, didn't matter now. Nothing mattered but her freedom. Prince or not, Westermark was now a target. She would kill him or die trying.

"We're here," he said, interrupting her fantasy of shoving a knife in his chest. "My summer lodge. This is where I go when I want some privacy, and I—I thought it might be an easier adjustment for you than somewhere more formal in the city."

It didn't escape her notice that he hadn't said *home* this time. Fresh air hit her face as they stepped outside, so different from the jump ship and prison on Cereth. It felt comfortable, and

Ryllis hated herself for giving Vilaria even the slight bit of grace. She inhaled as Westermark walked her through a security gate and through dark gardens, lit with starlight. No security challenged them. Not even a single servant confronted him. This was a prince's house? It didn't seem like it. On Cereth, no one was allowed within kilometers of the imperial family's on-world homes. Not even her father, not without a good reason and invitation.

Westermark pressed his palm against a pad by a large door. A shimmering force field became visible, then immediately disappeared; lights flickered on inside. "I shutter the place when I'm off-world," he said as he pushed open the door. "It'll be more alive once I get everything opened up. Don't let the tomb-like atmosphere frighten you."

Tombs on Cereth were a place of glory, a spot to celebrate the deceased's union with the Light. Not this dark, shadowy retreat. Ryllis stared up at the vaulted ceiling of the foyer as he waved on the lights. They were too intense after the blackness outside, sustained by the irradiated crystals Vilarians mined far away on Kenion, but they only served to make the shadows deeper where they didn't reach. Dim corridors stretched out from each side of the foyer, and in front of her and Westermark, through an archway, a large glass window covered the back of the house. She couldn't see what was on the other side, out in the vast darkness of the mountains. He'd called it a summer retreat, but now it was chilled, so much she couldn't hide a shiver.

"I'm sorry." Westermark slung his Fleet jacket on an antique table by the door and took her by the arm. "You must be tired."

Ryllis nodded, though her eyes had widened at how casually he'd thrown the jacket next to a vase that cost more than her father made in a solar cycle. Sleep meant she could put everything off for another day.

"Right, then." He glanced around into each dark corridor in turn, like he wasn't sure which direction to go, then pointed. "This way."

Her mind was too exhausted to care that he was leading her to a thin mattress on the floor of an outbuilding somewhere far away from this somber yet magnificent house. As long as she was horizontal and not shackled to the floor, it would be bearable. She'd need her wits about her tomorrow, so sleep would have to find her wherever her captor dictated it did. And then, in a few days, once she was well-rested and found her courage again, she would kill him.

"Here you go."

Westermark stopped in the doorway of a large room, lit by several dim chandeliers. Beside him, Ryllis almost ran into the doorframe. She squinted inside, at the large bed, the priceless statuary, the ornate rugs, the large circular tile fireplace that warmed her core despite being unlit. Must filled her nose; he hadn't lied about shuttering the lodge. She sneezed, once, and Westermark took a step back. If she'd offended him, she didn't care.

"What is this?" she asked, blinking. Besides a hallucination. Where was the stone floor, the dirty mattress, the sparse, cold room that might as well be a cell? Was she so tired that she was seeing things?

He shrugged. "My room."

This one will satisfy his needs.

Flames brushed her face as her legs tensed, ready to flee. His intent was obvious, and without realizing it, she'd fallen for his kindness so hard back on Cereth that it was the last thing she'd ever expected. Was there anywhere to run? Anyone to hear her if she screamed? She couldn't physically overpower him. She'd already tried that once, and it had ended in disaster, along with a few large bruises on her knees and hip.

"I—Your Highness—" Her gaze shot from the bed, draped in silk linens and topped with a dozen luscious pillows, to the dark corridor behind them. "Please don't do this. Not yet. Give me time. More than a few hours, at least. I promise I won't fight you then, but I need—I just need some time."

Horror crossed his face as he backed away from her. "Not like that," he said. "I'm sorry. I didn't mean to frighten you. It's just—you look exhausted, and I can sleep anywhere."

Her knees almost gave out. What he was saying didn't make any sense.

"But surely you must have somewhere else for —" She couldn't say the word. "For someone like me."

"Oh," Westermark put his hand on the doorframe, suddenly appearing less distressed. Nonchalant, almost. "I don't keep slaves, as a rule. Don't have a servants' quarters, either. I had to improvise, and this will do for now. For as long as you want, actually. Goodnight, Amaryllis."

With a quick smile, he shut her inside the opulent room and disappeared.

The sun hit her face the next morning, thin and weak so far up in the mountains, yes, but warmer than space and certainly warmer than her cell on Cereth. Ryllis rubbed her eyes and stared at the intricate wood ceiling. Carved starships danced between swirling galaxies interspersed with pine trees and singing birds. It was an odd combination, yet strangely welcoming, proof that nature and the cosmos could coexist in a way Cereth tradition taught it could. She averted her eyes before the scene became comfortable and pulled the quilt over herself again.

The design of the blanket was as bewildering as the ceiling. Instead of the expensive silk she'd supposed a prince would prefer, it was rough, almost coarse, covered in folk woodland creatures and flowers. She grudgingly admitted to herself that it did match what little she'd seen of the rest of the house, but it was at complete odds with everything she'd expected of Vilaria and of its royalty.

Exhausted from the jumps, she'd spent half the night pacing Westermark's room looking for an escape route before collapsing on top of the bed covers. Trying to find a way out had been a futile exercise. Each of the six large windows opposite the bed hummed with the unmistakable sound of a static field, and Ryllis hadn't bothered to check the door she'd entered through. There wouldn't be cameras in a prince's bedroom, but the corridor outside was no doubt monitored, likely by a security team or Westermark himself.

The door opened as she was considering the best way to defeat them. She grabbed the blanket against her chest, one more layer of defense against whatever came next, but to her relief, it wasn't Westermark who entered. Instead, an elderly woman bustled inside with an extraordinary sense of purpose and tossed an armful of clothes on a chair in the corner before pointing toward a door on the far side of the bed. Ryllis swung her feet to the floor and stared at her.

"His Highness said you have ten minutes to clean up." The woman wrinkled her nose as she headed to what had to be the washroom. "I told him twenty. You're lucky he agreed." She turned around in the doorway and motioned Ryllis toward her. "You'd best be fast, though," she added. "It'll make things easier if he's not kept waiting."

Things.

Ryllis walked to the bathroom as ordered, but her throat closed up at the implication that Westermark's civility the night before might not last. The woman didn't make a move to give her privacy, so she stripped off the gray jumpsuit she'd been wearing for weeks and stepped inside the shower. The hot water almost took her skin off, but there was no easy way to lower the temperature—and she would never humiliate herself by asking how to do something simple. It cleaned the dirt from the prison and jump ship off, anyway, and she would figure out this strange planet eventually.

"Hair, too," the woman called.

With shaking hands, Ryllis unwound the ribbon and let it dangle from her hand while she ran shampoo through her hair. She smelled like Westermark now, which was bad enough, but now there wouldn't be time to replace the ribbon before she was to report to him. Surely he would give her time to do it later, wouldn't he? He'd spent enough time on Cereth to know what it meant.

Shower complete, she wrapped a towel around herself and dressed rapidly under the woman's watchful eye, thankful the provided clothing didn't appear to be shabby or indecent. The slim leather pants were quite new and supple, though they didn't fit as well as they should have after the weight she'd lost on Cereth. A light gray sweater she couldn't keep from touching finished off the outfit, and a glance at the woman in the mirror told her she looked better than she had in ages. Yes, the clothes were good enough for now. Pride wasn't everything, but it helped, and less of her body Westermark saw, the better—at least until she learned his intentions for her. She dried her hair as much as she could and shadowed the woman back into the bedroom, her heart thumping with each footstep.

Westermark sat there, at a small table by the large window with two cups of something steaming next to him. He stood when she appeared and gave the woman a smile. "That will be all, Lina. You slept well, Amaryllis?"

Ryllis nodded—abruptly half-frozen—as the woman departed, leaving her alone with him. It was the first time she'd seen him out of his Fleet uniform, but the casual jacket he wore, embroidered with the imperial crest she hated, reminded her that he was someone worse. She could scarcely tear her eyes away from the fearsome bird on the left side of his chest, a crown above its head and a sword in its talons.

Though there was something else about it about well. Something strange and sympathetic, almost as though Westermark wore it with a disdain that was wholly unfamiliar to him. Maybe, just maybe, it was a reminder to himself of who he was. Coming home to Vilaria had to be a difficult transition for him, too, and a pang of compassion sparked through her.

"Again," he said, "you can speak to me. Whenever you want. I rather miss your past impertinence, even if it seemed the interrogators were growing tired of it." He sighed. "Though I suppose I understand your reticence now."

"I don't know what to say to you, Your Highness." She nearly vomited on the title, but it sounded like the right thing to add to her bold confession.

"I suppose not." He eyed her for a moment, then took a sip of his drink. "I would prefer if you thought of yourself as a guest here. With some restrictions, of course. You will have some freedom, more than you probably expect. But outwardly, things must appear . . ."

"The marking that man spoke of." She hadn't been able to get his comment out of her mind all night, even as she'd inspected the static fields.

"Yes." Westermark shifted uncomfortably from side to side, a strange movement from a prince who controlled her very life.

"What is it, exactly?" Ryllis fought the impulse to turn around and lock herself in the bathroom.

"A tattoo. My family crest. Required by imperial law." He seemed to gather himself, then pointed at the symbol on his jacket. "It is —I've only witnessed it applied twice, but it can be quite unpleasant. I thought you should know that before I begin. Being prepared might help."

"Unpleasant?" Her heart fluttered. What could be more unpleasant than the current situation? "How?"

Westermark hesitated. "It's quite painful, as you can imagine. Among other things." He didn't seem inclined to say more. "But there is an alternative. An only vaguely legal one, but some of us are able to get away with it, I suppose, especially up here in the mountains."

He shrugged and focused on her head. "You can lose the hair, Amaryllis," he said quickly, like he'd have second thoughts if he didn't. "That would mark you as slave enough for anyone who visits this household, and no one else would dare argue with me."

Ryllis reached for her hair, damp and loose around her shoulders. He might as well have asked her to cut off her arm. "I can't do that. You—you know."

"I would prefer the tattoo myself." Westermark's lips thinned. "It would be quick, placed wherever you'd prefer, and afterward, hidden by clothing. You wouldn't have to subject yourself to the procedure every few weeks as with your hair."

"But it's permanent."

"Yes." He frowned at her. "That it is. But what does that matter? You knew of the permanence of this situation when you were eradicated from

Cereth, and there are far worse things to be marked with. No one will bother you as long as you wear the symbol of the Westermark family."

He sounded so bewildered at her reluctance that she almost laughed. Could he not see the difference? She couldn't be branded the whore of one of the emperor's sons if she were to ever return to Cereth—or even escape this house. It seemed Westermark had no idea of her rebellious thoughts, though, and that was the one bright spot of the entire situation.

With that realization, she made her decision.

"The hair," she said, clenching her hands into fists. If she reached up and touched it, she would lose her nerve and agree to his original offer. It would grow back, and she would appear outwardly normal again, even if the trauma of being eradicated would remain for the rest of her life. "Please."

"You understand this will be a weekly routine as long as you remain in this household, and that if you choose not to cooperate in the future, I can make it permanent as well?" He ran a few fingers over his clean-shaven chin, and she took his meaning at once. "Do not think I'll forget this agreement."

"I understand—Your Highness."

She tried to swallow the lump in her throat, tried to imagine what her father would think if he could see her without the ribbon. Would he think she'd surrendered to this captivity too easily? Or simply that she'd disappointed him just like she always had?

Westermark gestured toward the bathroom without another word. Ryllis sat on the edge of the tub and stared at her feet. The ribbon caught her attention, lying where she'd dropped it before, and she grabbed it and wound it between her hands as Westermark dug through a few paneled cabinets for his tools. By the time he approached her, holding a razor and sharp pair of scissors, the tips of her fingers were as purple as the silk. She loosened it and bit back a gasp as the blood flowed toward her hands again.

"Ready?" he asked. "Slide down into the tub—it'll be easier to clean up."

Ryllis closed her eyes and climbed inside the deep bath to face the timber-edged window, rewrapping the ribbon around her fingers as she did. It hurt even more than the first time, but the new pain couldn't distract her from the sudden sound of scissors that filled the room. She wanted to put her head down on her knees, to hide from everything, especially Westermark, but the blades were so sharp that moving was out of the question. She stared straight out the window instead, at the birds that alighted in a tree as she watched, at the leaves rustling in the breeze, at the faraway highlands that barely showed through the dense forest.

The prince's mountains were beautiful.

The view was a balm to her breaking heart. She might be a slave, but oh, if she could only catch glimpses of the wild outside every so often, she might eventually heal. She'd never been grateful for her perilous gift before, but now . . . yes, it meant she would heal. For it went both ways, this power of hers that the Star Realm forbade —her presence nourished nature and nature sustained her soul. She would survive without it, naturally, and had in the prison, but she couldn't *thrive*. She couldn't feel joy.

But here? Yes, even here, she could sense delight waiting on the edges of her emotions, and not for the first time, she hated her power. She had to hate her situation. Had to. Tears spilled over at the realization that she couldn't, amplified by exhaustion and the sudden change in her circumstances. From behind her, ignoring her emotion, Westermark continued cutting as the trees danced and sang their obliviousness; a weight lifted off the crown of her head. Ryllis chanced a look at the bottom of the tub.

So much hair.

"Don't look," he said. "It's mostly gone, but it's rather ragged. Let me clean it up first."

Even the mountains couldn't heal the hurt that time. She put her head on her knees and squeezed her eyes shut to stop the tears, then flinched as the scissors hit the counter beside her. The razor began to whirr, and she recoiled as it touched her almost bare scalp.

This was wrong. She should have fled. Struck Westermark once more after she'd learned of his identity. They'd have had to kill her then, wouldn't they? Death would have been better than this shame. The razor brushed over her head a few more times, then the bathroom became silent, except for birds protesting something outside.

"Relax, Amaryllis," Westermark said. "It's all done."

She looked up at him, dizzy.

"Do not cry over this." His gentle tone turned harsh when he noticed the tears. "I will not have an outburst over a decision I allowed you to make out of compassion."

"No, Your Highness," Ryllis whispered, pressing the ribbon against her mouth. She put her head down on her knees again and prayed he didn't say anything about how much she was shaking. He was asking too much. He had to know that.

Westermark's shadow moved in what was left of her peripheral vision. "Clean yourself up and meet me in the courtyard," he said. "Lina will show you the way if you get lost. There are no other servants here, so I suppose I should find you something to eat."

She was crying too hard to hear him leave.

CHAPTER FOUR

Kresten stalked from his bedroom, brushing loose hair from his hands. It clung to his pants, and he swore under his breath at both the mess and the situation. The Cerethian woman should have chosen the tattoo. He'd only offered the alternative—an ancient ownership symbol scarcely accepted on Vilaria anymore except in the most rural of areas—because he'd been dead certain she would decide against it. Ryllis was right—he knew what being able to advertise her district meant, since it was one of the few pieces of their culture the Star Realm allowed. It was harmless in the grand scheme of things as far as the emperor was concerned, so it was something the subjugated planet clung to. He imagined he'd be in the same way about his uniform in her situation.

Of course, he'd practically talked her out of the tattoo, so it was no wonder she'd chosen the way she had. He wanted to kick himself for that. Telepathy in the confines of the Shadow Force's medical center was easier, but even out here in the wildness, it would have been a simple enough matter to add the nanobiotes that allowed him access to her mind to the ink, and she wouldn't have had any idea until it was too late. He had a canister of them locked in a safe in his office, like every telepath, just in case. Ryllis might have known he'd done *something* to her, might even have guessed what, but by then she'd have been in too much pain to fight back. Why had he emphasized how painful and permanent it would be?

It's nothing. Just a few pricks. You'll barely feel it.

That wasn't true, but that was what he should have said. Why hadn't he? That was a decision he was not going to analyze yet—except to tell himself it had everything to do with the blackouts that were becoming more and more frequent each time he accessed a prisoner's mind. It had absolutely nothing to do with the strange feelings she'd stirred in him since the very first time she'd looked at him with that desperate need to hope. Yes, that was it. Who wanted to end up on the floor their first night on-world after almost a solar cycle?

In any event, it was done, and as long as he didn't have to fight her once her hair began to grow back, he could convince himself he didn't care how badly he'd messed up. The Eradication Council man had been right, anyway. Ryllis's dark hair had been too much of a reminder of Elise, and there could be no mistaking what she was here for. It wasn't for sex, and it was not for love. She was here for information, and nothing else. He'd never needed to use telepathy for that. It was a shortcut, nothing more, and he had no deadline.

And when he was finished with her? Well, he'd have to see about that.

He cornered Lina on his way to the kitchen. She'd seen the lights the night before from her cottage up the hill, and like each time he appeared at his hideout without notice, she'd begun to open the lodge before he woke. Her loyalty was almost enough to bring him to tears. His brothers could wonder all they wanted how he'd managed to maintain such a faithful housekeeper since his age of majority, but it wasn't a mystery. Treat them well, and they stuck around. Treat them poorly, and . . . well, there was a reason Vidar in particular couldn't keep a manservant, much as he insisted he couldn't understand what the problem was. Not a soul would remain in his household of their own free will for long, and even Vidar wasn't stupid enough to employ captives in his private quarters.

Lina charitably ignored his grumblings as she searched through the cabinets in the small kitchen. "No produce right now, sir," she said, pulling a few bright yellow objects from her bag and laying them on the counter. "But I sent a request, and you should have fresh food later this afternoon. I brought eggs to tide you over until then."

Kresten rolled one between his fingers. The hens Lina and her husband kept were vicious creatures he wanted to shoot whenever they appeared on his land, but he couldn't deny how much he missed the taste of their eggs when he was off-world.

"Eggs are fine," he said. "Plain is fine, too. Add one to the coffee. Find some honey, too. I don't care if you have to hunt all over the mountain for it. I'll be in the courtyard when it's ready. No, not alone, before you ask."

The orders were curt and rapid. He knew what was coming and was desperate for escape before it did, but Lina didn't blink.

"Honey? It's rather early in the sea—"

"Just find some," he grumbled. It was too early for an interrogation, and he could tell when a welcome was about to turn into one. Lina had served him long enough to know better than to ask for details of his missions, so she usually shifted her innate curiosity to more personal matters. Good for operational security, bad for his sanity.

"Honey. Of course, sir. Your . . . guest is Cerethian, then," she said to his back.

Kresten bit his tongue and began to walk off, then turned. "My new slave is Cerethian, yes." He forced normalcy into his tone. "She's also a reward for my time away, so I intend to enjoy her company as I eat breakfast."

"You've never accepted a slave before. Never even asked for one, especially such a trophy from the Eradication Council." Lina raised her eyebrows—and the pitch of her voice—in feigned innocence. "Did they force her on you, Your Highness?"

"Oh, for pity's sake. What's with the questions this morning?"

He darted away before she could answer—or ask him anything else. Escape was a pathetic means of resistance for a member of an elite a unit as his, but no one ever thought to train soldiers for a nosy housekeeper. The sound of dishes being slammed around in the kitchen echoed down the corridor, and unpursued, he pushed open the door to his courtyard refuge, safe at last.

While the house itself was locked while he was off-world, the gardens weren't treated nearly so shabbily, and he was pleased to find the evergreen shrubs trimmed and new flowers sprouting from the damp ground.

"I didn't expect it to be so green. It's lovely."

Kresten spun at Ryllis's voice. Her wide gray eyes were swollen, but they weren't red anymore, and he had to give her credit for that. The shapeless prisoner uniform she'd worn on the jump ship must have been gone when he'd cut her hair, but he hadn't bothered to notice, as long as she had been suitably clothed when she'd exited the washroom.

Now he noticed. Governor's daughter or not, the outfit Lina had provided was likely the most expensive clothing Ryllis had ever worn, and the change from prisoner to pretend imperial houseguest was remarkable. He'd been a little off on the measurements he'd given Lina, and the pants were a little large, but they clung to Ryllis's hips just fine for now, and the sleeves of her gray sweater were detailed with a clematis vine she probably hadn't noticed. They would need to order better-fitting clothing for her later, but this second, all he wanted to do was to kiss Lina for trying to make Ryllis feel better.

"It's been cold," he said, forcing his gaze away from those hips. "If you think it's lovely now, you won't believe what it'll look like in six lunar cycles."

A shadow crossed her face—mentioning the future was a mistake. He noted that for later. Today's mistakes led to tomorrow's victories.

"Come. Sit." He flopped to the ground on one of the cushions set back by the fountain and extended his hand. "Breakfast is on the way."

Ryllis followed, much more gracefully than he was capable of, and leaned away from him, toward the laciniata shrub. "I'm not hungry, Your Highness."

"I'm not surprised. The jumps will do that to you, but it won't last." It was true, and also a brilliant segue. "You've never jumped before, have you?"

She shook her head.

"Haven't ever left Cereth?"

"No. Not even for other parts of the system. But you know this. I told them over and over." She fiddled a bit with the decorative trim of her cushion. "Maybe you really were sleeping against the wall all that time."

"Idle conversation," he lied. "I want to make sure you're well and don't require a doctor. And I'm surprised at how limited your travel has been, given—"

He slammed his mouth shut, quickly, before he could end with *given who your father is*. Ryllis didn't have a father anymore. Like all Vilarian slaves, she had no family at all—not legally, not emotionally. She'd been erased from legal records on Cereth, and when she died, mourning would be forbidden, for who grieved a person who didn't exist?

"The governor never took you off-world?" he asked instead, in a more diplomatic manner than felt comfortable. Maybe it was the way his chest tightened and his stomach turned at her plight—*hypocrite*, his brothers would say. *Sanctimonious coward. You say no to slaves until you find one pretty enough?*

"I rarely left Therus." Ryllis met his eyes. "And you know he never took me off-world. Even if we'd wanted to explore, the Star Realm kept us from doing so."

"Did we, now?" Her lashes fluttered as she stared at a point just beside his ear. She was clearly trying to be the last to break the stare, and he let her win. "I hope you like yellow gold coffee," he went on, stretching out his legs in front of him and focusing on the silver ash across the courtyard. "And eggs. They're bright orange, which is a little strange for me, but don't let that concern you."

"I like coffee. And eggs"

"But?" he prompted. "I know there's a 'but' here."

"But I'm really not hungry."

The tinkle of glass charms in the doorway interrupted further protests. Lina hurried through the cutout hedge carrying a tray loaded with more food than he'd expected. She froze at the sight of them, and her mouth parted as her attention landed on Ryllis. *On Ryllis's head and swollen eyes.* Kresten didn't need to be able to read her mind for him to recognize her disapproval—and without reading her mind, he knew what she was thinking.

If you miss Elise, there are better ways than acquiring another human being.

Ryllis noticed the expression immediately as well, though Kresten was certain she mistook it for reproach of her very existence. Cheeks red, she looked away from both of them, then sprang to her feet and bolted through the nearest door. He moved to follow her, but Lina set the tray down in front of him before he could budge.

"Eat, sir. She's not going anywhere."

Kresten ground his teeth, preparing to lash out at her for her insubordination, then made the mistake of glancing down at the tray. His mouth watered, and he settled back on his cushion, temporarily diverted. Lina was right. Eat first, then deal with his problems. His mother had always laughed at how predictable he was regarding that order.

"Will there be anything else?"

"No." He could already taste the coffee. The freeze-dried kind the jump ships stocked never compared to the fresh plants that grew on the other side of this very mountain. "Not now. Let me know when the food order comes in." He'd hear the shuttle, but he wanted to inventory himself.

"Very well, sir. Enjoy your breakfast." Lina shot an appraising glance at the eggs, took a few steps back, then stopped. "She was quite beautiful before you cut off all her hair," was her parting remark, flung over her shoulder.

"I had no choice!" he shouted after her. "You know that."

The door chimes sang again, and he glared over his cup at the door that slammed shut behind her.

And she's still quite beautiful.

Not for the first time, he was grateful no one was allowed to hear *his* thoughts.

Ryllis pressed her face into the bed and cried.

It wasn't the humiliation of the servant woman seeing her, not exactly, but the way she'd reacted. Like Westermark had done something truly horrifying, and worse, that she'd agreed to let him do it. Maybe he'd done something wrong in his culture, offering an alternative to the tattooed imperial symbol. Perhaps she'd been wrong to accept. A hidden mark would have let her pretend to be a guest, like he'd said. She could have enjoyed the garden. Spent most of her time out there, working, if he agreed to let her do so, and then things would have been fine. She could have pretended she was happy.

But no.

She wasn't Westermark's guest, and perhaps that was why she'd chosen the way she had. It was a reminder to herself, as much as anyone else, that she wasn't on Vilaria of her own free will. That she'd been dragged, not kicking and screaming, but close enough, from her home. That this very outcome was possible over the course of her life hadn't mattered—no Cerethian ever thought it would happen to them. The Eradication Council was something that turned its eye on others.

Until they found themselves caught up in a rebellion.

Until they couldn't pay the taxes that seemed heavier and heavier each season.

Until they spoke to someone under suspicion, if only a greeting on the street.

Until they caught the eye of a noble one.

The heavy realization made her ill. Westermark's job as a security officer placed him in a position to meet dozens upon dozens of Star Realm subjects in trouble. Some would be all too grateful for his assistance, and some— well, if they weren't grateful and willing, that wouldn't matter to him, would it? She'd come along with him under duress, prodded on the jump ship by shock sticks, and he hadn't so much as blinked. Maybe he liked choosing from that second group.

She shivered as the door opened. If he preferred women like her, then she would need to kill him as soon as possible, before he hurt her. Before he learned her secret, and something much worse happened. The door closed again, the bed moved underneath her, and she shifted away from Westermark's weight.

"I had to come check on you, Amaryllis," he said. "I'm sure you want to be alone, but I was worried."

The name was the final indignation. "Do not call me that. I know you know better." Her voice cracked.

Silence. Not even the bed made a sound, like he was sitting as still as death.

"You're right," he said finally. "I'm sorry. I do know better. I suppose I—well, it's just that you look so alive when you're angry, and back on Cereth, I wanted to see you alive, whenever I could make it happen. You were so lifeless even as you argued with them and denied everything, and it killed me. It was wrong and selfish to prod you for a reaction, but I did it, and I'm sorry for that."

Could he hear himself? Ryllis pushed her face harder into the linens, then stopped. Even the audacity of the innocent silk angered her.

"Wrong and selfish?" she said to the pillow. "Bringing me here was wrong and selfish. Your entire existence is about being wrong and selfish, Your Highness."

"You're misunderstanding something—I had no choice. You grew up on Cereth. You know how the galaxy works."

At that, she sat up. Westermark was sitting cross-legged on the foot of the bed, farther from her than she'd initially thought.

"I know it's unfair," she said. "I know it's wrong. You don't have to explain it to me. You're the one who needs it explained to you. Do you know what it's like the first time you hear the words Eradication Council? Can you understand what it's like to hide your feelings? Have you heard your mother's voice shake when she tells you what *eradicate* means? Has your father"—her voice cracked again—"ever had to explain to you that sometimes people are taken and they never return?"

"We have to maintain control of the dependent planets one way or another, and sometimes that control requires drastic measures. Has it ever occurred to you that the Eradication Council prevents the indiscriminate slaughter of entire towns? That pulling out the weeds is nobler than burning the entire forest? This exile is punishment for your wrongdoing, yes, and as such there will be aspects you find humiliating and distasteful"—he waved at her hair—"but I have no desire to treat you cruelly. You will grow used to living here, and while doing so, you will have the opportunity to atone for your crimes in a manner that benefits both you and the Star Realm. What more can you ask for?"

"I've committed no crimes." Ryllis clenched her jaw, trying to forget about the flower in her cell. If the Fleet found out, if Westermark remembered, it would be a certain death sentence. "I hated your father, like any other Cerethian would, but I was loyal."

His stare was measured, even. Not even his breath quickened.

"If you hated him," he said, "then you were not truly loyal."

His soft indictment fell as heavily as a sword across her neck. Westermark thought she was a criminal. It didn't matter that she had no control over her power, that she'd never asked for it or used it intentionally. It didn't even matter that she'd never spoken a word against the emperor and the Star Realm before five seconds ago. Now she had, and as far as he was concerned, she was the traitor the Eradication Council had said she was, and she would never convince him otherwise.

"I did the best I could as a Cerethian," she said, "within the confines of centuries of oppression we've experienced. You can't possibly understand."

"I don't claim to understand. Only to obey, same as you."

"I did obey." she said quietly. "This shouldn't have happened."

"But it has." He studied her face for a moment until she looked away. "So, what about a truce?"

"A truce?" What was he talking about?

"Of a sort. A small one, to begin with, and later, perhaps, when you're willing, we can negotiate other terms."

"And the current ones?" Her hatred and fear were already beginning to falter in favor of his unexpected mercy.

Or maybe not so unexpected.

"Just one," he said. "You smile every so often, and I make every effort to give you a reason to —and call you Ryllis."

She couldn't smile so suddenly after insulting his father. She wouldn't smile, knowing the awful things he'd just said. But as her lips tilted upward, his did too, and she found she couldn't contain her emotion. It wasn't happiness—not in the least—but relief had much the same results, didn't it?

"That's an agreement?" he asked, the widest smile she'd ever seen on his face.

His earnestness won her over. "That's an agreement."

CHAPTER FIVE

The scream woke him from a restless sleep. Kresten rolled over and rubbed his eyes with the heels of his palms. The house fell silent again, but he struggled to his feet, anyway. He wouldn't have been able to explain why—he wasn't supposed to care one speck of stardust for Ryllis's comfort, after all, but leaving her alone to cry in that dark cavern of his bedroom wasn't appealing either.

He sighed as he pulled on an embroidered caftan. Moving his entire wardrobe to a spare room hadn't been difficult—it wasn't as though he stored much at the mountain lodge, but it did limit his choice of middle-of-the-night clothing. He hoped she wasn't offended.

An oppressive feeling overcame him as he made his way to his—her!—bedroom, and he searched his mind for anything that might have happened recently to make her feel like this. She'd have to be feeling strong emotions to both have a nightmare enough to wake her with a scream and for his insignificant empathy to notice. He came up with nothing, though truthfully, he'd scarcely seen her for the past few days.

The lights were on inside when he knocked on the door. Ryllis's soft voice replied, and it was clear she didn't want to see him, though her words said otherwise. He stood there for a moment, his forehead on the door. It was an almost impossible decision—leave her alone like she claimed she wanted, or console her.

In the end, he pushed it open. Ryllis was sitting on the chair by the fireplace, her knees drawn up to her chest, her arms around them. She looked up when he entered, then swung her head to the side. The oppressive feeling he'd sensed on the way there vanished, and he only felt relief. He wouldn't wish embarrassment on her, but it seemed she preferred that over fear and pain, and it wasn't his place to argue.

"I heard screaming," he said.

"I had a nightmare." Her voice broke as she stood, her long gown flowing about her. "I'm so sorry I woke you, Your Highness. Let me help you back to bed."

By the stars, what did she think this was? He could put himself to bed, hadn't needed a servant for that since he was ten solar cycles old.

"I was up anyway," he lied. "Couldn't sleep." Ryllis just stared at him. Finally, he spoke again. "The night is mild, and there is no moon. I know what Cereth thinks about them, but perhaps the stars would settle your mind."

He'd expected an argument, but she nodded, and, grabbing a cloak, followed behind him through the dark house. He was familiar with the turns and furniture, but she was not, and he had the constant thought he should guide her to the back deck. He decided against it but put his hand on her elbow to stop her once they reached the kitchen.

"Tea?" he asked.

She bobbed her head, her eyes red and glassy in what little illumination shone from the hallway, and moved to wave on the light. "Yes, Your Highness. What kind would you prefer?"

"Not for me. For you. Would you like tea?"

Her mouth opened and shut in what dim light remained from the security lights outside. "Your Highness, that's not appropriate."

"If you'd like to do something to help, don't argue with me."

Having frozen her feet to the floor in confusion with that order, he made short work of her tea, then gestured her outside, still holding the cup.

It wouldn't do for her to fall with it in her hands. She watched with something akin to apprehension and curiosity as he led her onto the stone patio, far enough away from the house that the sky above was unobstructed, sparkling in the dark. The night was cool, but he couldn't see his breath, and she looked warm enough in the wool cloak. He handed over her tea as she sat on one of the rounded cushions on the ground, and she looked away, blinking rapidly.

"The nightmare," he said, pulling up his own cushion and sitting next to her.

"It was nothing." Ryllis stuck her nose in the cup.

"It didn't sound like nothing." In truth, he didn't particularly care what she'd been dreaming about, but anything that came from her mind was potentially useful to him.

She craned her neck up at the stars she claimed to despise, then looked around the garden, avoiding his gaze. "I dreamed of what would happen to me on Vilaria."

"And?"

"It wasn't this," she said softly.

"What was it?" He forced himself to sound idly curious. Not desperate for information. Never desperate. Amazing how easily it came back to him.

"Your Highness, please—"

His tone grew firm. "Tell me."

Like he'd expected, Ryllis jerked up straight and clutched at her cup, her cheeks paling. She hadn't been allowed to be evasive in the prison on Cereth, and he wasn't too proud to use those enduring memories to his advantage. She swallowed, and her voice grew even quieter.

"Once, early on, they came by and opened all the cell doors but left the fields up. They told us to stand there, right in front of the field, that if we moved, we'd be punished. It was the strangest thing, and I knew right away that something was very wrong. And before they'd finished going down the corridor, I heard a sound. Not screaming. Not even crying. More like—more like keening. And then they were parading him along. Another prisoner. They'd whipped him so badly he couldn't walk. His back—" She looked up at the stars again, like she was desperate to escape into them, no matter how much she hated the wide-open galaxy. "It was shredded."

Kresten didn't say anything. It must have been during one of his shifts off. He'd have remembered otherwise, wouldn't he? Was he so far gone that something like that would have seemed like nothing more than another day?

"Once he passed by," she said, running her fingers anxiously around the priceless china in her hands, "I threw up. I was too scared to turn around, to even move, so I just stood there, and —anyway, one of the guards noticed, and he came in. He grabbed me by the throat and told me the same fate was waiting for me on Vilaria if they didn't kill me outright. He said I would never survive slavery here." She shifted the cup to one hand and wiped her eyes with the other.

Guilt. He could feel it, deep in his gut but also light, on the top of his skin that had just recognized how cool the night was. He didn't remember that unfortunate prisoner, but he remembered the bruises on her throat. The guards had told him she'd done it to herself. That was what the medical report had said, and like a fool, he hadn't questioned it. That was why his hairs were on end, wasn't it?

"He was mistaken." Kresten leaned back on his elbows to better see her response. "Or lying to upset you. Whipping slaves hasn't been legal on Vilaria in fifty solar cycles."

If he didn't know better, he'd have sworn the look on her face was pity. But it was just the starlight. No one could tell a thing in such darkness. He could only go by her voice and her words, which made this all a fascinating exercise. That was all it was. Training. Education. Learning her weaknesses and non-verbal clues.

"I am not so naïve as that, Your Highness," she replied.

His entire body grew heavy at her reprimand, like it had during his tour on the high-gravity planet of Candis. Ryllis wasn't stupid. And she wasn't wrong. Lashing a prisoner was permissible in the Fleet for even minor offenses, and most of the planet agreed that treating a slave better than the Fleet treated its men was unconscionable. Illegal or not, the law was openly defied. He'd seen it happen to palace slaves and a few of his own brothers as a child, hadn't he? He hadn't experienced it, thank the Realm, but he knew enough to know it wasn't something he would ever do to Ryllis. She didn't know that, though, and in a piercing burst of emotional pain, he found himself desperate to convince her of that.

"Maybe so," he said. "But it does not happen in this household. None of what you fear does. Ever."

Her eyes widened at his sharp denial. "I never suggested you—"

"You didn't." He wrapped his arms around himself. "I walked you into it, and I'm sorry."

"If that doesn't happen here"—she looked down, and he tried not to imagine the way her hair would have fallen in her face otherwise—"what does?"

Kresten looked up and tried to identify the flickering stars that weren't at all familiar after so long away. Realm's sake, why did she have to bring this up now? He didn't want to deal with it—ever. Punishing slaves had always fallen to the imperial palacemaster. Disciplining the few troops that had ever reported to him fell to his chief. He only meted out their sentences, then hid.

"Behave yourself," he said, "and we won't have to find out."

It was the wrong answer, he knew—she was dying for some knowledge about her future, but he hadn't thought the conversation would turn to this when he'd knocked on her door.

"Behave," Ryllis repeated. "By behave, you mean . . ."

He didn't know what he meant. Whether he'd considered this future somewhere in his subconscious or not, his actual decision to bring her here had been impulsive, and he hadn't truly considered what he'd do with a slave. By the stars, but having servants was an annoyance. Lina was capable of running the house on her own—more than sufficient.

He waved his hand. "Be helpful. Do what Lina asks of you, bring me tea in my office every morning. Don't try to kill me, don't steal anything, and don't even think of trying to escape."

It seemed a reasonable set of rules to him, but Ryllis recoiled a bit, then nodded. That strange feeling crept across his skin again. He'd brought her here; he owed her more guidance than that—guidance she was clearly crying out for.

"He mentioned an auction," she said. "Is that what will happen if I do?"

"If you escape?"

I'll never send you away.

He nodded anyway. If that's what she was afraid of, he'd let her be. Still, he cringed as he spoke. "Yes. Likely. I don't have the time nor inclination to deal with a disobedient slave. You'd be wise to remember that whatever new household you end up in will not treat you as benevolently as I do. And if you try to kill me, that whipping you're so terrified of will seem a mercy."

He could see her struggle with that, try to reconcile his lack of tact with the man who'd said the first night that he didn't keep slaves. Her fingers brushed the silk embroidery on her cloak, and he was relieved he didn't need to point out she wouldn't be wearing something like that wherever the Eradication Council auctioned her off to next—not that they ever would. Resignation and relief warred on her face, visible in the way her shoulders sank as she rubbed her eyes.

"But that's enough talk about that. You like the gardens?" he asked.

"Yes." One corner of her lip curved upward; she pulled her cloak tighter around her. "I am"—the smile fell away—"was a horticulturist."

"I know."

Kresten held his breath. Why hadn't he thought of this back on Cereth? It was an arrangement that would make her happy, and if she was happy, she might grace him with another smile.

Idiot. She might become comfortable enough to talk.

"Then they're yours," he said. "Iria—my gardener—has been talking about his retirement for a long while. I'll let him know that you're to be allowed to do whatever you want out here, whenever you want. After my morning tea, of course. Will that be satisfactory?"

"It would be wonderful. Thank you, Your Highness."

Even in the inky darkness, he could see the relief in her eyes. Finally, he'd done something right for her. The one thing he didn't see was sleep, and he suppressed his own yawn.

"The stars here look different from Cereth," she went on, then covered her mouth. "That sounded so stupid. Of course they do."

"It's not stupid. You're tired, and they're unfamiliar."

"Everything's unfamiliar—the moon, the stars, the sun. I didn't realize how much I recognized in the night sky until it was gone. I can't even find Etult."

She'd probably been looking out the windows for Cereth's main navigational star—the star that had allowed them to colonize the entire planet via its oceans—since she'd arrived. But Cerethians weren't space travelers, didn't study astronomy except as their own planetary history, and Ryllis was no exception. It was no wonder she couldn't find it.

"It's low, behind the mountains this time of night." Kresten pointed straight out, low on the horizon, where the ridgeline was scarcely visible in the dark. He didn't point out that Cereth was just above them, twinkling like it didn't even realize she was gone, sending out its light from millions of solar cycles before she was born.

"I should have known a Fleet officer would be familiar with the stars constellations." Ryllis picked up her tea and eyed him over the cup, this time with vague interest. "You learned of our local group, too."

He smiled, confident she wouldn't be offended by his cheerfulness now, if she could even see his expression. "Yes. But I'll tell you, I prefer the old explanations for the stars. The tales the women at court used to tell."

Her obvious interest grew more intense. "I can't imagine you sitting around listening to people tell tales. Tell me one?"

Was she—was she curious about Vilarian folk lore? Kresten crossed his legs and propped his head on his hand. Curiosity was better than apathy or hate.

"A long time ago," he began, "before the constellations kept their watch on us, there were no stars in the night sky. Only the sun and the moon, and sometimes the moon disappeared for a time. It bothered people, but the Light had decreed we live in night until he decided otherwise, so it was something they accepted and lived with, even though it frightened them. And then one day, a witch—" He broke off and laughed, like he always did when he told the story. "Some stories call her Ingmar, others call her Signe. We're not all that good at the oral traditions in my part of Vilaria, and the written stories were mostly lost in a flood thousands of solar cycles ago. Anyway, Ingmar heard from a traitorous footman in the palace that the princess would be traveling through the forest that very night. Alone, in the absolute darkness of the new moon. And, the footman said, she would be carrying a pouch of the imperial diamonds with her."

"Why?" Ryllis asked.

He drew his eyebrows together, even though she couldn't see. "Why what?"

"Why would a princess traverse the forest in the middle of the night, by herself, carrying what must be priceless jewelry?"

Kresten chuckled at her tone, disapproving and confused at the same time. It was—he hated to admit it, but *charming* was the only word for it.

"I suppose she wasn't very smart," he said. "Anyway, she came to a creek, and the thin court shoes she wore became stuck in the mud. She cried out for help, but her pleas only reached Ingmar's ears. The witch, who'd been trailing the princess all evening, could scarcely believe her luck. She transformed into a handsome young man and told the princess she would take the diamonds to safety and come back for her later."

He pointed his finger at Ryllis. "But the princess wasn't as stupid as you think, for she noticed something strange about the young man—when he reached out his hand for the pouch, she saw that his fingers were crooked and knotted. When she realized he was not a man at all, she flung the pouch into the air, hoping it would become stuck in a tree. She would have done anything to keep them from Ingmar, you see, for rumors were that Ingmar used them for nefarious purposes only whispered about in polite company and certainly never at court. But neither of them knew the diamonds were enchanted, charmed by the Light for just that moment. And when the princess threw them, they landed in the heavens, where they remain to this day, giving us light when even the moon disappears—and reminding us that the timing of the universe belongs to the Light, not we mortals."

Ryllis had gone silent, and after calling her name a few times, Kresten leaned over and gently shook her shoulder. She made a few soft noises, then tucked her hands under her chin. He squinted at her, but her eyes were closed and her breathing was regular. With a sigh, he stood and watched her, debating to himself. She was too peaceful for him to move back inside, or even wake up. Maybe it didn't matter. The shielding field was up at night, and she could neither escape over the wall nor fall prey to any number of animals that prowled the forest at night.

It was settled, then. He hadn't slept outside in much too long, anyway, and it reminded him of good things. Comfortable things. Walking carefully so as not to wake her, he made his way to the stack of blankets on a cushion by the door and draped one over her. Ryllis didn't stir, so he curled up against the wall a safe distance away, his own blanket over him, and closed his eyes.

CHAPTER SIX

*L*ina tossed a bag of flour on the counter and gave Ryllis a mock glare. "You will not help me with this," she said, slicing open the top with a sharp knife, "and I won't have any further argument about it. I don't allow people in the kitchen when I'm working on pastries, not even His Highness. No, don't look at me like that. You can find something else to do, I'm sure." The knife clattered on the smooth stone, and she crouched down out of sight, searching for something else.

"Lina." Ryllis stood on her tiptoes to see over the counter. "It's too cold to be out in the garden. I wouldn't be surprised if it began to snow. Surely there's something I can help you with."

She glanced out the large window, toward the low clouds that hung over the mountain and shrouded the lodge in fog. True to his word, Westermark had introduced her to his gardener Iria almost immediately, and she'd spent the past lunar cycle amusing herself in the gardens. How she wanted to be out there now, running her fingers through the dirt and letting the mountains sing peace into her soul, but there would be no way to explain that choice of activities.

"Then don't go outside if it's going to snow," Lina said. "I don't care what he told you, but there's no need for you to work in that garden every day. Explore the house. Sleep. Have a cup of tea. You don't need to be constantly busy, and even if you did, you've earned yourself a bit of a break."

"Tea? I can't sit around and drink tea. Won't the prince be angry with me if he sees?"

If she was honest with herself, she still wasn't sure what she was supposed to be doing, but if Westermark saw her lounging around drinking tea, he would—well, she didn't want to know what he'd say to that. The gray had settled on the mountain two days before, and the delay of spring hadn't helped anyone's mood. She was exhausted, Lina was brusque, and Westermark spent most of his time in the office, waving both her and Lina off when they offered to tidy it. He wasn't snappy with anyone, not in the least, but she wasn't about to test him.

"You haven't figured His Highness out yet, have you? He is a fair man, and I suspect he'll only be angry with you if you keep me from finishing these pastries." Lina filled a cup and tossed a tea bag inside. "Here, take this—no more excuses. Now off with you."

Ryllis reluctantly accepted the tea and wandered out of the kitchen, only to stop in the large living area. Lina's dismissal wasn't quite the same as the way her father had taken to dismissing her after he'd remarried, yet it certainly had felt like it. But it was only the weather. It had gotten to even kind, encouraging, Lina.

She looked around the open living area. Westermark didn't need her help today. The mansion was practically spotless—no surprise since he'd spent so much time on Cereth, leaving it empty, and the two of them were absolutely incapable of putting it in disarray, especially with Lina around. With the tea cooling in one hand, she arranged a few pillows on the sofa and gazed up at the vaulted ceiling, lined by wood beams, carved in a pattern just as complicated as the ones in her room. There wasn't much else to do. Why in the Realm had he requested a slave? The answer, of course, the one she kept pretending wasn't the truth, was obvious. He wanted a woman to satisfy him after such a long deployment. That he'd waited as long as he had to make his move spoke of his compassion, not his motives.

A few snowflakes caught her attention, and she pressed her nose against the window to watch them sail in the wind, landing on the deck and newly sprouted crocuses. They melted away as soon as they hit the ground, but the chill in the air outside was unmistakable. There was real snow coming, and it would put the spring thaw behind by at least a dozen days. She would have to be careful. Westermark couldn't notice his gardens were coming to life faster than the weather would suggest.

"I can't believe it's snowing. It's supposed to be spring."

Ryllis jumped at Westermark's voice next to her. "Just flurries," she said, "So far." She shivered anyway. Despite the warmth of her first few days, the mountain had since cooled, and it was only the fire she started in Kresten's bedroom fireplace most nights that kept her the least bit warm. Spring needed to come, and quickly. For so many reasons.

"Cold?" he asked, leaning against the window beside her.

"Not horribly. I found some warm clothes—thank you for that." She smiled and brushed her fingers across her leggings, heavily embroidered with metallic teal and gold thread. It wasn't the fashion in Therus, or likely anywhere else on Cereth, but they were beautiful, nonetheless. "And Lina made me some tea."

"It smells good."

Ryllis glanced out the window one last time, then back at him. "I could make you some. But Lina is—well, she doesn't want me in the kitchen right now." Westermark looked at her curiously, and she took a step toward the kitchen. Anything to escape. "But you know what, that's all right. I'm sure she'd understand if I told her you asked for something. I'll—I'll be right back."

He put a hand on her arm, then dropped it. "Not so fast. Kicked you out, did she?" Something cheery lit in his expression. "A little secret for you? That means you're going to be very happy in a few hours."

"That's good to hear." She felt like a fool standing here in her captor's luxurious living room, holding a cup of tea, but there wasn't anything else to say, anything else to do, anywhere else to escape. "I'm looking forward to it."

"Until then . . . you've been spending so much time in the garden that you haven't had a proper tour yet, have you?"

She could hear the realization in his voice. "No. Not really. But you don't need to do—"

"I know I don't need to." He smiled. "I want to."

"Then I'd like to see it."

Ryllis set the tea on the nearest table and shrugged agreement at him, even though she wanted to flee and hide under the covers. But if a prince of Vilaria wanted to show her his home, who was she to say he couldn't?

He gestured down a corridor, and she followed along next to him, listening to him explain the history of the mountains and the people who'd lived here until a series of eruptions had devastated the hillside three hundred solar cycles before. Thousands had been killed, he told her, and when the forest began to regenerate, most stayed away. Even though the god of fire was no longer worshiped on Vilaria, people were afraid.

"The volcano's quiet now, though," he added, as her eyes widened. "And we're advanced enough now that we can see anything coming many lunar cycles before it happens. I promise you're safe here."

"I believe you." The irony of his insistence almost, but not quite, made her laugh. She would never laugh again.

"Do you?" he asked, stopping in front of a large picture window. "I need you to know I won't hurt you, via a long-dormant volcano or otherwise."

Ryllis frowned at his earnestness. He'd already hurt her so much, first by his easy acceptance of the interrogators' accusations, then by bringing her to Vilaria and standing by while his Eradication Council made her a slave. What did he care if she was afraid of being hurt? Silent, she looked out the window, at the snow accumulating on the deck outside. The beauty of the wild shouldn't come this easily when she was so sad, but it did, like always. Today though, she hated it for its faithfulness.

Westermark sighed. "Ryllis—"

"I want to believe you," she told the window. "Surely that must count for something."

"It counts for a lot."

She spun around and faced him, suddenly brave. "Why am I here?"

His forehead crinkled. "Because you've been accused of—"

"No," she said, barely managing to keep her voice from breaking. "That's not what I mean. I know why I'm on Vilaria, even though you're wrong about me, about what you think I've done." She cast a glance outside, at the early spring flowers poking through the rapidly accumulating snow. "I mean why am I here in these mountains? In your home? With you? You told that man you'd requested a slave which implies the request was made before you went to Cereth, but since I spend most of my time wandering the gardens here, I doubt you've ever been in any need of a servant beyond Lina. And —and please don't take this the wrong way, but you don't seem the type to do anyone a favor, especially if they're Cerethian. You look exhausted all the time, and a favor would be a hassle you'd rather not deal with. So why?"

Westermark leaned against the window next to her and ran a finger down the chilled glass. "What do you want me to say?"

"I want to hear the truth, Your Highness."

"That's quite a demand."

Ryllis shivered, not knowing if it was from the cold or the change in his tone. "I haven't demanded anything. I've asked, very politely, why you've shown me the mercy you have. I think I'm entitled to that answer."

"Entitled?" He gazed at her for a long time. "Does my mercy frighten you?" he asked at long last.

"A little," she replied, with honesty forced into her soul. It hadn't, not until this very second, but now her mind was spinning in circles.

"It shouldn't." He turned away, then stopped. "I have a better idea than a tour. I'm sure you've seen enough houses in your time. But when's the last time you saw snow?"

"Snow? I don't know." It'd been so long. She'd spent most of the prior winter on Cereth in that prison.

"Long enough to make it novel, then." Westermark looked her up and down. "I wish I'd known you would need warmer clothes, but I wasn't expecting such a late spring storm. Let's see if we can find you something warm enough to wear."

He was clearly changing the subject, but she followed him back to his bedroom anyway, where Westermark dug through the closet and tossed her a scarf and an oversized man's coat. Ryllis struggled to roll up the sleeves as they snuck out the front to the front deck, now coated with a thin layer of snow.

"Here. Let me do that. Your nose looks cold already." Westermark stopped her with a hand on her shoulder as she tried to juggle the fabric and remain upright on the slick ground. With a practiced hand, he draped the scarf over her head and face, then stepped back and admired his handiwork. "Yes. That'll do for a while, I think."

He was too close as he smiled, and in the gray of the lowering clouds, his odd blue eyes, so foreign on Cereth, looked unnervingly and comfortingly like hers. Ryllis pulled her hands inside the sweater, even though outside of the snowflakes lingering on her eyelashes, it wasn't all that cold. Being exposed was simply uncomfortable somehow. With Westermark at her side, she leaned against the railing and watched the snow dance.

"The snow would just be starting again at home." Ryllis glanced at him. "I think."

"Maybe. I can hardly keep track of the seasons here."

"I don't doubt it, as many planets as you must have visited." The very idea hurt. Westermark couldn't possibly understand her pain, because he'd lived the opposite of her quiet, insular life —the identity that had already been stripped from her, along with her hope. "It must be confusing to be so powerful."

"I doubt you know what kind of power I have or lack."

The admonition wasn't unkind. It was as if he'd read her mind and was gently correcting her misconception, and that was more disconcerting than the attentive way he was looking at her. Westermark wanted her to think better of him?

"I'm sorry. You can't help who you are, and you're right—perhaps I don't know who that is." She focused on the flurries. Did she want to know? "But I know you have influence enough to have brought me here."

"This again. And so soon?" He raised his eyebrows. "Surely you know I owe you no explanation for my decisions."

"I don't believe you're the kind of person to answer like that," she said, and to her surprise, she believed it.

"Really?" Westermark's chuckle was softened by the falling snow. "Then perhaps you know me better than you think you do."

"Not enough. Tell me?" Her own bravery surprised her, but then, what else did she have left?

"About myself?" He stared at her for a moment, then raised his arms into the air and stuck out his tongue, letting the flakes fall on it. "I like snow," he said. "And I've missed it. A lot."

Ryllis shook her head at his evasion, but it was almost impossible to fend off his joy. "You look like a child, Your Highness."

"Do not say that." Westermark pointed a bare finger at her, then darted down the stairs to the meandering patio that wound between the shrubs. Without looking away from her, he brushed his hand over the most snow-covered of them, creating a small blizzard. "This is looking like a child."

Again, she wanted to laugh. Again, she stopped herself. He would have to settle for a smile. Covered in the white remains of his prank, he dashed back up the stairs to her, and Ryllis stared at his outstretched hand. She raised her eyes to his and saw something there, something that captivated and frightened her at the same time.

He's making you think it's your decision to warm his bed. And you're falling for it.

Tentatively, she reached out her fingers. Westermark's were warm, and as he interlaced them between hers, her face heated as well. Before she could jerk away and cover her cheeks, a gust of icy air rustled through the early spring leaves, and she took a breath as snowflakes hit her face, cooling her in an instant.

Westermark didn't say anything about the way she'd flushed. "Come on," he said, pulling her toward the stairs. "This is the last time in a dozen lunar cycles you'll get to experience this."

"This? Snow?"

"No. Not snow. This," he repeated as her feet hit the stone pavers.

Letting go of her hand, he scooped up a pile and tossed it at her. The snow was too dry to stick together, and instead of hitting her shoulder like he'd doubtless intended, it fell apart in a cloud in front of her, showering her in powder. Ryllis spit it from her mouth, brushed it from her shoulders.

"What—you—" *You just threw snow at me.*

He laughed. "Got you."

"Got me?" She could feel her face contorting into some kind of odd and unattractive expression, but she couldn't stop it. What kind of bizarre Vilarian game was this? "With—with snow?"

Westermark's laughter was the loudest sound in the clearing in front of the house. "Yes, with snow. Try it. I won't even run."

Ryllis reached down, grimaced at the burn of the ice on her bare skin, and tried to pack it into a weapon the best she could. It was too cold on her hand, so she gave up and tossed the powder at Westermark—who, true to his promise, didn't blink when it hit him.

"Fun, right?" he asked, wiping his face.

"I don't know about—"

His next shot was more accurate than the first. Ryllis shrieked as the snow found its way down the neck of her coat, then crouched down and padded her own ball together. It didn't stick any better than the first, but that perhaps wouldn't matter as long as she could get close enough—

Her screech echoed through the trees as Westermark hit her again, on the back of the head this time, then danced a few steps back, still laughing.

"I'm sorry," he said, gasping for breath. "It's just —it's been so long so I've done something like this. But I shouldn't have done it twice without you hitting me in return. That wasn't fair."

"No. It wasn't fair."

She approached him, holding a huge pile of loose snow in her hand the best she could. He didn't move, and the glint in his eyes told her he knew exactly what she meant to do and wasn't going to fight her when she did. Ryllis smiled back—then dropped the entire handful down the front of his shirt. Westermark's teeth caught his lip, then he began to shiver as the snow melted on his chest.

"See?" he asked through gritted teeth. "Fun."

"You have an interesting idea of it, Your Highness." She brushed the remains off her palms, then pulled her hands back into her sleeves.

He reached out and brushed the snow off her scarf, his expression less giddy. She knew that look. She was sure of his intentions now. Combined with his excuses to touch her, even under the pretense of helping to warm her, she knew, even if he'd denied it that first night on Vilaria.

And she would do what he wanted, likely this very night, if not out of love, out of fear and a grudging respect. It would never become love, that much she knew as well, but perhaps it would turn to something pleasurable. She wouldn't need to dread it any longer if it did. Maybe she'd even benefit from it. Westermark had said it best once—there were worse places she could be at this very moment.

"I have a lot of interesting ideas," he said, taking a step closer.

Ryllis could scarcely breathe, and it wasn't from running away from the snow he'd thrown at her. She had asked him for more time that first night, hadn't she? And he'd complied with her request, longer than she thought he ever would. That compassion had to count for something.

"Like what?" she asked, hoping she sounded sensual instead of naïve.

He tilted his head to the side. "Well—"

"Sir!" Lina stood on the deck above them, arms across her chest, shivering. "I heard screaming. Is everything all right?"

Westermark gave Ryllis an apologetic look, then turned his attention toward Lina. "Just a snowball fight. We were having fun."

"Was that all? It sounded like someone was dying out here. Well, get inside and warm up before you both freeze to death." Lina stomped back into the house.

Westermark raised his eyebrows at Ryllis. "I think we've been ordered. Ready to taste whatever she was baking in there?"

Ryllis nodded. He brushed his fingertips against hers as they climbed the stairs, but she didn't let his touch affect her that time. She could only think of one thing.

Dying.

Lina had reminded her, inadvertently, of her real desire. She would escape. Either by his death . . . or hers.

CHAPTER SEVEN

Ryllis ran a finger down the edge of the knife. It wasn't as sharp as she would have preferred, but it was long enough, and that was all that mattered. Lina hadn't noticed when she'd slid it up her sleeve last night, and Westermark had retreated from dinner early, muttering something about checking in with work. Yes, it would do. She stared at it for a few more moments, then slid it down her pant leg, outside her thigh, into the makeshift holder she'd fashioned with the purple ribbon earlier that morning.

Perfect.

She reached back in her pants to remove it again, jerking her hand away at the knock on the door. Westermark wouldn't barge in on her, but he'd become suspicious if she didn't answer. No matter. She would hide the knife somewhere after he left.

"Yes?" Her heart was racing; it was the only thing she could say.

"May I come in?" he called.

No.

"Y—yes."

Westermark swung open the door with a grin. "I came to see if you'd care to join on a walk. A short one, because it's about to storm—but the clouds are lovely right now, and I have the perfect place to watch them roll in."

"I don't think so." There were a thousand other things she could find to occupy her time within the confines of the house. *Alone.*

"Ryllis—" He leaned against the doorframe and sighed. "I wish you would come see this with me."

Her heart sank. How could she argue with someone who looked like he did, pleading for her company, even if he was a prince? Without a word, she grabbed a cloak and followed next to him through the dark house and courtyard. The clouds he'd mentioned were dark and low, and there wasn't any thunder in the distance, but as she watched Westermark struggled with the rusted gate that led outside the high stone wall, she had a certain sense of dreary foreboding.

"Is this safe?" she asked. "It looks bad."

"Mmm. No lightning right now, or I wouldn't take you up here." He yanked harder at the gate, almost falling backward when it finally came open, and she smothered a laugh as she watched.

"Laughing at a prince is considered uncouth, you know," he said, turning toward her. "On any planet."

Ryllis covered her mouth.

"I reprimand you, and yet you do it again." His eyes sparkled. "I don't believe you hate me nearly as much as you pretend to."

"Perhaps not, Your Highness," she murmured. It surprised her how much she meant it, and that only made her more determined. She had to hate him. Had to. And if she attacked him, even if she didn't quite manage to kill him, they would kill her. Westermark would never forgive her, would never grin at her like this again, and then she would be free, if even in death.

The knife shifted a bit in its holster as she followed him through the gate, swallowing the rest of her misgivings. On the other side of the wall, the wild of the mountains gave them no freedom; only a narrow, rocky trail leading up a slope broke the dense underbrush.

Ryllis eyed the climb warily. Westermark hadn't said anything about a rough climb, and the shoes she saved for the garden didn't look nearly sturdy enough for what he intended.

He'd said a walk, after all. Not that they'd be climbing a mountain. She took a step, testing the gravel beneath her.

"It's not so steep the entire way. Only the first bit. Here." Westermark slid backward toward her, scattering gravel as he did. He let her lead by a half step as she clung to his hand, let her control the pace uphill, and she had the wildest realization that it was the first time since arriving on Vilaria that she hadn't been following along behind him. Was that what being royalty was like? Being so assured of your safety that even your enemy could walk a step behind and be trusted to not harm you?

The knife flew into her mind, and she stumbled.

"Careful." He put a hand on her back to stop her fall as she slid down the rock-strewn path, almost into him.

"I'm sorry. It was slick right there." He was so close she could smell him, sweaty despite the chill in the air, but with an underlying warmth of vanilla that warmed her. "I didn't mean—"

"To almost push me down a hill?" Westermark appeared next to her, tightening his grip on her hand.

"I—" She was considering throwing herself to her knees and begging for forgiveness when she noticed the humor creasing his eyes. "Don't joke with me like that!"

"But I get such a reaction from it."

Ryllis shook her head to hide her grin and continued up the hill. Away from the house, the woods became sparser, the trail wider, and Westermark was able to walk beside her, though he didn't let go of her hand. *In case you fall again,* he argued when she tried to reclaim it. *You might knock me over next time.*

"I don't understand the Cerethian problem with full names," he said abruptly, as the small rocks beneath them turned to smooth pink granite. The change in the ground and her own ragged breath suggested they'd made it to the top of whatever mountain stood next to the mansion. "Why does it matter? On Vilaria, not a single soul would think twice about using any form of my names if I wasn't who I was."

"All your time on Cereth, and you didn't learn such a major custom?"

"I suppose I didn't."

She sighed, concentrating on the wet stone beneath her. It wasn't raining, but a damp mist hung about them, covering everything in wetness. Next time she'd have to cover her head.

Next time?

"It's too intimate for casual use," she said. "Our parents call us by our full names as children, though some choose to use nicknames, then no one calls us the same until much later. Not until we meet that one person."

He frowned. "I don't understand."

Naturally, he wouldn't. "Only our betrothed can know all of us. It's a part of our reserved society, I suppose."

"It's beautiful. Truly."

Unexpectedly, she wanted to lash out at anything Cerethian. "It's a silly custom," she said.

"Silly enough that my unwillingness to participate in it upset you? Love and intimacy aren't silly."

Easy for him to say when he had his choice of women. There hadn't been anyone on Cereth for her, not for over a solar cycle. She'd been grateful for that lack of a connection ever since she'd been arrested, but the idea that there would *never* be someone now was unthinkable.

"No. For some of us, it's become nothing more than a dream." No matter how dangerous it was to show emotion, she couldn't hide the bitterness.

"You're right. And I can't begin to imagine how painful that is." He fell silent as the trail curved and the rush of water filled her ears. "Though I had that dream once, too."

Had?

"And?"

"She died."

"I'm sorry." And to her surprise, she was.

He gave her a quick smile and pointed to a small waterfall falling from the cliff above them. It wasn't anything like the Carnraine Falls in her district on Cereth, just water running down the rocks, but the young spring ferns and lichen clinging to the rock nearby transported her somewhere familiar. A stone bench sat a few paces away, a strange thing on the side of a mountain, and Westermark sat, gesturing for her to be seated with him. After a few wary glances back down the trail, she did.

"After my wife died," he said. "I escaped to this mountain. Hauled this bench up by myself and sat for hours, watching the water. Sometimes Lina came with me, and we'd just sit and watch the water. I think she was afraid I'd throw myself off a cliff and that she needed to protect me from myself as some kind of obligation toward the empire. So yes. I know loss. Maybe not like you, but I'm not altogether unfamiliar with the concept." He shot her a quick glance. "I hope that doesn't offend."

It made her heart ache instead. Ryllis tried to smile at him but couldn't quite manage to make it happen. "No. It doesn't offend me. It humanizes you."

"Humanizes?" Westermark smiled. "I'm glad for that, being human and all."

"We forget that on Cereth, I think. Vilarians, as a whole, don't seem human unless you take the chance to talk with one as a person, and no one wants to do that. If we look at one of you the wrong way, say the wrong thing, even accidentally . . ."

"I hope you're not still that frightened of me. You don't need to be afraid of saying anything to me."

Ryllis shivered as the mist turned cold. "Let's just say I'm wary."

"That's an improvement of a sort. I'll take it."

"It's strange," she said, boldened, "to think of a Fleet officer as a widower. No one Cereth would believe me if I told them."

She glanced beside her, amused despite the solemn conversation. If she so much as mentioned to anyone at home that a Vilarian prince had been so depressed over his wife's death that his housekeeper had had him on an unsolicited suicide watch? No. They would laugh at her if she told Westermark's story.

"We all have our histories. Even me. Even you." His gaze grew intense. "Who were you before?"

Her brow furrowed before she could stop it. "You already know all that."

"Perhaps I want to hear you say it here instead of an interrogation room," Westermark replied, staring at the water.

She shouldn't talk to him, if only because her life's story would bore him to tears and having him cut her off would be humiliating. But she needed to feel like that person she'd been once again. Needed to be reminded that she'd existed as a person before the Vilarians had brought her here as a slave.

"My mother died when I was a baby," she said. "My father remarried ten solar cycles later, and his new wife and her two daughters are the center of his existence now."

She didn't bother to hide her bitterness. Zaella —she refused to think the woman's name most of the time, much less say it—doted on anyone in the room, as long as it wasn't Ryllis. It was the one part of Cereth she didn't miss. She sighed and moved to brush her hair behind her ear before she remembered.

"I love gardens, but I'm only a horticulturist by training. The Realm denied me a work permit because it was considered redundant for the governor's daughter to hold a job. So, I worked in his office when I felt like it and worked in his gardens when I didn't. Without pay, of course. I was lucky he loved me enough to oblige."

Westermark shuffled his feet on the hard granite below. "Not much different from here, then."

"No. Not much different from here." She should have felt bitter, but her reply was gentle. His comparison made too much sense. "Even the waterfalls."

"Not so," he said. "I've seen the Carnraine Falls. They're amazing."

Westermark was lying. Why would he find anything on Cereth impressive, even the soaring cataracts that people came from a world away to see?

"I'm sure Vilaria has similar falls," she said.

"Yes, but the natural ones here aren't as impressive anymore, thanks to Carl Hellquist."

Ryllis wrinkled her nose. "Carl Hellquist?"

Westermark shifted on the bench. "Generations ago, when innate powers were much more common than they are now, he had the power to control water. Decided the river nearby his home in Bruket could do with a little . . . drama. The resulting falls and farmland flooding killed hundreds and changed the landscape until the end of time. Thankfully, powers like that are genetically rare outside my extended family—Hellquist was a fluke, but a dangerous one. He's why the law forbids anyone besides the royal family from having gifts like his."

The back of her neck prickled as she remembered the flower. Everyone knew the Vilarians had bred magic out of almost everyone by force. She hadn't sustained the flower intentionally, but being in her presence had extended its life. Had Westermark noticed it never died?

"Maybe he couldn't help it," she said.

"He chose to flood that land. But even if he hadn't, if his gift was that uncontrolled, he had to die."

Ryllis gulped down a breath of fear.

He couldn't know.

She'd begun the conversation about the waterfall, and it'd flowed naturally into this discussion. Hadn't it? The interrogators on Cereth had been adept at trying to walk her into confessions, but everything had always been about the resistance. Even so, it had been exhausting, and too far removed from being constantly on edge, she'd let her guard down just now, wrapped in the false sense of security Westermark had exuded since they'd arrived.

But no. This wasn't an interrogation. It was a conversation she'd directed. She was safe, as long as she didn't do anything conspicuous. And even if she couldn't control her power completely, it was spring, wasn't it? Everything on the mountain was coming to life. By the time she needed to worry about it, he'd be dead—or she would be.

"Do you have a power?" The idea of him starting the woods around the lodge on fire with a flick of his finger was terrifying, but her curiosity was overwhelming.

Westermark hesitated. "No. I used to be bitter about that, but then I grew up. I like it that way now, believe it or not—unnatural powers cause more problems than they solve." He smiled at her and gestured down the cliffs. "Rain's picked up earlier than I thought it would. Are you ready to head back down?"

The cold mist had made the granite even slicker than before. Ryllis focused on each measured step she took. To fall now would hurt, and more importantly, it would humiliate her in front of Westermark. It wasn't too far until the narrow trail that led back to the house, and the pebbles, though an annoyance on the way up, would give her a little more grip, at least.

"Wear different shoes next time. We'll find something that will work better." Westermark trailed along behind her, paying no attention to his treads. She couldn't help her jealousy.

"Next time?" she asked.

"Wasn't it nice to get out the house and get some fresh air?"

"It was." Ryllis shot him a sideways smile and promptly lost her balance on the slippery rock. Westermark reached for her as her feet slid, but she slammed into the ground hip-first, crying out in surprise as she slid down the small boulder. It felt like she tumbled forever, but sooner than she expected, she crashed to a stop at the bottom of a pile of boulders. Westermark's voice called her name, and she rolled to her knees, feeling around to make sure nothing was broken.

"I'm all right," she called to him. "Just a little—"

Westermark's voice became steel. "What is that?"

"What's what?" Ryllis pulled herself to her feet and looked up the trail at where he was pointing.

The knife. It lay above her on the trail where she'd first slipped, dislodged from its ribbon holster. Her heart, which had settled after her fall, began to pound again.

"I—"

Westermark swiped it into his hand and held it up as he walked toward her. "Don't even bother making excuses."

He jerked her to her feet, wrenching her right arm behind her. The knife disappeared into his pocket. Terrified, she tried to spin from his grip, but it only tightened. She couldn't say anything else. All the worry about accidentally making a plant come back to life, and she'd gone and done this.

"What else are you hiding?" he asked.

"Nothing. Nothing! I swear to you!"

Westermark searched her anyway as she struggled to free herself. The ribbon was still half around her thigh, and she cried out as he reached down her pants and seized it. This had been a bad idea. She hadn't wanted to kill him, only harm him enough they'd have to kill her, but now, with the way he was handling her, perhaps she'd made a mistake. It was one thing for the emperor to order her execution for assaulting his son. It was quite another for

Westermark to abuse her out of anger before he did.

He shoved her forward, even as he pulled her arms tighter behind her. "Walk down the hill. Now."

"You're hurting me." The protest came out breathless.

"Like you intended to hurt me? I don't care. Now walk."

She did, though it was difficult stumbling downhill with him right behind her, limiting her stride. As the wall around the lodge came into view, fear took control, and she made one last-ditch attempt to swing her leg backward at him. If she could catch him off balance, they'd both fall on the steepest part of the trail, and then she could get away. Westermark blocked the kick with a leg between her knees, like he'd known it was coming, and pushed her forward toward the gate, the pressure on her wrist increasing.

She gave up after that. Westermark might be an overindulged prince, but he was also a Fleet security forces officer. He could thwart any move she made, anticipate anything she could try—and he was stronger than she. She stumbled through the dim hallways, soaked and on an ankle that hurt more by the second. Lina was nowhere to be found as he walked her into his office and pushed her to the floor. She reached for her bruised hip as he slammed the door shut, locked it, and held up the knife again.

"Tell me why I shouldn't use it on your throat this very second."

Ryllis managed to make it to her knees for the second time in five minutes, panting too hard to answer. Standing would make it harder for him to do what he'd threatened, so she stayed down. It was revolting to think he might assume it was out of deference, but she didn't care. She'd won. Dying would hurt, but she'd won. She'd escaped. As soon as he moved toward her, as soon as the knife sliced into her skin, she would be gone.

"Well?" he asked.

Tell him what you can do. He'll have to kill you then.

But what if he didn't? What if her gift made her useful enough to keep around despite the laws she violated by simply existing? What if Westermark wanted his pretty gardens more, or his father decided to keep her around as a useful toy?

No. She couldn't risk living. Westermark couldn't know what she was capable of.

"Do it," she succeeded in spitting out. "Just do it and be done with it. I hope it stains your rug, and every time you see my blood, for the rest of your life, you remember what you've done here."

Westermark lips thinned. "What I've done here?" he snarled at her. "You mean how I saved you from the Eradication Council? How I've treated you with nothing but respect, even though I could have easily done the opposite and not a soul would have challenged me? How

I gave you a home and shelter and a pleasant afternoon's walk?"

"You expect me to be grateful for that? You expect me to forget how I came to be here?"

"I expect you to—" He swore under his breath. "I don't expect a thing from you, Ryllis, except that you not try to kill me in my own home!"

"Do you feel that blade, Your Highness?" she screamed at him. "It wouldn't have killed you. But it had the power to remove me from this place, and I don't regret that decision. So do it. I won't fight you."

Westermark strode toward her like a wild animal, lithe and dangerous. He stopped, just short of where she knelt, and ran his finger across the length. Something sparked in his eyes, and she knew she wasn't going to like what he had to say—though she suspected he thought she would.

"I was planning to cut your hair tonight," he said, "but I think it's fair I use this instead of the razor. And for the next two weeks, whenever you see how ridiculous you look, you will have a reminder of how inexcusably you've acted and how merciful I've been."

Her chin fell forward. He didn't know what he was talking about. This gift of life wasn't mercy. It was anything but.

"Lift your head," he ordered, laying the knife flat across her scalp. "And hold still. I don't want to cut you too badly, but you know what they say about a dull knife."

Ryllis raised her head but closed her eyes. She didn't care that he'd forbidden her to cry. She knelt there and sobbed, waiting for him to begin. And when her knees became sore and her body was out of tears and the first cut never came, she looked up.

Westermark—and the knife—were gone.

CHAPTER EIGHT

ood splintered into the air as the knife met its sapling target. Kresten yanked it out, examined the blade, and flung it once more. It missed that time—probably due to the vodka he'd downed and the now-torrential rain. He stared at where it had fallen, lying in the bushes next to the courtyard wall.

Ryllis had planned to kill him. Or at least tried to harm him enough that she'd get herself killed, and contacting the Eradication Council —or at least someone in the Fleet—about her actions was the first thing he should have done. He couldn't explain why he'd nearly destroyed a tree and his liver instead.

Only his liver would survive, and the tree would, too, but his soul would not. This morning had been a futile dream, and taking Ryllis to that special place up the mountain had been a mistake, but for a brief moment, he'd felt alive. He'd felt happy. He'd felt—well, something that he hadn't felt in years. Not since Elise. And he'd been almost certain Ryllis had felt it too.

And then he'd seen the knife. Then she'd had to bring him back to real life by reminding him who she was and who he was.

He pulled himself to his feet and began to search through the bushes for it. He could guess where Ryllis had found it, and Lina would be none too thrilled when he informed her that she'd have to start counting cutlery.

Lina.

He jumped up as her footsteps echoed across the pavers through the rain.

"What happened?" she asked, adjusting the hood of her raincoat. "She came out of your office, shaking and pale. Wouldn't tell me what was wrong. And now you—are you drunk, sir?"

He waved away her concern about his liver. "Wouldn't tell you what was wrong, would she?"

Lina shook her head.

So he told her, starting with his and Ryllis's walk, how she'd laughed at him and made him warm inside, the waterfall, how his heart had nearly stopped when she went sliding down the granite.

About the knife.

"She tried to kill me," he finished petulantly. His mind heard how peevish he sounded, but he couldn't stop himself.

Lina gave him a patronizing smile. "Did she? And it never occurred to you it's unlikely she's capable of that? Look at her. Look at you. Look at the training you've had. You could snap her neck with one hand and your eyes closed. She never had a chance, and I suspect she knew it."

"Do not dare defend her!" Lina didn't flinch, and a better excuse sprang into his head. "She could be a plant, Lina. A Cereth rebel sent here to kill me. Maybe that was her plan all along. I had to protect myself."

"Do you hear yourself?" She crossed her arms and sighed, and he felt like a wayward child. Lina and the thirty-odd years she had on him always had a talent for making him feel that way. "You sound paranoid."

Sullen, he tossed back the rest of his glass. "And you sound naïve. She could very well be an assassin."

"The vodka has addled your brain, Your Highness. If that woman was a Cereth rebel sent here to assassinate you, you'd be dead already. She'd had dropped you the very second you told her who you were."

Kresten opened his mouth. Tried to pour the empty glass into it.

Dakk.

Lina was right. And he'd let Ryllis get into his mind so badly that'd he stopped thinking like a Fleet officer and started thinking like a—well, that didn't matter, any longer. After what he'd done, Ryllis was no longer the woman who'd taken his hand and laughed at him and said he was just as human as anyone else. She was the girl kneeling on the rug in his office in tears, begging him to kill her because she couldn't stand to be on his planet—in his presence—one more second.

"Lina." The vodka made him bold. "I threatened to kill her. She must have been terrified, and she —she told me to do it. She hates being here so much that she would rather die, and there is nothing I can do to make that better for her. Even if I defied the Eradication Council, even if I defied my father, what good would it do? If I financed a luxury cruiser back to Cereth for her, she'd be in danger. And I can't allow that."

Lina stood there, the rain dripping down off her hood, dispassionate. The door charms jingled as he stared at her. It couldn't be Ryllis, but when Kresten swiveled toward the noise, there she stood underneath the portico. Her expression was flat, and her eyes were red, and he decided he couldn't look at her.

"Lina, please," he said. The vodka hadn't given him the courage it promised, for now he was panicking. "Tell me what to do."

"You got yourself into this situation, sir," Lina said. "You can get yourself out of it. I suggest you start by considering why her actions made you so angry." She disappeared inside as he stood there silent, giving Ryllis a pat on her shoulder as she did. Kresten stared at her, unable to move.

Because she was afraid of me, and she shouldn't have been.

Because while I was baring my soul, she was thinking about killing me.

Because my training kicked in and I couldn't stop myself.

He had dozens of excuses—but they were only excuses, and he knew it.

Ryllis took another few steps toward him, into the rain, then stopped. "Your Highness, I'm so—"

"Don't." She went so pale at his order that he almost ran to her, but he stopped himself just in time. "Don't apologize. It is I who should be doing so."

"I wanted to hurt you." Her eyes were bright, but she didn't cry as she stepped out from under the portico into the rain. "I am sorry for that. I could tell you how much pain I've felt, that I didn't feel I had any other choice, but I have no excuse."

"Ryllis, you have nothing to be sorry for. You may have wanted to do it, but you didn't."

She brushed the water from her face. "I would have. I wanted to, so badly. I was waiting for the right time, and then you—you were so kind up there on the mountain that I forgot what I intended to do."

That strange warm feeling slunk through his belly, and he was certain it wasn't the vodka this time. "I hope I can keep being that kind. Not for myself. For you. You deserve—"

Ryllis began to shiver. "I tried to hurt you. Wanted to kill you. I deserve nothing."

She had no idea, did she? She deserved everything beautiful and good, and she would never see it now, not on Vilaria. Not anywhere, not any longer. The snare they'd both been caught in made him want to scream, made him want to throw something, anything. Instead, he took a deep breath. What he was going to do was cruel and harsh, and it would hurt more than almost anything she'd experienced so far— but it was the only thing left.

He was going to call her on her lie.

"And you believe that lie so fervently that you decided you'd rather die than live here, don't you?" he asked.

And it was his fault.

Ryllis jerked her head up at that. He saw it there, in her eyes and the way she held herself—the awful truth. The truth that she hadn't even known, perhaps, and didn't want to admit now. But he knew. He knew, and it wasn't that maddening heightened empathy this time, though there was some of that, too. It was because she spoke to his soul and didn't even realize it.

"That's right. I know why you did it. You think that would make everything better, but you're wrong. Death won't fix anything—it ends only life. It's not what you want. Do you understand me?"

"Your Highness—"

"There's no argument to be had." She wasn't listening to him, and he was growing frantic now, could feel it in the way his neck was tensing and his gut was twisting. "Promise me you won't ever try anything like this again. Promise me, Ryllis. They will hurt you if you do, and even I won't be able to protect you."

"I can't promise that."

By the stars, he loved her spirit and her backbone, but if she didn't stop arguing, he would lock her in a small room until he didn't need to worry about her anymore.

"No argument. Swear to me." He hated giving her an order, but the very idea of watching her die for what she'd done made him ill. "Or I—I won't allow you alone in the garden any longer. You'll bring my tea each morning, and then you'll sit at my feet in my office and wait until I need something else from you."

Her eyes widened. That had done it. He didn't just hate what he'd said, he hated himself as well. But it'd worked, and the relief was more important than his guilt.

"I won't swear anything to you, prince or not. I told myself that when you brought me here— the only thing I have left is my word, and you're not getting that, too. But I promise I won't try to kill myself." Ryllis swayed on her feet as she spoke, slowly, like each word required effort.

He narrowed his eyes. "You're injured, aren't you? Where?"

She shook her head, even as she lifted her foot just a hair off the ground, probably hoping he couldn't see. "I'm not. I'm fine."

"You're lying. How bad does it hurt?" She shivered harder as he approached her, and he hated himself for it. Whether it was the fall down the granite boulders or from when he'd thrown her to the floor didn't matter. He'd done this. Not the blood he saw around the hem of her pants, but he'd hurt her, in every other way.

"Not badly." She bit her bottom lip. "It's my wrist. And my ankle. I think I twisted it when I fell down the rocks, but just tell me where I can find a medical kit, and I'll take care of it."

"No. That's not going to happen."

He wound an arm around behind her back, then, meeting no resistance, slid the other under her knees. Something strange sparked in her expression, and she stiffened at the contact at first but relaxed into him as he lifted her. By the stars, but holding her felt good, even though she was trembling and half frozen. He wanted to stand here, just like this, even with the rain, but the way her lips were turning purple meant he needed to get her inside.

If only the trip to his room wasn't so brief. With the greatest reluctance, he laid her on the floor and propped her against one of the chairs, then stuck a pillow behind her head and a few more under her ankle. While Ryllis stared at him, wide-eyed, he retreated to the bathroom to find the medical kit.

"You shouldn't be doing this for me," she said.

"Why ever not?"

Kresten set the kit next to her and switched on the fireplace. Fixing her ankle wouldn't matter if she froze to death right in front of him. The glowing embers sparked immediately, and he twisted back toward her. She was staring at him, and judging by the way she turned her face, she had been for some time.

"Because—"

"I knew you wouldn't have a good answer for that," he interrupted as he knelt beside her. With all the gentleness he could muster, he lifted the hem of her pants leg. Her ankle was swollen at least twice the size of the other, and a long gash ran down the side of her leg.

And he'd hurt her further, out of nothing more than anger and fear. The influence of the vodka was gone now, leaving him sick.

"Your Highness—"

"Kresten."

"That would be inappropriate." Ryllis flushed. "You are my enemy. I am your prisoner."

"Enemy? I doubt your enemy would be healing your sprained ankle in front of his bedroom fireplace."

Her cheeks grew redder. "A prince, then. And I am still your slave."

Realm's sake, he needed her. He dropped his focus to the cut, lest she recognize the look in his eyes. Shadow Force ought to be grateful for his service. Most of them had no idea the kind of sacrifice required when someone like Ryllis was right in front of them.

"A prince serves his people," he murmured as he wiped the blood away. "All of them."

"You forget I am Cerethian."

"And you forget my father also rules Cereth."

Ryllis struggled a bit more upright and looked out the window. The storm had to be right over the lodge now, and the torrents of rain outside darkened the room, making her eyes almost black.

"I have never forgotten that, Your Highness," she said softly.

"I wish you weren't here, either," he said, attaching the leads of the pad around her ankle. How long would he have to bear her pain? "Do you know that? I wish you were home on Cereth, growing wine or researching fertilizer or whatever it is a horticulturist does. I wish you'd gotten that work permit, and I wish—"

He'd almost said it.

I wish your father hadn't turned you in.

"I wish you were happy, too," he said, stumbling over the truth. "I would do anything to make you happy."

He hadn't known how true that last was until he spoke the longing. The little sparks of happiness he'd seen were a taste of something he—and she —could never have.

"Send me home."

"Ryllis." He switched on the box and moved next to her. She was still shivering, and her clothes were still soaked, so he pulled the blanket from the nearest armchair around her. "Let me see the wrist."

She offered her hand with tentative grace, and his body threatened to rebel against proprieties when he brushed his fingers against her soft skin. Ryllis looked toward the rain, but he could tell from the flush that wouldn't go away that it wasn't because he was hurting her.

"I want to send you home. I wish I could. But the Council—even if I did, you'd end up right back here. And not with me. Worse, certainly. Thinking of you in that situation makes me sick."

He dropped his gaze to her hand again. Her wrist was only bruised where she'd landed on it. Reluctantly, he released her, and she immediately brushed her cheeks with her palm.

"It does?" she whispered.

He nodded.

She shivered again.

"You need to get into some dry clothes." He checked the timer on her ankle, grateful to the excuse to look away. "I'm sorry—I should have let you change first. Another half hour, though."

"I'll be fine." Ryllis gave him a half-hearted smile. "I once got frostbite checking some vines for rot before they were harvested late. Turns out I just don't do cold well."

"Yeah? Why didn't you tell me that before I dragged you outside to watch the flurries?"

She smiled, and Kresten readjusted the blanket around her and edged just a bit closer. Why was he so afraid? He might be involuntarily chaste for the most part, but after four years of idyllic marriage, he was hardly inexperienced. And by all rights and laws of the Vilarian Star Realm, if it hadn't been for his bothersome oath, he would be allowed to do what he wanted with her.

He knew the answer to his self-control, of course.

"Ryllis?" he asked.

She looked up at him, questioning.

"I can't watch you like this anymore. You're making me cold. Come here."

She couldn't, of course, not without dislodging the pillows under her ankle, so he scooted closer to her, lifted the blanket, then rewrapped it around them both. Ryllis went rigid, like when he'd first picked her up outside.

"I'm warming you up," he said. "Nothing more."

"You could have found another few blankets to do that," she said, reproach tinging the suggestion.

"Is that what you want? Another few blankets?"

Please say no.

Ryllis opened her mouth, then shut it. She looked out the window, like it was a way to escape, then stared at the fire.

"No," she said, so quietly he could barely hear her. "I don't want another blanket. But this—"

"Is just warmth. That's all." But how he wanted more. So much more.

"Really?" she asked, focusing on him. "That's all?"

It was disappointment he heard, despite her earlier protest. Not innocence, despite her wide-eyed look, and not coyness. Even without reading her mind, after knowing her for as long as he had, he knew. Kresten pushed himself back toward her, and this time she didn't move, didn't stiffen, didn't pull away. Just stared. He wrapped his near arm around her, drawing her against him the best he could without moving her leg, then let his other hang loosely across her.

Ryllis's head settled against his shoulder and he held his breath, afraid he'd break the spell she'd put him under if he moved. Slowly, as he became chilled from the frost of her body, she stilled.

"You were right," she said after a few minutes of watching the fire. "This is better than a blanket."

He risked moving his free hand to stroke her cheek and gave a short laugh. "Believe it or not, me being right does happen every so often. And I do love hearing someone else say it."

A noticeable shiver ran through her at his touch.

"I thought you weren't cold anymore." Kresten traced a few gentle circles on her skin, just to watch her tremble. How could such a movement affect him like this? It was intoxicating, in a delightful manner the vodka hadn't been able to match. "I think you lied to me."

Ryllis looked up at him from behind the longest lashes he'd ever seen. "Whatever could have given you that idea, Your Highness?"

It was all he could do to keep his jaw from falling open in shock. She hadn't looked at him with the fear he was all too used to, she hadn't sniped at him about Cereth or the Star Realm, she hadn't reverted to the flat expression that always killed him. She had *flirted.*

He pulled back and gave her a look of mock horror to cover his desire. "Lying to a prince of Vilaria is considered just as uncouth as laughing at him, you know. I could throw you in the dungeon for that." He furrowed his brow. "If I had one."

Ryllis burst out laughing.

By the stars.

He didn't know what kind of reaction he'd been expecting from her, but it hadn't been this. His heart swelled at the sound of her happiness, all sunshine and birdsong and joy. He wanted to kiss her. On her ears, on her lips, on her neck, on her collarbone, on her—

You are going to make yourself insane.

He settled for the only proper thing he could do. "Your laughter is beautiful," he said. "I hope you let me hear it again soon."

Her smile fell. "You're not the first to say so."

"And?" She'd said there hadn't been anyone on Cereth, but perhaps she'd lied. Maybe he'd taken her away from him, too.

Ryllis squeezed her eyes closed.

"Ryllis, what—"

"I've betrayed them," she said, hunching over as far as she could manage with her leg in front of her. "I can't do that."

"By—"

He didn't finish the question. It was all too clear. Merely being happy, if even for the briefest of moments, must be devastating for her. The snarling and fear and revulsion—those were comfortable. They meant she saw him as the enemy, and as long as he was such, she had a chance at changing her circumstances. Accepting them? Letting herself admit there might be a life waiting for her off Cereth? Laughing was the first step toward that, and, he knew, that was the last thing she wanted.

"You're allowed to be happy."

Ryllis shook her head, furiously.

"It doesn't mean you don't miss home, or that you want to be here. It just means you found something worth living for, even if it's nothing more than a joke. And I promise you there will be more jokes, more happiness, more things to live for."

"I'm not sure I'll ever be able to believe that," she whispered.

His promise had fallen flat, he could tell. He would work on that happiness, later, when she wasn't half frozen and upset.

"I'm going to have Lina make you some tea." He sighed at the thought of moving away from her. "Don't get up. I'll come back and move you to the bed when the machine is done. And then you're going to rest, no arguments about it."

"No." Ryllis pressed against him. "Please don't go. This is—" She looked away and chewed on her lip before continuing. "I think this might be one of those things. Please stay. I'd rather have you than tea."

Her invitation—unexpectantly audacious and oh so welcome—was all he needed. Carefully, keeping her leg straight, he turned her to her side and laid her head in his lap. Her eyes flickered closed when he settled his palm on her head, and as he stroked his thumb across her temple, thrilling at her warmth, he realized just how much trouble he was in.

CHAPTER NINE

*K*resten placed the chip in his wrist against the decoder on his computer and keyed in his authorization code. The computer came to life, running through the list of messages unread since the last time he'd bothered to check.

It had been almost two lunar cycles since Ryllis had arrived, almost two lunar cycles since he'd pretended to do a modicum of work. Oh, sure, he questioned her here and there, but he never pushed very hard. She'd know something was amiss if he did, and then what would be the point? She spoke more to him every day, and that was a step in the right direction—even if her discussion was about such innocuous things as the harvest timing in Therus, her father's fear of not being elected during the next governor cycle, or the fact she still had nightmares about how she couldn't move her body while they'd jumped. Kresten had done his best to combat those nightmares, certain he felt them himself some nights.

That was nonsense, of course. The only nightmares he experienced were his own.

He'd cut off her hair for the sixth time last night, and at last there had been only a few tears from her, though the bottle of spiced vodka he kept in his desk had been considerably less full afterward. How else was he supposed to deal with the look of anguish she'd favored him with before retreating to bed? Perhaps she could be trusted to do it herself in the future, because he was, apparently, too weak to handle upsetting her.

Kresten shook off the thought of her tears and turned his attention to the comms. Three lunar cycles of leave after an interstellar mission of any length was policy, and though he was only two-thirds of the way through his time, the real world never stopped because one officer was on leave. No one in Shadow Force took the allotted amount.

His eyes landed on one message—not marked urgent, because that wasn't how Major Dahl did things—but for his boss to contact him on leave, it had to be important. He almost dreaded opening it.

Lieutenant Westermark,

I trust you had a good trip back. Colonel Löfgren is looking for a report. I know you're busy, but give him some kind of status, okay? I'm tired of fending off questions.

Major Ivar Dahl

Tapping his fingers on the desk, Kresten closed that one. It could have been much worse. It could have also been better. He'd known Dahl long enough to know that the breezy, casual tone of the message was anything but. Löfgren, he knew, was simply curious; Dahl was wondering just what was going on with Ryllis— and he would never let that question go.

The next message caught his eye as he was debating how to tell Colonel Löfgren he had absolutely no update whatsoever. It had been, sent, it appeared, while he'd been reading Dahl's.

Kresten,

I hear you're back on Vilaria, even if you ran right off to the mountains and couldn't be bothered to come say hello to your cherished family. I also hear you have a new slave. This I have to see. Tomorrow, say? I still like Cerethian sweet wine, so I hope you remembered me.

Vidar

Kresten wanted to reach for his own bottle of vodka that very second. Disaster. This was a disaster. His second eldest brother and his network of family spies had found out about

Ryllis somehow—likely the food orders, so different from his usual meals, had raised questions. Or maybe Lina had talked, though it wasn't as though anyone ever contacted Vidar on purpose. Well, however it'd happened, his quiet solitude and slow mission was about to shattered by the member of the imperial family who cared the most about tradition and laws and putting outworlders in their place. Ryllis would have a panic attack when he told her.

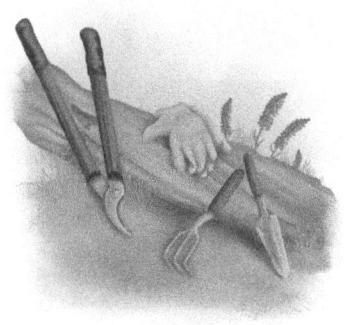

He found her in the garden, an old jacket around her shoulders and a trowel in her hand. Iria had fought her assistance when he'd first learned the gardens had been turned over to her, at least for the summer, but even the old gardener had finally admitted her worth when he'd last stopped by to check on things—none of his employees he sent to various locations in the hillside were interested in hearing his stories for the thousandth time, while Ryllis, he told Kresten, listened with rapt attention while she dug.

This afternoon she was alone, though, and Kresten gave a short cough so he didn't startle her. She hesitated for a moment and brushed her hand across her eyes, then turned and smiled faintly at him. Her skin was pale, too much for someone who spent as much time outside as she did. It was clear she'd had a bad night.

He should have expected it. He could forbid her from crying in front of him when he cut her hair, but he wasn't so cold-hearted as to ban it entirely. From the way she looked, she'd made the most of her isolation afterward.

"The dove-worts haven't been growing like they should," she said by way of greeting. "I dug one up to see what was going on and half the roots were frozen, so I'm going to move some of the youngest ones to the greenhouse until it warms up a bit more. I transplanted them a bit too early, I suppose. Iria says it's silly, that they need to acclimate to the weather in order to survive, but I want to see them flourish. So what if they need a little help to do it?"

Kresten couldn't help but smile, more at how she didn't seem to realize what she'd said than at how the garden looked better than it ever did so early in the season.

"Then the greenhouse is where they need to go. We all can use a little help sometimes. Though"—he glanced around—"you've worked a miracle here already. It's beautiful."

He wasn't exaggerating. Iria had started an assortment of bulbs in the small greenhouse over the past winter, but Ryllis had planted them. She must have an eye for this sort of thing, because with apparently little effort, she'd recreated an untamed mountain meadow right here behind his lodge. Sunshine glinted off heavy cones of pines, and the scent of early honeysuckle drifted on the breeze. He wanted to park himself here under the blossoming trees and never leave.

Ryllis turned even paler at his compliment. "Yes. Perhaps I can convince Iria of that." She frowned at him. "But something's wrong."

"It's not you. At all." He couldn't decide if her recent aptitude at reading his expressions was an advantage or not. "But we need to talk, unfortunately."

She brushed the dirt from her hands, still frowning. He sank on to one of the lounge cushions and she sat next to him, almost shaking, the questions in her eyes. Too late, he remembered what *we need to talk* would mean to someone in her situation. Would she think she'd displeased him? That he meant to send her away?

Curse Vidar for making me to do this.

"One of my brothers is visiting tomorrow," he said.

Her breath hitched. "Oh."

Kresten wanted to wrap his arms around her. He'd just turned the one safe place she had into something else she needed to fear. Barely, just barely, he managed to restrain himself.

"It was bound to happen, sooner rather than later. He usually stays away from the lodge —it's far too provincial for him—but he—"

"Heard about me?"

"Yes."

At least one of them was relieved, as ashamed as he was that she'd done his thankless task for him. A mid-grade officer of the Vilarian Imperial Fleet shouldn't be afraid of giving someone bad news.

Then why did he care?

Kresten shoved the question away to debate in bed that night.

"And?" she asked.

"And he's coming to call me a hypocrite, I'm certain. And to leer at you, though that's not something he'll get away with." It was a blunt assessment of his brother, but Ryllis needed to be prepared. "I'm not thrilled about it, but there's no way I can avoid it."

"Which means I can't avoid it either, can I?"

He shook his head. "Vidar is—well, let's call him determined."

"Then I will survive."

As I have before, he could have sworn he heard floating on the breeze. She didn't seem inclined to say much else, and he pointed up the mountain.

"Care for a walk?"

Ryllis picked at a paver that was flaking apart. "I don't know, Your Highness."

They hadn't been up since That Afternoon, as Kresten had taken to calling it in his mind and he couldn't blame her for her reluctance. Eventually, sometime far in the future, he'd take her back there, and she'd see the beauty instead of the bad memories, but that would be a long time from now. She needed to heal, needed to learn to trust him, and that was something he couldn't rush, as much as he wished he could.

"Not the waterfall," he said. "But Lina and Aared live just up the way, and they have these hens that I think—"

"The hens? She's told me about them. And"—Ryllis's eyes lit up—"that you're afraid of being attacked."

"Well." Would she think less of him if he looked afraid? Probably. He pushed the thoughts of their sharp beaks from his mind. Having Ryllis tend to him if they mauled him again wouldn't be the worst thing in the world, especially if she did it while looking at him like this. "Perhaps you should meet them before mocking me over that."

"Perhaps I should." Ryllis laughed. "Let me change first, Your Highness . . . then let's go for a walk."

The well-worn trail to Lina's house looped through a meadow instead of the dense forest Ryllis had expected, and Westermark's house was never out of sight as they made their way up. The spring weather wasn't as warm as she'd expected, but the sun felt good on her face. She'd become used to the static fields protecting the windows in her room, but it meant they didn't open, and the lack of a fresh breeze was one more thing she missed about Cereth. It was partly why she spent most of the time in the garden, as risky as that was. She never stayed in one area of the garden for very long and, except for very short trips to gather supplies, kept out of the greenhouse that contained the young plants. It was the young ones which were the most responsive to her power and always had been.

Kresten chattered at they walked, her arm on his, pointing out the early wildflowers and spring lilies that didn't seem to mind the fact the snow had just recently disappeared. Ryllis cataloged them all in her mind—there was an unused side garden near the mansion she hadn't yet touched, and Westermark wouldn't object if she worked in it when she was finished with the courtyard. The natural look of the meadow would be beautiful there if she could properly recreate it.

"This trail is partly why I shut the place up when I'm gone, especially in the winter,"

Kresten said as he helped her over a small ditch. "Lina doesn't need to be hiking through here in the snow."

"I'd imagine not. How long has she been with you?"

"Since my age of majority, when I inherited this place. I came up here to see it, took one look at it, and decided there was no way I could make all the necessary repairs before I left for the academy. The next time I visited on a break, well, I couldn't believe it. My mother had been here and met Lina prowling around the mountains, and between the two of them and a whole lot of contractors, they'd made it beautiful."

It hadn't ever occurred to her that Kresten had a mother. It was a strange thought. "Does your— the empress still visit?"

"No. She's rather ill. Intractable dementia." He glanced at her, and she couldn't read the look in his eyes. "She scarcely knows me anymore, and visiting usually makes things worse for her. Kresten is her baby, not a man."

"I'm sorry."

"It's all right. I was the youngest, and I don't think there was ever a time I didn't see her as elderly. It's why she and Lina got on so fabulously."

"And Lina just stayed on all this time."

"It works for her. She and Aared love the mountains and will live out the rest of their time here, but she also loves having her hands busy. Judging by the way she watches down the hill for the lights to turn back on, I think she lives for the day I show up again—and dreads the day I leave."

An uncomfortable emotion she couldn't identify right away sank in the meadow, dulling the spring blooms. Westermark was too caught up in his own plans to notice the change in their luster, but she wasn't.

He would leave this place.

Of course he would. He had a career that required he be off-world more than he was home. He had family of the worst kind, somewhere in Carilles, the capital of Vilaria, and they wouldn't let him camp out here forever. And when he was forced to return to his real life? The uncomfortable feeling turned to panic. Would he take her with him when he left? Loan her to someone else in the imperial family? Or, perhaps, would he send her to Carilles, to one of the numerous palaces there, to work the laundry machines or in the kitchens, far away from this lovely meadow?

"When will that be?" she asked, hoping she sounded idly curious.

"I have another lunar cycle of leave," he said, shoving his hands in his pockets. "And no one has pressed me for a visit yet. They know I need the recovery time."

"And then?"

What will happen to me?

"I report to Fleet headquarters in Arvika."

The sun suddenly seemed so much hotter. Was it better to be taken to some Vilarian Fleet base where her circumstances would be visible to dozens of Fleet officers? Life was bearable enough now that dying was no longer at the forefront of her mind, but the very idea made her want to hide in her room and never come out. No one could survive that kind of humiliation.

Only on Vilaria, they were forced to.

"Your Highness—"

He chuckled. "Don't look so anxious. You'll come with me, of course. I have a flat there. There aren't any gardens, but I have space for some pots. Anything you want."

It was an answer, but was it the answer she wanted?

"That doesn't please you?" he asked when she didn't reply.

Ryllis focused on her feet and the damp earth underneath them. "Does it matter what pleases me?"

"Of course it does."

"Just not enough." She looked up at his face, twisted in confusion. "That was a rhetorical statement. It doesn't require an explanation or cursory argument from you. I know where I stand."

"Legally, perhaps." He took her hand and pulled her to a stop. "But do you know where you stand with me?"

"Beyond a doubt. I've known since I realized that my father is governor in name only. Nothing but the desires of the Star Realm and its imperial masters matter—we conquered ones do not, especially on planets like Cereth. We are only to yield unquestioningly to whatever is ordered of us, and if that demand is slavery, well—we yield to that, too, without any argument. It's always been that way. I know how the galaxy works."

"Ryllis."

Her eyes began to burn, and she ducked her head so he couldn't see the tears. It wasn't anger in his voice. She'd wanted anger, not pain, and certainly not guilt. But anymore, anger wasn't Westermark, and she couldn't fight someone who treated her with kindness like he had over the past few lunar quarters. She tried to pull her hand away, but he held firm.

"No," she said, brushing her cheeks dry. "Fine. I suppose I don't know. I thought at first you meant to force yourself on me. I know it happens. We all know. And you'd been on

Cereth for such an extended time, your wife gone so long . . . Then I thought perhaps you were trying to seduce me, make me believe it was my idea, so I'd give in easier, and you could assuage any guilt you felt about what you were doing. The way you looked at me in the snow and the way you comfort me after I've had a nightmare—it doesn't make any sense, and that was the only explanation I could come up with. Only you haven't touched me like that, ever. When you do, it's respectful and warm and kind and exactly when I need it. You let me while away my time in the gardens, where I want to be more than anywhere except Cereth, and you somehow act like this is a normal situation for a prince with a slave he doesn't seem to need."

"You make me happy," he said. "You always have, from the very first day I laid eyes on you. Why wouldn't I want to do the same for you?"

Ryllis looked away from him, out toward the mountain. He put his palm on her cheek and drew her face back toward him. His touch flooded her with warmth, a strange feeling on this unprotected and breezy hillside. She should have hated him for manipulating her emotions, but instead she hated herself for feeling the way she felt.

"Listen to me," he said. "Lina was shocked when she saw you that first morning at breakfast. And she reacted that way because she knows I've never used slaves since I reached my age of majority, indentured or otherwise. I barely use servants. You've probably already figured out that I misled you before about the house being filled with them—she's the only one here now that Iria is retired for good, and at my flat in Arvika, it's just me. I like it that way, the quiet and the solitude, but I enjoy your company more. So much more."

He ran his thumb down her neck, and the meadow grew warmer. Over his shoulder, the snowdrops grew more vivid. Ryllis closed her eyes. The flowers didn't understand. Westermark couldn't be making her this happy —could he?

"Even so, if you don't wish to accompany me to Arvika, I won't force you—and the idea of sending you to the palace in Carilles never crossed my mind, if that's what you're worried about. Lina would be thrilled for the company if you stayed here, and I would survive by imagining your smile. I'd miss you more than you could ever imagine if you chose that option, but I suspect you'd have too much to do here to feel the same about me—I expect that wild, overgrown garden will be a paradise when I return."

It was a bit of her self-sovereignty back, and Ryllis wanted to throw herself at him and kiss both his cheeks for the unexpected compassion. She pried his hand off her face instead and gave it a squeeze.

"Can I think about it?" she asked. Suddenly, with a sliver of long-desired freedom right in front of her, she wasn't sure she wanted it. Was it the mountain she wanted—or was it him?

"Until the very second that shuttle departs with me on it. Now," he said with a smile, "let's go see these chickens."

CHAPTER TEN

*A*ared greeted them with a wave when the house came into view, a leaf green wooden thing with steeply angled sides that met on the top to shunt off the heavy winter snows. The front was almost completely covered in tinted windows, the large front deck swathed in pots filled with whatever Lina could grow this high up. Kresten had always loved it for its mountain charm, from the very first time he'd visited.

The chickens? Well, the chickens were another story, but there were only a few in front pecking at the spring ground. They looked too busy to harass him. Kresten waved at Aared in return, deftly sidestepping a trio of hens as he came down the stairs to greet them.

"Your Highness." Aared nodded respectfully, but his eyes were on Ryllis. "And Ryllis. My dear, Lina severely understated how lovely you are. But come, come. I'll make you some tea—it's cooling off, and we wouldn't want the ladies to peck the prince to death."

Her laughter rang out as they followed Aared inside, and Kresten poked a finger in her ribs.

"You just wait," he said, "until they lay their beady little eyes on you. Keep laughing at me, and I won't bother coming to your rescue when they do."

"It's a good thing, then," she retorted, sitting next to him on the sofa in the main room, "that I can handle myself among a bunch of birds."

"Not these. You have no idea."

She laughed again and turned her attention to Aared. He waved off her offer of help with the tea and eyed them both while he bustled about the open kitchen. "It's been a long while, Your Highness."

"I was on Cereth for almost a solar cycle."

"Ah." Aared focused on Ryllis for a moment and frowned. "Right."

"Aared," Ryllis said, "tell me about the hens. I hear His Highness is . . ."

"Terrified of them?" Aared chuckled. "Yes. Six years ago, he was visiting, and for some reason, offered to take the feed out to them."

"And they attacked me." He could still feel their beaks breaking through his skin, could still hear how he'd hollered at Aared like a child.

"The prince slipped in the mud," Aared said, ignoring him. "The feed went flying, and they came running, naturally. Only they were a little confused about what was food and what was royalty."

"You can say that again." Kresten glanced at Ryllis, who looked horrified and amused at the same time.

"We *did* get rid of the roosters after that," Aared said. "It was the least we could do—and you didn't argue about dinner that night, either."

"Too little, too late. I still have scars, believe it or not." He hitched up his pant leg and pointed. "Seven years in the Fleet, and the only marks I have to show for all my pain are from a bunch of birds."

Aared shrugged and placed two cups of tea before them. "And how is the Fleet drudgery going?"

Next to him, Ryllis reached for her tea like nothing was wrong, but he felt her tense more than he saw it. He couldn't blame her for not wanting to hear about the Fleet. "Nothing new to report. You know how it is. Drudgery is drudgery."

"Except for Cereth."

His blood chilled. After so long, it was obvious when he was being questioned. But Aared was no threat. Just curious—a quality he'd picked up from his wife.

"It was a routine deployment," he said.

"Not so routine, it seems." Aared picked up his own cup. "You returned with a slave."

"I did."

"Then all your pretty talk about freedom and autonomy was just that?"

He should have known his straightforwardness would come back to bite him. Well, better a hypocrite than Aared and Lina—and Ryllis!—

knowing his secret. He was behind enough questioning her as it was, and that would bring things to a screeching halt.

No. You've brought things to a screeching halt yourself.

"Really, Aared," he said. "Could you at least have the decency to not question my decisions to my face? Especially in front of her?"

"I'm not questioning anything, Your Highness. I'm simply perplexed at the change in you."

Kresten looked at Ryllis again. She'd clutched the tea in her hands like it was about to be torn away from her, and her lips were pressed closed, like she wanted to say something but couldn't trust herself to stay silent.

"There's nothing to be perplexed about," he said. "We've eradicated thousands from various planets over the years. You know that. I knew Ryllis on Cereth, and I wasn't about to subject her to who knows what kind of future when I had the opportunity to bring her here. It seemed like the best option for all concerned."

"Knew her? I'd assumed she was assigned to you when you arrived on-world."

"In the prison." Ryllis's shaky voice cut in. "He was one of the guards. And he—he was good to me, as much as he was allowed. He gave me hope and has continued to do so since I arrived."

Kresten couldn't believe what he was hearing, but she'd never talked of those lunar cycles in front of him before now. She spoke to her hands, but even so, it sounded like she was defending him—or maybe thanking him.

Aared raised his eyebrows. "Ah," he said. "Of course. Sometimes I forget what he does off-world. That does sound like His Highness."

"And yes," Kresten added, "I requested her when we arrived on Vilaria. Why wouldn't I? Is that clear enough?"

"It is, Your Highness." Aared turned toward Ryllis. "What do you think of the Kebnekaise Mountains?"

"They're cold," she said, after a short look at Kresten. "But beautiful."

She didn't look as flat as her voice sounded, and she didn't look lifeless, but she didn't look happy, either. Kresten didn't blame her. He wasn't all that pleased, either. It was too bad grabbing her hand in front of Aared was out of the question—not that there was a chance Lina had kept her observations to herself. Aared likely knew of the furtive glances, how they brushed fingertips, and how Ryllis ate in the kitchen with him every night.

"Has he told you about the cave behind the house?"

She shook her head. "The cave? No."

His chance. Had Aared given it to him on purpose? Kresten stood. "I think I'll do that now, if you don't mind. If you'll excuse us. . ."

Aared nodded, even though Kresten could feel his stare on his back as he led Ryllis outside. He stopped her on the back deck after they'd escaped out the door.

"I'm sorry about that," he said. "I should have known, should have warned you. Aared is a little too forthright for his own good."

"He was just curious," she said.

"Yes. This way." He pointed out toward the tree with the misshapen limbs. "But he hurt you."

"He is Vilarian." Ryllis darted away from a chicken that had made its way around the house. The bird squawked, then half flew, half jumped to a perch in a low bush and eyed them warily. "He can't help it."

"He should." He stuck his hands in his pockets and gave the ground a morose look. "I help it, don't I?"

She favored him with the cautious smile he'd come to expect when she meant to taunt him. "Most of the time."

"Ryllis!"

She laughed out loud at his mock exasperation and brushed another curious hen from their path. The bird scattered without protest, and

Kresten frowned at them both. "Don't tell me the chickens love you, too."

His face went red in horror, but he caught himself before he stumbled to the ground in humiliation. Maybe she hadn't heard him. Maybe she'd forget immediately. Maybe he hadn't completely humiliated himself.

Ryllis froze for the briefest moment, her fingers at her throat, then recovered. "They know you're afraid of them, Your Highness. They'll take advantage of that. They won't follow us into the cave, will they? If you think they might, we can just head back now."

"No." He felt like gasping for air—or digging a hole and burying himself in it. "They're curious, but they won't stray that far from their food."

"How far is it to the cave?"

"A fifteen-minute walk."

"It's nice weather for it."

Kresten wanted to hug for her letting his blunder go. He couldn't love her. He barely knew her, and not a single Vilarian made the mistake of falling in love with an off-worlder, especially not from Cereth and the like. Well, it did happen, he supposed, but not among Fleet officers. Not among his family. He might enjoy her company and find her appearance pleasing and be thankful their paths had crossed, even in such a manner as they had, but he didn't love her.

Love isn't an emotion, and you've always been an expert at fooling yourself.

Elise's voice echoed in his head as clearly as it had when he'd been inside hers. Some things never changed, even her affectionate reproach. Was she right? Perhaps. Things between them hadn't always been easy—between his disclosure of his telepathy, his almost-pariah status in the imperial family, and the frequent partings due to his Fleet work, no one would have blamed them for going their separate ways. He and Elise had never entertained the thought, though.

Desperate to forget her memory, if even for a moment, he grabbed Ryllis's fingers by the tips. They swung their arms between them as they walked, even though his misgivings were growing by the second. Her touch calmed him, and more importantly, it reassured her that he wasn't angry, but this was a bad idea. The worst idea he'd ever had—if not only for him, for her. He couldn't lead her to believe they had a future together. He wouldn't hurt her like that.

"The entrance is just around this corner," he said. "It goes fairly deep, but without a light, we'll need to stay by the entrance."

He pointed her toward the hole in the rocks, surrounded by gnarled trees and the ever-present ferns. Ryllis hopped across the last few roots covering the trail and stared up at the ceiling.

"It doesn't look that big," she said.

"Not from here." A few drops of water dripped on the back of his neck when he joined her, and he suppressed a shiver. "But if you turn right after that large pink vein of granite, you can get lost. There's a cavern about a hundred paces down that passageway, and if we'd planned better, we could have visited. But not now."

"Getting lost doesn't sound appealing."

"No." He smiled. "I used to come up here when I didn't want Lina to find me at the waterfall. I bet there are still cans of water back there."

"Let's not find out." Ryllis brushed the water off his neck and smiled back.

By the stars. Her silhouette, dark in the backlight illumination of the cave's entrance, sent flashes of something unfamiliar through his body, and her touch—he couldn't remember this kind of haziness in his mind. Ever. He took a step closer, and she didn't move as he reached a finger toward her cheek in a silent request for her blessing.

She met his eyes, licked her lips, and nodded, as if she'd understood him without words. Heart racing at the vulnerability and strength in her expression, he slid his free hand around her waist and drew her against him. He'd held her before, yes, but not like this. Her soft body fit against his perfectly, and unlike the night when she'd slept with her head on his lap, she was clean and warm and dry. His breath quickened as he watched her breathe, firing off a desperate longing he hadn't realized he possessed. Before he had the chance to think better of what he was about to do, he leaned in and gently tilted her head toward him.

She tasted better than he could have ever imagined, like pine and honey and yellow gold tea. He gripped her harder, unable to let go, and she sighed against his mouth. Her hands found the back of his neck, and suddenly she was running her fingers through his hair, returning his kiss with a ferocity he'd never expected. None of his dreams had prepared him for this.

He broke away after too short a time, certain his heart would explode if he didn't. Ryllis glanced at the dirt at the interruption, and he lifted her chin with a shaking finger. In the twilight of the cave, her eyes were dark, but the delight she'd tried to hide in whatever misplaced embarrassment she felt was unmistakable.

"I should regret that," he said with some difficulty. "But I don't."

She shook her head, looking almost dazed. "Will you regret it a second time?"

He didn't deserve her. With a smile that almost split his mouth, he lifted her onto a small ledge in the cave wall. At his height now, she cupped his face between her hands, and he had the futile thought that perhaps he should have shaved, but she didn't seem to mind. When she wrapped her legs around his waist, he knew.

"I doubt it," he replied. "But we should try once more, just to make sure."

She smiled at him, exquisite and shy, then her lips were on his again, warmer and gentler than before, like she'd quenched her desire the first time and could now linger as long as she wanted, savoring him. He wasn't nearly as satisfied, but he let her lead, reveling in the innocence of her touch. If only this could last forever. If only he could do it whenever he wanted. If only they could go further. If only—

Ryllis pulled back, then leaned her forehead against his. "I can scarcely breathe."

She had no idea. He caressed her cheek as he waited for his breath—and the rest of his body —to return to normal. "Me either. But if it's the choice between breathing well and you doing that to me, I know which one I'll choose, every time."

"Men are so predictable." Her laughter rang off the walls of the cave, light and breezy, as she closed her eyes and pressed her cheek to his. "I was afraid at first."

"Are you still?" When she didn't answer, he leaned back and looked into her eyes. The tears took him by surprise. "Ryllis? What's wrong?"

"I'm afraid that this was a mistake, perhaps."

"Oh, my darling star." He wiped off the tears, but she tilted her face away from him. "It wasn't a mistake."

"But I can't let myself feel anything for you," she said, more to herself than him, he suspected.

"Why not?" He chanced a smile—along with everything else. "Have you already forgotten what I asked about the chickens?"

Her cheeks grew red. "You didn't mean it."

"One doesn't accidentally lie." He knew that. Accidentally telling the truth was what got people in trouble. Accidentally lying? If it happened, he'd never seen it.

"If that's so"—her voice broke—"then perhaps it was you who made the mistake, Your Highness."

His chest tightened. "And you don't mean that."

"You may think you love me, but love isn't always enough. It's certainly not enough to overcome our realities. It's not enough to change who you are or how the Star Realm sees me"—her hand brushed across her scalp—"or that love born in our circumstance is hopeless from the start."

"I don't care about any of that," he said stubbornly. "I want you. And even though you won't admit it, I think you feel the same way."

"Are you used to always getting what you want?"

She couldn't possibly think—well, she did, and no surprise. But even outside of the oath, that wasn't him.

"I won't pressure you into anything. I swear it on my father's name. But can I ask that you not rebuff this immediately?"

Ryllis rested her head on his shoulder. "I care for you. I could love you, easily. But I refuse to be someone's secret—or worse, their mistress. I know what that means for my future, and while it breaks my heart to think of the years of loneliness ahead, I knew that was the outcome when I left Cereth. I've had plenty of time to accept my fate. I know you'll marry again, and that I'll be sent from your household to who knows where, and that you won't waste another second thinking of me after I leave."

She had no idea. She didn't understand, and he couldn't blame her for that. He could still feel her lips on his, and yet he wanted more. He wanted to tell her why having her as a mistress was never going to happen, that he wanted to wake up every morning next to her and see her brilliant smile beside him, that he could do whatever he wished with an Eradication Council slave, even free one, and that there wasn't any reason he couldn't marry her if she was cleared, if that was what she wanted.

But those dreams would mean breaking his cover. It would mean forcing her to talk, and if she confessed to the wrong things, her current standing would be academic, because he would lose her, anyway. She might lose her life.

For all this to work out? She'd have to be as innocent as she claimed, and what were the odds of that? He was caught now, trapped between his desire and his need to protect her.

"I won't accept that," he said.

"It's best if you accept it," she said, just as he was beginning to fantasize about running away and changing his name. "For both of us."

"What if you married me?"

He'd half expected her to laugh, but she went deathly pale instead. "Is this a joke?"

"No. No joke. If you won't be my mistress, be my wife."

"That's unfair to ask of me." Her voice shook. "You know I don't have the power to walk away from anything you propose. That's not love. It's —it's control. So please, don't suggest it."

Her answer, too logical and heartbreaking at the same time, broke the magic. Still, he couldn't help thinking that if she felt for him like he did for her, such things wouldn't matter.

He looked at the ground. "Then answer one question for me." He was burning with the need to know. "Can you ever love me?"

"Kresten." His heart sped up at what her use of his name had to mean to her, but when he looked up, there was nothing but sadness on her face. "Stars help, but . . . maybe I already do."

CHAPTER ELEVEN

*H*is brother swept into the hilltop mansion the next morning, scorning Lina's offer of tea. *Just the sweet wine, please,* he'd said when he arrived, and Kresten was so relieved at the rare use of the word *please* that he hadn't argued that getting drunk before breakfast was unbecoming of anyone, much less the emperor's second son. It was a waste of breath to argue with Vidar most of the time, and with his brother on some kind of mission, hopefully not assigned by the emperor himself . . . well, his only goal right now was to finish the visit and have Vidar depart as quickly as possible, leaving as little damage as possible behind him.

"So?" Vidar asked, perching on the hearth of the great room's fireplace, his glass of wine in hand. "Where is she?"

For some reason, his brother had chosen the hearth instead of the half dozen chairs scattered around, like he intended to spring away once his task was accomplished. Maybe the large stones that made up the chimney would collapse on him, running him and that ridiculous formal jacket off quicker. What kind of man wore silk to a rustic cabin in the mountains, anyway?

Kresten waved an idle finger over his shoulder at Lina in reply. No small talk after the Cereth assignment was disappointing, for family was family, and on some base level he did love Vidar. At the same time, it was the best he could have hoped for—Vidar would do whatever he planned to do, then leave. Thank the Realm.

Lina's footsteps clicked in the hallway, then disappeared. Kresten took another sip of his own sweet wine, grown and cellared in Governor Camden's district, of all places. It was too strong for so early in the morning, so he closed his eyes as he swallowed and prayed Ryllis wouldn't fight the summons. A few doors hissed in the background, and he took a bigger gulp as two pairs of footsteps returned. Lina led Ryllis into the center of the room, nodded at both him and Vidar, and disappeared. There was no doubt she was returning to her own drink somewhere far away from the whole scene.

Vidar approached Ryllis as she stood with her eyes on the floor, absolute fascination on his face. Something had surprised him, that much was clear, though whether it was the fact Ryllis existed at all or that she was wearing a dress completely inappropriate for a slave was anyone's guess. They'd picked it out together that morning, a gray-colored piece of silk that matched both the mountain clouds and her eyes, with a skirt that hung just below her knees and enough delicate lace flowers on the hem to make one wonder about the price.

Traditional Vilarian costumes were still popular in rural areas like this, and Ryllis's contemporary dress looked as out of place on the mountain as Vidar's  jacket did, but Kresten hadn't been able to breathe when she'd come out from her room, a shy but exhilarated smile on her face. He'd thought the outfit ridiculous when he'd purchased it last lunar cycle on a whim, but looking at her now . . . no, he hadn't made a mistake. How women could walk in shoes like the ones that clung to Ryllis's feet, he'd never understand, but the things they did to her calves made it worth it—for him, at least.

He looked away before his emotions became evident. Drooling all over himself would be all too humiliating, especially in front of Vidar.

"I can't believe it," Vidar said, looking her up and down. "I thought it was a joke when I heard, but it turns out you're just as much of a hypocrite as the rest of us. It's lovely to see." His gaze swung to Kresten. "Have you not had time to educate her in basic manners? Or at the very least, remind her she's not on Cereth any longer?"

Couldn't he tell she was too terrified to remember her own name, much less court etiquette? Kresten steeled his tone, ignoring the shame that flooded through him. He'd warned her. She'd play along.

"Amaryllis."

Ryllis's head jerked up at his voice, then down toward the floor again. "I am sorry for my rudeness, Your Highnesses," she whispered in a tone clearly intended for only one of them. She went down on one knee, as flawlessly as she'd likely been taught as a child, and Kresten took a breath. Even Vidar couldn't find fault with that, even though the sight of her prostrating herself before his brother made him sick.

Vidar sniffed. "Best work on that, dear brother, if you plan on having her seen anywhere near Mother and Father. They would be most displeased to be treated so casually—and by a Cerethian, no less. Get up, girl."

Ryllis rose more gracefully than Kresten would have been able to after that reprimand, the lifeless expression he despised so much on her face. It'd been a dozen, perhaps more, days since he'd last seen it, and he'd forgotten how much he hated it. It would take a long while before he forgave Vidar for making her look like this again. He clenched his fists, lest they meet his brother's nose of their own accord.

Vidar circled her as she stood, his eyebrows raised. "No mark?"

"No mark." Kresten took a breath and ran a finger up the arm of his chair. The motion quelled his rage, but just barely. "We do things differently in the mountains."

Vidar laughed as he brushed a finger against Ryllis's scalp. She flinched, and her breathing grew rapid, but she didn't move otherwise. Something, deep down, told Kresten she would have reacted differently to such a brute a solar cycle before, prince or not. How he wanted to see her that spirited again.

"I see that. What a charming anachronism." Vidar's hand fell to his side, and before Kresten could do a thing about it, he'd cupped it about her bottom. "But personally, I'd have chosen to put it right"—he squeezed—"here, if I were you."

Rage rushed through Kresten's entire body, but he forced himself to stay seated. He couldn't do anything about the horror and disgust in Ryllis's gray eyes, and he couldn't murder his brother and get away with it, but he could pretend he didn't care. Vidar was aiming for a reaction, and the more of one he got, the longer this ghastly show would continue. He took another sip of wine, though it was more like a swig this time around. Foul stuff.

"If, later on, I decide to mark her in that way," Kresten said, forcing calm into his words, "I promise you'll be the first invited to watch."

But thankfully, Vidar, you are not me. And she'll never be marked.

He looked out the windows before Ryllis's wounded gaze swung in his direction. If he saw the pain and betrayal there, Vidar would lose some teeth, and then . . . well, he didn't want to know what would happen then. Princes didn't fight over slaves—it was unbecoming. Most importantly, any kind of argument would keep Vidar around, and all Kresten wanted to do was comfort her for what he'd already said and done.

Later. He'd console her later, in private, away from Lina's prying eyes. He'd tell her how beautiful she was, and how much she meant to him, and how he loved her more than she knew, and that his bastard of a brother didn't speak for anyone but himself. And then he would listen to her scream or cry or whatever else she wanted to do, and then he would kiss away the tears and stroke her cheek as she fell asleep.

His gut tightened at the thought.

Focus, man.

"But until then," he went on, the very picture of a Vilarian noble he usually disdained, "keep your hands off my property, if you would."

Vidar jerked his hand back like he'd been burnt.

"Then you've had her." His eyes glinted with approval. "Not that I'd blame you. She really is something, isn't she? Even for a Cerethian."

Kresten glared, his noble façade too difficult to keep in place after that remark.

Vidar burst into laughter. "Or maybe you haven't." He put a finger under his chin, pretending to think. "There must have been enough eager women on Cereth to keep you occupied all those lunar cycles you spent there, and whatever I think of your numerous dalliances, you've never lowered yourself to prisoners. Or slaves, for that matter. So, what in the Realm is she doing here? This is fascinating. A true mystery."

His brother dared utter the word *dalliances?* Like his brother wasn't as bad as what he'd just accused him of doing? He had a reason for pretending to indulge in his own casual romances. Vidar, on the other hand, liked to throw his power around, enjoyed the physical pleasures of a woman. Not that the women were unwilling, but his brother had a tendency to promise things that would never come true, and not a single young woman on Vilaria would risk saying no to him.

On one hand, it made his cover story easy if his brothers, Vidar included, lived their lives as if that kind of thing was normal, but on the other, though Kresten desperately wanted to judge, he never let himself forget he'd have been just like them if things had gone differently.

"I wonder . . ." Vidar went on to himself. "But no, that would be nonsense, wouldn't it?"

Kresten didn't think he'd ever clenched his jaw so hard. Vidar was up to something, and he was the last to know what. By the stars, if Vidar had any kind of surprise going on . . .

"What would be nonsense?" he asked.

"I think you're compensating for something. Over-compensating, if one wishes to be technical. But for what, is the question. Elise would have never tolerated a lack of marital relations, so I have to assume you do prefer women. Yes, I think we can safely rule out a fondness for men," Vidar said to himself.

Kresten raised his eyebrows. That speculation was nowhere near where he'd thought Vidar was going with that comment. Ryllis, he noticed, didn't appear to know what to do with the suggestion except to furrow her brow. He didn't want to imagine what was going on in her head.

"Now, it's possible you truly are the womanizer you hold yourself out to be. I don't know that Elise would have tolerated that either, but I do suppose it's always possible. The benefits that come with marrying a prince can outweigh a great many drawbacks."

Vidar shrugged before Kresten could stand up and defend the woman whose death had put him in a deep depression for almost a solar cycle. "But you know, the strangest thing happened last week," he went on. "I ran into Liala at this new club in the Ericha Quarter. You remember her—the charming young lady who attended Father's naming celebration ball just before you left for Cereth. I of course considered her off-limits since the two of you were seen cavorting about in the southeast gardens, but do you know what she said? She told me you never touched her. Not even on her lips. It does make one wonder."

"Liala was so drunk that night she couldn't possibly remember what happened."

With that, Kresten leaned back and let his almost-empty glass dangle. Vidar had no idea what he was talking about, and after a half glass of sweet wine, listening to him speculate was turning out to be more entertaining than he could have ever imagined. Maybe this visit wouldn't be so bad after all, for now even Ryllis was listening to his brother's ramblings with undisguised interest. He wanted to laugh, but that would give Vidar too much information.

"Perhaps she was, but she seemed rather lucid about the entire thing, even remembering how your uniform had a snag on the left shoulder. Said she'd pointed it out as a chance to get closer to you, and you'd all but run away from her. You broke her dear, crown-chasing heart, Kres, not that she waited very long for you to come around."

Vidar chuckled. "And there's also the matter of your position within the Fleet. It's not normal for someone of our lineage to be as content as you are about being a glorified jailer. You could have done anything—commanded starships, become a military barrister, even flown fighters if that was your thing. Instead, you're a security officer."

He held out his hand in a mock appeal. "Oh, don't mistake me. You people are necessary, just like the cooks. It's just that it's a rather humble career decision for a man of your pedigree, don't you think? Though"—his finger hit his chin in thought again; Vidar had always had a bit of drama in him—"it would make a brilliant cover for something else."

Kresten flew to his feet. "Amaryllis, out." She fairly raced from the room, taking all the warmth with her, and he faced Vidar. "Was that necessary? If you feel the need to blab about something that I've successfully kept confidential for a very long time, you can blab to me and me only."

"Then I'm right!" Vidar's eyes sparkled. "Oh, don't look so angry. You work isn't classified. It was your own decision to not tell anyone, and Mother mentioned a few solar cycles ago that your security cover was just that. To your credit, it took a while to figure out what you needed a cover for, though. Your lovely new slave was the final piece of the puzzle."

"Mother's suffering from dementia! She also insists Father has six other wives on Holiv that he visited in his dreams and that Lina's chickens speak to her through her pillow. You shouldn't have listened to her."

"She was right about you, though. Maybe Father as well. Who knows what he really does on those vacations—or naps—of his? I wouldn't put it past those chickens, either."

Kresten pinched the bridge of his nose, hard. Vidar was right, as much as he hated to admit it. Neither his Shadow Force position or his telepathy were classified, exactly, but keeping his skills secret made for a more normal life. People understandably became uncomfortable when someone who could access their thoughts was in the room, even when they knew how complicated the procedure was, and he wasn't the only Shadow Force telepath who had a cover position in the Fleet. Elise herself hadn't been thrilled with the idea, even though she'd eventually come around. It helped that reading the mind of a spouse wasn't anything like reading the mind of a prisoner. If only he could convince Ryllis of that.

"Yeah," he said, wishing he'd poured himself a larger drink. "Fine. So Mother was right about me. Why are you here harassing me about it now?"

"Well, it's a rather concerning revelation, don't you think? Are you reading my mind right now? Have you in the past? I want to make sure you're not a danger to me."

Kresten wanted to drill a hole in his own forehead. "If you believed I was a danger to you, you wouldn't be such a pain in the rear end."

"Indeed." Vidar flopped back on the hearth and regarded him with interest. "The truth is, I have a bet going."

"A bet? A stars-blasted bet? Who did you make a bet with?"

"Austet, naturally."

"For pity's—Austet knows, too?" Kresten all but hollered. Vidar was bad enough, but their eldest brother and the emperor's successor couldn't keep his mouth shut about anything. Austet would squeal to the entire palace—blast it, the entire *planet*—if he knew.

"No, he thinks you prefer men, and I'll let him believe what he wants. Your secret is safe with me, though it would be the brotherly thing to do if you'd transfer me the credits I'm losing by protecting it."

"Vidar, homosexuality isn't illegal. Why would I be pretending to sleep with dozens of women to hide it?"

"Sixteen hundred crowns. I'm sure it's a drop in the bucket after your hazard pay from the Cereth mission."

Kresten jabbed all of his fingers against his skull. "Yeah. Fine. Whatever. Send me an invoice."

"Gladly." Vidar grinned. "So? What's she really doing here?"

Kresten straightened. "Now that *is* classified."

"She's a subject, then." Vidar shrugged and yawned before jabbering on. "I was afraid of that—you could have just come right out and said it. By the stars, what a bore this turned out to be. I was hoping I was wrong about you. Or at least that Austet was right. Though I have to admit, you've done a great job. You've had us all going with the reputation you've worked so hard to maintain. And rest assured, I'll continue to maintain it for you. Are you going to keep her after you're done with her? If not, I might be interested."

Kresten pressed his lips together. *Not in a million solar cycles, Vidar.*

"Well. Think about it—I think my work here is done. Tell your new friend it was wonderful to meet her, and I'll see you when I see you." Vidar finished off his drink in one gulp, pushed himself off the hearth, and headed for the front door. "Oh . . . but Kresten?"

Kresten looked up.

Just go home.

"Sex is great. You should try it some time."

Kresten blinked backed the memory of how the gray dress showed off Ryllis's waist. "Vidar, I was married. Believe me, I'm well aware."

His brother just winked.

CHAPTER TWELVE

*L*ina had brewed her a cup of Kresten's expensive yellow gold tea, and Ryllis didn't want to offend her by not drinking it, but she could do nothing but push the china cup around the kitchen table as it grew cold. Kresten's brother's reaction wasn't a complete surprise—she'd heard stories of the imperial family, after all, and they weren't much different from any other Vilarian—but still, she'd never expected him to touch her. *To grab her.* She would never be able to wear this lovely dress again. Not with the reminders of what had happened when she did.

And for Kresten to do nothing about it but watch with that indifferent look on his face? It was unconscionable, especially after what had happened in the cave. Yes, he'd warned her she'd have to follow along with his brother's game, but he'd also promised to protect her from any leering, and he'd failed miserably there. And then to send her out of the room for them to talk about her? He was hiding something, and that bothered her more than the creep's hand on her bottom.

Lina stood, her shadow growing smaller as she left the kitchen, and Ryllis glanced up to see Kresten standing a fair distance away from her, hands clasped behind his back. As much as she wanted to flee—to punish him for what his brother had done to her more than anything else—she needed answers more than she needed revenge, so she pushed her tea to the center of the table and nodded at him to sit.

Kresten sat and sighed, then grabbed her cup and took a long swallow of what had been hers. Ryllis stared at his lips, then at her hands.

He rubbed his neck, frowning at the cup. "Ryllis . . . why do you think you're here?"

That was an easy question.

"Because this is how the galaxy works."

Unfair, yes. But she could feel the prince's hands on her, still. That was also how the galaxy worked when one was a slave, even though everyone pretended it was not.

"Yes"—was it her imagination, or did he flush as she threw his words back on him?—"and I apologize for my brother's actions. They surprised me as much as you, and they won't go unpunished, even if I have to speak to my father about it. But specifically, why do you think you're here, as opposed to that prison back on Cereth, or a prison here on Vilaria, or living as a slave in a household that wouldn't treat you nearly as well as I?"

Or dead, she was happy he didn't add.

"I—I don't know," she whispered. Had he lied in the cave? All his words and promises and talk of love—had they been false? She touched a finger to her lips, suddenly ashamed of what they'd done. "Because you wanted me."

She'd make him deny it again and again, especially after what his brother had implied.

"My darling star, that's not why. I want you now, more than you can imagine, and I don't blame you for being hung up on that, but that's not how this works." Kresten shook his head. "I shouldn't be telling you this, but since my wonderful brother has already spilled my secret . . ."

He pressed his fingers against his eyelids and groaned in what sounded like frustration. "The truth is, I can't sleep with you, no matter how much I'd like to. It would be detrimental to my health, and even worse for my career. It's not an option I can entertain. You see, I won't ever have a mistress, and I won't keep you as some kind of secret lover. Even if I wanted to, even if

I thought you were worth that little, I can't. It's not allowed."

It was a shot of relief, even if the rest of his words made no sense. Kresten still loved her. He still thought highly of her. He hadn't lied.

"But then I don't—I don't understand. What does this have to do with anything? Why can't you—" She slammed her mouth shut, confused.

"You asked me if I was gifted with an innate power. And I lied you to when I said I wasn't." His jaw clenched as he pressed his palms against the table. "I do, though it's not one I like to talk about, and I think you'll understand when I tell you. I'm not a Fleet security lieutenant. Not only, anyway. I'm a Shadow Force officer."

Shadow Force?

His admission hit her like an asteroid smashing into an oblivious planet, like when he'd pulled her toward him and she'd known he was going to kiss her, only this was painful and frightening and raw instead of pleasurable. Her stomach flipped, and she placed a hand over it, glad she'd declined Lina's tea.

Kresten was a telepath.

Like others with different innate powers, they popped up on Vilaria every so often—and having been banned from using their power if they'd been born outside the imperial family, they usually ended up just where Kresten was— in the military, where such things were not only allowed, but encouraged and sought after. Masters of reading emotions even when they couldn't directly access a mind, the telepaths made for expert torturers.

And interrogators.

And regular security guards who leaned against walls during interviews and pretended to sleep.

And she'd kissed him.

Kresten's secrets all fell into place as she struggled to keep her emotions in check. It was just as he said—why he hadn't forced himself on her, why he couldn't have her as a mistress, why he'd lied to his brother about his sexual liaisons to keep his family from the truth.

Shadow Force telepaths were chaste, for the most part. Sex bonded a telepath to their partner just like accessing a mind did, only deeper, and the Fleet didn't allow it for obvious reasons. If Kresten had connected with her in that way, it would affect his ability to access others. A wife was one thing. Numerous other involvements and mistresses were another—a proportional reduction in the number of prisoners a telepath could read over the years. The Fleet was nothing if not demanding of its officers.

"I see you've figured it out."

Ryllis grabbed her temples, then dropped her hands, the feeling of stubble almost as horrifying as someone *existing* in her brain. Kresten had spoken out loud, hadn't he? Had his lips moved? She didn't know where to focus anymore.

"You're not—you're not reading my mind," she gasped.

He chuckled, without any humor. "No. Sometimes people's emotions are obvious, and your expression is usually enough. Trust me, you'd know if I was doing it."

Her stomach dropped at how matter of fact he sounded. "But I wouldn't be able to stop you."

"That's right. You wouldn't be able to stop me." Any impression of amusement fell from his face. "But it doesn't work like you think. I can't just walk up to a stranger, touch them, and read their thoughts, much as we've tried to experiment and make it work. There's a pragmatic reason we limit the use the military applications and prisons—it's just too difficult otherwise. And in my case . . ."

Ryllis stared at him, wide-eyed, unable to process his confession, and waited for him to continue.

"There was a rebellion on Izonus four solar cycles ago," he said. "Endless work. I spent over a solar cycle there, and toward the end I would collapse when I accessed a mind, every time. It began to take longer and longer to recover from the blackouts, and that's when I was sent to Cereth. It was meant to be a mental break in the hopes I'd recover and be just as useful again."

"I was a break?" It was insulting, in some twisted way.

Kresten shrugged. "Telepathy isn't the only way to get information from someone, and we prefer other, less invasive means to begin with. You were supposed to be easy, the pampered governor's daughter, in over her head, not knowing who she was dealing with. The interrogators you spoke with were trainees, so I watched the interviews and gave them input afterward on how to improve next time around. Of course, I hoped you'd see me as an ally, as well, give me some bits of information I could use to help them force a confession. It happens more frequently than you'd ever expect."

"The gifts? The candy? The flower?" *Why had she mentioned the flower?* "You were only trying to make me see you as a friend?"

"No." He reached across the table but stopped before he touched her. "Ryllis, no. I wanted to see you smile. I wanted to see you alive. I suppose, yes, if you'd have decided I was someone to trust, I would have used that to my advantage, but that wasn't the intent. And when you didn't talk . . . I didn't make the decision to bring you here, if that's what you're asking. The Fleet ordered it, and I complied."

"You brought me here until I decided to talk?"

"Not exactly. You truly were eradicated. My superiors suggested I ask the Eradication Council for you, and I . . . I saw no downside to doing so."

Ryllis took a few steady slowing breaths. "You stood there and watched as they made me a slave. You did nothing to prevent it. All so you could *practice* on me? You—you—"

No epithet, even the vilest Cerethian one, was suitable for what he'd done. The kitchen faded into a cloud of fog while she struggled to herself, fought to keep from lashing out at him.

Maybe Kresten could feel her emotions, perhaps he couldn't, but she didn't care. How could—how could someone who'd professed to love her allow this?

"It was going to happen one way or another. Would you have preferred to bide your time in a cell while they decided who to give you to?" he asked sharply. "As I said when you first arrived here, that can still be arranged. I did you a favor, the best I could under the circumstances."

"A cell wouldn't be much different from being here, Your Highness."

It felt raw, and unfair somehow, but his threat had terrified her. She reached for the tea to wash away the sour feeling in her mouth, then drew her hand back. It was sitting too close to him.

"Ah, Ryllis," he replied. "Everything I've told you, everything I've done for you . . . Has it been that bad?"

He sounded almost broken, and his use of her name disarmed her. The feel of his body against hers had changed everything. Her thighs began to shake as the adrenaline retreated, and she pressed her damp palms to them, leaving marks on the silk.

"I'm sorry. You've been kind," she said to the table, shaking her head. "More than kind. I didn't expect to feel—"

"Then never compare my home to a prison again."

The words and the way he'd interrupted her apology were harsh; the underlying pain was not. She stared at him for several seconds, but he didn't speak again.

"If you can't just walk up to someone and touch them," she said, pulling her hands closer to her chest, "how do you do it?"

Kresten looked out the window and her gaze followed. A small brown bird was sitting out on the garden wall, singing its heart out. She wished she were that bird, wished she could fly away and worry about nothing but building a nest somewhere safe.

"A tattoo," he said, eyes on the bird. "We add a special type of nanobiotes to the ink, and once it enters the bloodstream, it opens a channel to the mind. For most prisoners we access, it's a black circle, sized for the dose of nanobiotes needed. Some need repeat treatments—their arms have a line of circles up the inside. But I couldn't imagine the sight of you like that. You didn't deserve it, and it would have destroyed me. The imperial crest I offered is detailed enough on its own for what I needed to do."

He paused. "I wasn't lying about it being painful. I went through it once. We all do, to make sure we understand what kind of power we've been honored with and what it takes from subjects when we use it. The original idea was that it would prevent overreach by Shadow Force telepaths, and they were right that it has. I still have nightmares about it every so often. The pain, the violation, it's something you can't imagine until it happens to you."

She felt faint, grateful for the steadiness of the chair beneath her and the table that mostly kept her from fleeing. "And people let you do this to them?"

Kresten laughed, even though she didn't think it was funny, and suspected he didn't either. "Of course they don't let us. No sane person would, but those subjected to the procedure don't have a choice. Usually strapping them down is enough to ensure compliance, though sometimes they need to be sedated as well. You —I had drugged your coffee that first morning. You wouldn't have known what was going on until it was too late, and you were in too much agony to fight me."

The kitchen was silent, except for the squawking of birds in the distance.

"You were going to do this to me."

He nodded. "Yes, but—"

"Then why didn't you do it that first morning? Why did you give me the chance to say no?"

"I don't—" He frowned at his hands. "I don't know. Maybe because even then, you did something to me. Made me feel things. And the longer you were here, the more I was able to forget what I was supposed to be doing. And then I saw the fear in your eyes that afternoon after the waterfall and questioning you that way became even harder. Almost every night, I dreamed of you screaming in pain while I forced my way into your mind, so I told myself it was unnecessary. They didn't care what I did with you, after all."

I can control plants. They grow better and stay alive longer when I'm around. It's why the flower you gave me on Cereth never died and why your garden looks like it does.

Ryllis tested the confession in her mind—tested *him*—but Kresten didn't so much as blink. Relief flowed over her entire body. He couldn't read her mind as they sat here. Or, at least, he had decided not to.

"Why are you telling me all this now?" she asked.

"Because it's nothing compared to what I told you in the cave. And because my brother put the question in your mind, and because I didn't want you thinking I was a womanizer, and because I feel you should know the person you've fallen in love with, blemishes and all."

Her stomach fluttered. "Then what do we do?"

"I don't know." Kresten's shoulders sank, like holding in the secret had cost him most of his energy, and he was going to collapse on top of the table. "You can let them do it. Prove you're not a traitor."

"Them?" She frowned. "Not you?"

"They won't trust me. Not if I bring this concern to them now. And I hardly think I can trust myself. It would have to be someone independent and unbiased. My boss, most likely. He's good at what he does, and if you're innocent, he would never say otherwise just for his reputation or record."

"He's a stranger. A Vilarian." Ryllis sprung to her feet and began to pace the kitchen. "I can't do this. What you're asking—to let him in my mind—it's—"

"Why not? I know you're not a traitor. Even though I haven't been in your mind, I know you, Ryllis, and I know you would have never done such a thing. I know you aren't my father's biggest fan, but murdering people, planning attacks . . . I just can't see it."

But the flowers . . . She clutched her hands together, desperate for an excuse. "You just told me how horrible it is. And now you're telling me it won't even be you doing it."

"I had to be honest. I won't let you agree to it without knowing what you're agreeing to. And you don't have to give me your answer now, but will you think about it? I want you cleared. I love you, and I want everyone to know it. My darling star, I want so much for both of us."

He was asking too much. Had he done it in the cave, while her lips were still tingling and her knees were barely holding her up—yes. She might have been silly enough to agree to anything he asked. But here, back in the mansion, with her senses intact and Kresten sitting across from her like a stranger, it was terrifying. She traced circles in the fabric of the silly gray dress, not knowing what else to do.

How was she supposed to tell him the truth which would ruin his dreams?

CHAPTER THIRTEEN

Kresten didn't know why he'd told Ryllis his secret the day before.

He did know that he'd made sure the static fields on the windows were fully functional when she'd escaped into her room immediately after their conversation. If it came down to it, telling her he could read her mind could be considered a tactic; allowing her to escape would be considered . . . well, he didn't want to know how the Eradication Council would consider it. Malfeasance at best, treason at worst. Ever since he'd sworn into the Fleet, his royal status could only protect him so far.

Kresten knocked on her door, twice. She didn't answer, and he stood there for a minute shifting back and forth from foot to foot, debating his next move. He wasn't going to barge in, not when she could be in the bath or doing a myriad of things he didn't—and did, at the same time—want to see. There'd been no tea waiting for him that morning, so he settled for asking Lina for a cup and parked himself in his office, feet on his desk and a book in his lap.

He was ignoring the words, though. A print of him and Elise sat on top, taken at the palace two solar cycles after their wedding. His hands were around her waist, and she was laughing up at him, her eyes squeezed shut. By the stars, but they'd been young. He wanted to laugh at the young couple who was so sure they'd last forever, more because of their naïve certainty than of how it'd ended.

But surprisingly, underneath his amusement, there was no pain. Sorrow, yes, and loss, but it didn't take over like it had at first.

"It's time," he said out loud. "I've pretended it wasn't, but now I think I was more afraid of going forward than losing the past. We cling to a lot, don't we, even when it doesn't exist anymore." With a quick glance at the closed door, he brought the photo to his mouth and kissed it. "I won't forget you."

There was a shuffle in the hallway, and he dropped the photo to the side of his chair and picked up his book once more. Lina kicked open the door with her feet as he pretended to read about the history of attrition warfare in the Theipra System, a tray in her hands. There was the long overdue tea, yes, two cups of it, but also an assortment of pastries he'd seen her making earlier. His mouth watered at the smell of sugar and cinnamon—Lina's baking was something he craved when he was off-world—but the two cups were concerning. Kresten sighed as she placed one on the side table next to him and perched on the upholstered bench under the window with the other.

"Why do I feel like I'm not going to like what you're here for?" he asked.

"You know, it's strange, Your Highness." Lina made him up a plate of pastries with her free hand and passed it over. "You don't want to see me, and Ryllis doesn't want to see me, and the two of you don't seem to want to see each other."

His stomach growled, and he grumbled out loud to cover the sound. "And I'm the loser, I see."

She chuckled and shook her head. "Just the one with the most information."

"Information?" He snorted and crossed his ankle over his knee. "Not exactly. I don't have any information, if we're being truthful. I don't even know where she is."

Lina took a sip of tea. "She's outside, in the side garden. You should see it. Crocuses, snowdrops, and she's even gotten some early roses to grow in that rocky soil. She knows what she's doing, sir."

Ah.

"I'd wondered where she'd been," he said.

"You haven't been wondering—you'd have looked harder for her if you were. Since I haven't even seen you in the kitchen since you came in asking for tea, I doubt you've searched at all, beyond knocking on her door. Almost as if you knew she didn't want to see you."

His jaw tightened. "You can stop this hedging. I know what she told you."

Lina leaned against the window with her tea and shrugged in a strange, cat-like manner. A sunbeam lit her face, exaggerating the wrinkles in her skin but making her look youthful at the same time.

"Shadow Force," she said. "I should have known. So many things make so much more sense now."

She sounded so matter of fact and indifferent to his true identity that he almost laughed. "You're not afraid of me?"

"Why in the Realm would I be afraid of you?"

Kresten shoved an entire tartlet in his mouth. "I don't know. Most people would be," he said, chewing. His mother would die if she saw him eating like this, which was why he was doing it. "She is. What if I'm truly a monster, and everyone knows it but me?"

"If Ryllis is afraid of you, it's because she has a reason to be." Lina set her cup on the coffee-colored silk of the window seat. "You brought her here as a slave, and then, if I'm understanding the situation correctly, intended to continue her interrogation on top of that. That would have been bad enough on anyone, but then you dumped some other, perhaps more frightening, information on her, I think.

Information that's much easier for you to accept than her."

He almost coughed out the pastry. "She told you what happened in the cave?" he asked, brushing the crumbs from his pants.

Lina smiled in the motherly way he'd grown to dread over the past few lunar cycles. "No. But I've seen the way you look at her, and Aared saw the way she looked at you when you left after your visit. We remember what that was like, and I took a guess. You just confirmed it."

Kresten wanted to swear. She'd walked him right into a confession. He should have known better—he *did* know better.

"And if I had to speculate," Lina went on, "I think she's more afraid of one than the other."

Her confrontation had already muddled his brain. "Which one?"

A laugh. Lina couldn't reach him from the window seat, but he wouldn't have been surprised if she had patted his knee in response if she could have.

"You've asked a lot of her," she said. "You've ordered her to abandon her home and her family, forget how you met, and now you ask her to trust you enough to give her a future. None of these are minor things. Then you tell her you're a telepath. For a Cerethian, you might as well have told her you can fly."

"I can," he grumbled.

"Automated shuttles don't count. Unless you've suddenly sprouted wings, she doesn't care about that. She cares that she's been brought here as a prisoner, and that she was raised to fear you and your kind. You're not a monster, Your Highness, and I know it, but you might grant her a bit of grace if she thought of you as one in fright. You know the stories they tell on Cereth and the others."

He did. On most colonized planets, Cereth included, it was said that telepaths could read your thoughts from across the room—and plant new ones at the same time. That they could scan a warship commander's strategy from light years away, giving them a substantial advantage in battle. That Shadow Force was known for sewing prisoners' lips together to prevent them from confusing the telepath with deliberately vocal falsehoods.

That last one, he supposed, wasn't too far from the mark.

"They're just stories." He stuck another little tart in his mouth, berry this time, and washed it down with some tea. Lina raised her eyebrows at his etiquette, and he waved her off. There was a reason he was here on the mountain instead of the palace. "You know how it works."

"I do. I also know you asked her to subject herself to it."

"I don't have a choice. Lina, I—fine, you're right. I don't know why I bother trying to lie to you anymore." Against his will, his lip quirked up. "I love her." The words were startlingly easy to say to someone else. "And now they'll never trust me to prove her innocent. They sent her here, they believe she's guilty of everything she's been accused of."

"But what if she is?"

"Is what?"

Lina shook her head. *Royal idiot,* he almost heard in her mind.

"Guilty," she said.

The pastry threatened to come up again. He hadn't considered that explanation because Ryllis couldn't be guilty. It would ruin her life —and by extension, his. He could marry a slave. It didn't happen frequently, especially among the imperial family, but it wasn't unheard of. Father would protest, but he'd eventually accept it. It wasn't as though Kresten had a chance of inheriting the throne, so such things were overlooked and tacitly celebrated. But a traitor? It was so hard to think of Ryllis as one to begin with, but he couldn't marry a traitor, someone who'd actively worked to overthrow his own family. Wasn't *allowed* to.

"Then I don't want them to know," he said. "I'd rather keep her safe here and never be able to consummate my love. She deserves that, no matter what she's done."

"And maybe that's what she wants, too. Let her make that decision, yes?"

Kresten ran his hands over his face and sighed. Would it make a difference to him if Ryllis was guilty? Before Lina had mentioned it, he hadn't realized he'd been presuming her innocence for a long while. *Why?* Was it a truth he felt deep down or simply misplaced hope and naïveté? It was the conundrum to end all conundrums.

The hub of the lodge's security system pinged as he was considering the effects of another pastry on his stomach. He waved at the screen and frowned at the dot there. A suborbital shuttle? No one was expected up in the mountains. Vidar had caused enough trouble, so he couldn't possibly be—

Kresten squinted at the ship's identification.

Shadow Force.

"Find Ryllis," he ordered. She'd panic if they appeared without warning. Would accuse him of calling them in. He needed to speak with her first, needed to calm her, needed to prepare her with how to act and what to say. Lina darted out the door, and he turned a few aimless circles in his office, trying to get his thoughts under control.

I should have sent that report to Colonel Löfgren.

But they wouldn't come all this way to reprimand him for that. It had to be something else. Were they taking Ryllis away? The thought was unbearable—and didn't make sense. The Fleet was done with her, and even if they weren't, they should have allowed him to bring her in to the Shadow Force headquarters at Arvika.

The security system beeped again the signal the shuttle's landing, and with a sigh, Kresten squared his shoulders and headed out front to meet them. He could see six men through the windows: Major Ivar Dahl—his immediate commander—Captain Erik Ahlund, and four regular security guards. Those last didn't bode well for Ryllis, but he wouldn't panic yet. Dahl was known for arriving with an entourage, especially when he was unexpected.

Dahl waved at him as he hopped out of the shuttle, and Kresten, after the briefest glance down at his white cotton undershirt, returned a casual salute. Dahl was lucky to be getting that much with this kind of surprise.

"Good morning, sir."

"Good morning, Lieutenant." Dahl sounded all too cheerful for someone who'd have to have been up before sunset to make a flight to the Kebnekaise Mountains. "Where's your slave?"

Kresten swore to himself. "In the garden around the side of the house, I believe. This way, sir."

He led Dahl, Ahlund, and one of the guards through the house, the long way to the Ryllis's new garden. It would give Lina time to calm her, and more importantly, would give him time to come up with a reason they had to let him keep her here. Because *the Eradication Council gave her to me* suddenly sounded more reversible that it was supposed to be.

Lina headed them off the kitchen, pale. "Your Highness—" She slammed her mouth shut when she noticed the rest of the group.

"Well, what is it?" Kresten asked. Panic had always made him rude.

"She's not in the garden. And I—"

"You what?" Dahl broke in.

"I can't find her anywhere." Lina's eyes flickered from him to Dahl, as if in apology.

Ahlund swore and pointed the guard toward the rear door and the garden, while he took off down the left corridor, toward the bedrooms. Doors hissed and slammed in the background; Ahlund was rapid and efficient as he searched. Kresten's knees grew weak.

"How could you let this happen?" Dahl asked him. "You actually lost her?"

"Sir, with all due respect, no one watches their slaves every second. She has her own duties, and I don't need to watch her." Dahl had to know that. "I'm sure she's here.

Probably somewhere else on the grounds. But why—"

Dahl shot a sharp glance at Lina. "Go home. If she's there, send her back here." He guided Kresten on to the back deck, in private. "New intel arrived from Cereth two days ago," he said quietly. "She's part of that resistance group that planned the attack on the emperor and empress six solar cycles ago—she wasn't involved in that particular assault, it sounds like, but we're not sure what she's been up to since. We're lucky we got her first."

"The attack at the transport authority building in Therus?" His gut twisted. His parents had escaped by minutes. "Says who?"

"The regional governor."

"Her father?" By the stars, his neck was aching, his muscles tense.

Dahl nodded. "I'm sure you've enjoyed having a slave, but you'll have to find another, because Amaryllis Camden is back in Fleet custody for now—at least until the Eradication Council can be given accurate and complete information about her crimes. I suspect they'll agree her sentence was too light."

Too light? Slavery was too light? Hot rage and something more fearful and visceral filled the kitchen, almost tangible, like it'd sucked the air from the room. Kresten pushed it away. They couldn't take her. He wouldn't allow it. Wouldn't allow them to torture her and imprison her and then, when they'd made their point, execute her.

"Sir, you know he's got it in for her," he said. "Why has he been so bent on proving his daughter a traitor? Doesn't that strike you the least bit strange? I hardly think we can consider him a reliable corroborator."

"He knows where his loyalty lies. Can you imagine his fate if we found out he was hiding information like this?"

"Still, sir, I—"

Ahlund rushed back in. "She's gone. Not outside, not in the house. Lieutenant?"

"I—Captain, she was outside." That palpable rage and fear was compressing him now. Maybe Dahl was right. Ryllis would have seen the shuttle from the garden. Maybe she'd known. Or panicked.

Perhaps she'd taken it as an opportunity.

"She escaped," Ahlund said. "Just as we arrived —that's a rather strange coincidence, don't you think, Lieutenant?"

"Excuse me?" He was living in some parallel universe where nothing made sense. "What are you saying?"

"Where are you hiding her?" Dahl asked.

"Hiding her? I'm not—" No, this wasn't a parallel universe. It was a strange nightmare brought on by stress. A hallucination. Had Vidar poisoned the vodka? "You're crazy. All of you. She's not a rebel assassin, and she hasn't escaped because I warned her you were coming."

"Give us the truth. Now," Ahlund said. "And this will be easier on you."

"What will be easier on me?"

Dahl jerked his head at the guard, and before Kresten could strategize a suitable response, they'd yanked his hands behind his back. He bit back a torrent of profanity as Ahlund and the guard handcuffed him and pulled him toward the door. Cursing would come later. Much later. Now he needed to keep calm. Not antagonize them. Figure out just what was going on here.

"Take him to the shuttle," Dahl said to Ahlund. "Then start searching those hills. Don't stop until you find her. Alive. I've got some questions for her, and she won't escape them this time."

CHAPTER FOURTEEN

*R*yllis lifted her head from the damp ground. The shuttle had been parked in front of the house for almost half an hour now, and a few Vilarians in uniforms were still prowling the side garden where she'd been working not an hour before. Luck was such a nebulous, fanciful thing, but it had been on her side—she'd made it out just in time.

It hadn't been an easy decision. The feel of Kresten's body was never far from her mind as she checked the small kit of belongings she'd managed to scrounge: some thread, a fire starter, a small flashlight, and a package of water purification tablets. It wasn't much, and it wouldn't give her a lot of time, but it was enough to let her hide in the cave and think about her next move. Kresten would find her there if she tarried, but she needed time and space to collect her thoughts.

I don't want to die a slave.

If only the Vilarians would leave. The cold from the spring earth was seeping through her clothing now, but it was too risky to stand and resume her walk up the meadow—they'd see her movement immediately, especially if Kresten had notified them she was missing. She dragged her fingers through the mud and wiped them on her leggings, running through her limited options. If they headed this way, she might not have a choice but to return with them. And then what? Would they remove her from Kresten's household? They certainly weren't up in the mountains for a social visit, especially since Lina had passed by her on the trail a while back. Thankfully, the weeds were high, and she hadn't seen anything amiss.

She squinted down the hill at the small group exiting the front door of the house. It was so hard to see from this far away, but she could still recognize the undershirt Kresten had been wearing that morning. He was in front, two men in Fleet uniforms behind him, and the way they were moving, shoving him forward every time he turned around to speak—Ryllis stifled a gasp. After the Fleet had dragged her out of her father's house at gunpoint, there was no mistaking the meaning of the situation.

They'd arrested Kresten.

But for what? Was that even allowed? Surely his status as a member of the royal family gave him protection—but it appeared it did not. For as he turned back and said something to the two strange Fleet officers one last time, and they pushed him onto the shuttle, she could see their weapons, both pistols and shock sticks, and how Kresten's hands were cuffed behind his back. She wanted to run down the meadow and scream at them to release him, but her legs had gone oddly weak and her throat strangely tight.

It was just as well. Wasn't this what she wanted? For Kresten to be gone and for her to be free? Vilaria was huge. She could flee the mountains, grow out her hair, and, somehow, disappear into society. Maybe even find work that would allow her to buy passage back to Cereth. That had always been her plan, and with Kresten out of the picture, it would be even easier. The Fleet would be looking for her for a while, but they'd eventually decide she'd fallen off one of the numerous cliffs out in these hills. She wasn't important enough for them to search for her body for more than a few lunar cycles.

She closed her eyes. It was too hard to forget how his lips had felt against hers, the things he'd said, and the way he'd shown her compassion, from the very first day. Prickles rose up on her skin as she remembered the way he'd looked at her in the gray dress, and it wasn't from the chill of the meadow breeze that time—he'd done something to her. Even with his lie about who he really was, she couldn't forget the parts of him that she *did* know, and that made the lie so much easier to accept. Everyone made mistakes. Weren't his forgivable?

He was gone now, yes, and she was freer than she'd been in many lunar cycles, but was that what she wanted? It'd been the obvious choice this morning when she'd woken up a slave in his bedroom, but now it was impossible to shake the concern in her heart. Her brain argued that escape was the only logical option, but her soul screamed for his. Was there a solution? She needed to be free, but she needed him as well.

As the shuttle screeched into the sky, Ryllis plucked a few blooms from beside her and headed up the hill.

The cavern was a hundred paces after the vein of granite, Kresten had said.

Except *paces* wasn't the right word. He'd been mistaken about that. Ryllis pressed her body even further into the cave floor as the ceiling lowered. It wasn't touching her back yet, but she said a silent thanks to the Light that she wasn't claustrophobic. As she'd stood in the entrance, trying to shake the feel of his lips on hers and the memory of his adoring words, she'd never expected the passageway to become this narrow. But then, perhaps, that was why Lina had never found him back here.

Fifty-two.

A sharp piece of stone jabbed into her back, and she froze, biting back a curse. Kresten was almost twice her size—how had he fit through here? Cautiously, she shifted her body to the side and managed to make it by without stabbing herself further. Water dripping on the back of her neck, like it had on Kresten's just before she'd brushed it off and he'd taken her in his arms.

Forget him.

Just for now.

Eighty-six.

A breeze blew across the top of her head, and she breathed a little easier as the darkness became less oppressive. Rolling to her side for a breath, she flicked on the lighter. It didn't reach far into the opening of the cavern, but she could see enough that she chanced crawling the rest of the way on her knees. If the Fleet did show up, they'd struggle to get to her. Just the idea of a squad of armed men fighting their way past that low ceiling raised her spirits.

Once she was certain of not smashing her skull, she stood and turned on the lighter all the way. It didn't take long to make a full circle of the cavern. The walls were smooth, and except for a small pool on the far side, contained by a low ledge, so was the floor. A few large boulders were scattered around, fallen from the ceiling many hundreds of solar cycles ago, no doubt, and she wished they could conceal her completely if the Fleet arrived. The source of the pool must have been an underground river somewhere below, because a soft rushing filled her ears when she held her breath.

The cans of water Kresten had left in some other life were stacked up beside a large boulder to the right of the entrance. A few were empty, but with the pool and the water purification tablets, hydration wouldn't be an issue. Food was another matter, but the new moon was only a few days away, and with any luck, she could sneak out and find something in the darkness. She stuck the flowers in one of the empty cans and set it on the ledge of the pool.

"I wish you were here with me." Her desire echoed against the walls, and she waited for a response that never came. "I miss your smile. I miss the way you brushed my fingers with yours, and I miss the way you held me, and I miss the way you pretended not to understand why I shivered when you touched my cheek."

She wrapped her arms around herself and shuddered, though the cave was warm.

"I don't know how you expected me to react when you told me. I'm sorry I handled it so poorly, but I think I did the best I could. I'd almost let myself forget how we met, and it was a shock to be reminded of it."

The memory had become hazy since she'd arrived on Vilaria, but not hazy enough to forget. Five or six days into her imprisonment, after a brutally long interview, the guard had walked her outside, and she'd braced herself for the feel of his hands as he walked her back to her cell. If she was lucky, he'd only grope; if she was unlucky, he'd push her against the wall, grope her, *and* whisper all sorts of revolting things in her ear.

That day, she was neither, for Kresten had been leaning against the corridor wall opposite the interrogation room door, his arms folded.

I'll take her from here, he'd said, and the guard had blinked, then walked off without any argument. Temporarily freed from his hold, she'd stared at Kresten like a fool, wanting some kind of explanation for this interruption in routine, but he'd merely grabbed her and marched her back to her cell, professionalism personified. For a heartbeat, she'd let herself believe he was a savior come to rescue her, but as the static field buzzed to life and the door slammed shut behind her, she realized what an irrational hope that had been. And as she'd lain on her bunk the rest of the day, she'd decided she hated him. She'd told him as much two days later when he'd returned.

I don't give a flying dakk what you think of me. Stand against the wall and put your hands on your head.

His response rolled around and around in her head, long-forgotten yet now remembered against her will. Had he been lying that first time they'd met, or had he simply changed his mind about her? The flower had appeared under her mattress not a lunar cycle later, so the answer, was obvious. Perhaps it wasn't affection he'd felt then, or even attraction, but he'd respected her. He'd cared.

So no, it didn't matter if he'd hated her at first. He didn't now, and that was all that mattered. And she loved him in return. She repeated it over and over to herself as she paced the cavern, finally stopping by the pool for a drink. She downed an entire can before she noticed the flower. Ripped away from both the sun and her proximity, the petals had already started to wilt.

Ryllis sank to the cavern floor next to them, closed her eyes, and began to cry.

It was impossible to tell how long she'd been in the cave, though the growling of her stomach and the drastic improvement in the flower's health gave her some idea. The new moon had been just a few days away the last night she'd spent in Kresten's home, so even if it wasn't quite gone, it should be dark enough outside for the forest to hide her. Without even knowing if the sun was showing or not, Ryllis slipped back out the narrow passageway and toward the cave entrance with the blooms behind her ear.

It was an easier crawl out, though that might have been desperation from the hunger. Kresten's house was likely alarmed, or worse, guarded, but there was enough food in the forest she could scavenge for a small meal. And when Lina and Aared made a trip to town? She'd sneak into their house for more supplies.

Only a dim sliver of moonlight shone through the trees when she reached the entrance, and as carefully as she could, Ryllis picked her way through the rocks to the trail. Faster than she'd expected, her eyes adjusted, and she breathed in the deep scent of pine. She'd missed it, deep in the cavern, and reached up for one of the lower boughs. It wouldn't cover up the entire damp scent of the cave, but it would be something fresh and clean. She tossed it inside the entrance to take with her on her way back.

Her footsteps were scarcely audible over the sounds of the forest at night. Birds chirped, wolves howled, and the wind—was there a storm coming or was it always this loud? She could scarcely hear herself think, and her heartbeat, which had kept her company in the echoing cavern, was no longer her companion. Ryllis quickened her pace, and far sooner than she wanted, the lights of the Lina and Aared's house came into view.

Eggs would make a decent meal if she could figure out a way to cook them over the fire starter. Ryllis crept closer to the house, staying just off the trail. The hens would be in their own little house or roosting in the trees above, and they'd seemed to like her—though there was always a chance they wouldn't be happy with an intruder. No matter. She only needed a few, and she could be in and out before anyone noticed.

The soft clucking from somewhere near the house gave away her targets. Ryllis followed the sounds toward a small clapboard building set off in a clearing. Some sort of Vilarian anti-predator technology surrounded it, and judging by the noise the hens were making, they knew they were safe, even at night. She wanted to call out to them, get them to stop scratching around on the ground inside, but that idea could easily backfire. Lina would notice if they fell silent, anyway.

Instead, she felt around the sides of the coop, looking for an opening to the nests. Kresten's fear of the hens poked about in her mind as she did, and when she tried to laugh at it off, sadness took its place.

Don't tell me the chickens love you, too.

She leaned her head against the coop and took a breath. Kresten would laugh if he saw her here right now, sobbing over him rather than worrying about the chickens. Especially when they were laughing at her, too. She was too distraught to hear what they were saying in her head, but they were talking about her more than to her, that was for certain.

"You know," she said to herself, "for someone who managed to escape a situation you didn't want to be in, you're awfully upset about missing him."

"Escape?" a voice behind her called. "Is that why you're up here stealing my eggs?"

The living area was dark. Not even a fire glittered, and Ryllis wrapped the blanket Lina had given her tighter around her chest. She hadn't been able to touch the tea Aared had made for her, her gut sour and her hands shaky.

"Now tell us what's going on," Lina asked from beside her. "Why aren't you on the way to Dannerth?"

Ryllis's heart began to slow. "Dannerth?"

"His Highness left a day and a half ago." Aared crossed her arms and frowned at her. "A two solar cycle mission to Dannerth. He sent Lina a message. They didn't allow him to take you?" Confusion spiked his question.

She shook her head, willing tears away. "He's not headed for Dannerth. Not of his own free will, anyway. They took him," she said. "And I—"

Aared's eyes narrowed in the dark. "Took him?"

"Fleet officers." Her throat began to close up, and she moved to tuck her hair behind her ear before she remembered. "I watched them, from high up in the meadow."

"Escorting him, likely," Lina said. "It's not though a prince of Vilaria is expected to carry his own gear. Though His Highness may have argued with them about that. He always does."

Kresten carried his own bags all the time, and the Fleet let him. He had when they'd returned from Cereth. Why weren't they believing her?

"No. No one was carrying any bags at all. They had their weapons out, and—" Ryllis held her hands up in front of her, even though they hadn't stopped trembling. "And his hands— they'd handcuffed him behind his back. He wasn't going with them willingly. Lina, I know what I saw. It was the same when they came for me on Cereth."

Aared scratched at the floor with his bare foot, looking guilty.

"Have they been up here looking for me?" She was finally able to make a move for the tea.

Lina nodded. "Two days ago. They poked around, asked a few questions and left. We assumed you had fled and His Highness sent them to find you and bring you back."

"But they might be back again, if what you say is true," Aared pointed out. "Where have you been hiding?"

Ryllis gripped the cup tighter. Aared was Vilarian. She didn't dare trust him—and even if she did, the Fleet telepaths wouldn't have a problem torturing him or Lina if the two sided with a slave. *Their prisoner's slave.* "There's a clearing on the other side of Azov Creek. And a hollowed-out log. It breaks the wind and keeps me warmer, at least."

"That's a long way to come in the dark for some eggs." Aared cocked his head to the side, then seemed to accept her lie. "What can we do?"

"I don't want to get you in trouble."

"Nonsense," Lina said. "Besides, if you're right, they'll be right back up here as soon as they find out I work for him. We're already involved."

"But I don't know—"

That wasn't true, was it? She knew exactly what she needed to do, what kind of help she needed. She couldn't hide in a deep cave for the rest of her life—Kresten needed her. She couldn't have ever predicted that when he'd led her on to the jump ship on Cereth, but he needed her now, and that wasn't something to be discounted.

And maybe, just maybe, she needed him, too.

Aared sighed as he stood and headed to the kitchen. "We can talk about it tomorrow night —but I'll come get you after the sun comes up, and it's certain the mountain is clear. You don't need to be wandering the hills in the dark."

"No. Wait." Ryllis looked up at both of them and took a deep breath. "Lina—can you contact Prince Vidar for me?"

CHAPTER FIFTEEN

There was something ironic about being manacled to a table just like the one he'd once restrained Ryllis to—in a room she would be all too familiar with. Maybe he dreaded the punishment for snickering at her way back then, or perhaps it was how the universe seemed to come full circle sometimes, but whatever the reason, Kresten could scarcely breathe as he waited for whatever was to come. It shouldn't have frightened him after several lunar cycles of training for just this situation, but there was something totally and completely wrong about the whole thing, and that set him on edge.

He glanced around at the bare walls and locked door before focusing on the scratch in the center of the table. Exploring his surroundings, if only with his eyes, was a risk,  because he could see the cameras that kept watch on his every move, but he'd never experienced it like this, and his training was difficult to remember. It was strange, in a way, to know he was innocent and yet treated like this by people who would have been kneeling to him in his other life. He wasn't hiding anything, after all. He hadn't done anything wrong besides fail to make Ryllis talk, and that was an administrative issue if the Fleet even chose to make it one, not a criminal matter. Loving her? Even that should have been a slap on a wrist, a letter of reprimand in his file, and an end to his enforced telepathic respite. Yet here he was with an empty steel chair across from him, waiting on Dahl, most likely, to come in and accuse him of—what?

Besides not realizing Ryllis had escaped, he hadn't done anything wrong, and that was an Eradication Council problem to begin with. Even kissing her—like the chocolate and other gifts he'd given her on Cereth, that was easily explained away. He'd needed her to trust him, and what better way to make her feel vulnerable yet safe?

The lie, even in his own mind, made his stomach turn, and he tried to lay his head under the table. That strained his neck too badly, so he finally gave up and let himself slump. The very idea of lying to protect his own ass made him sick. What had she done to him to make himself second-guess everything? And why did it bother him so much?

The answer was obvious. Because if he had failed to protect her, the Fleet would bring in someone else to work her, or the Eradication Council would give her to someone else, and he couldn't subject her to that. Not any longer. Not even if she was guilty. He'd protect her from further pain with his dying breath, that, he was certain of. No matter how Vidar might laugh, or his father might rage, or the Fleet might accuse him of who knew what. If he had anything to say about it, she would never be afraid again.

Or sad.

Or in pain.

Or alone.

Or despairing.

Frantic to forget the feel of her body against his and the ways he'd already let her down, Kresten twisted in his own metal chair as much as he could and swore at the door. They couldn't hear him through it—the doors were manufactured to dampen a man's screams—but the cameras would.

"If this is a joke," he called out, "I'm well over it."

Another few seconds ticked by, then the door hissed open. Dahl entered, wearing a crisp blue uniform that had just come from the laundry, knife-edged pants and all. Realm's sake, he shouldn't care—he'd smelled worse during field exercises in the marshes near Arvika, but the disparity was enough to make every muscle in Kresten's body tighten.

Accentuate your difference in hygiene with the prisoner. Put them in their place right away, if possible.

Dahl had said that once, when he'd first come to Shadow Force, and Kresten had never forgotten it. Now, he gave Kresten only the briefest of looks, then sat down across the table and brushed imaginary dirt from his sleeves. And stared.

How predictable.

It was also, unfortunately, effective. Not as an interrogation technique—Dahl was much better at telepathic questioning than anything else— but being stared at by one's boss tended to make any situation uncomfortable. Especially when one could smell their stink, could sense their own unfamiliar facial hair growing in. Was it his imagination, or did Dahl's nose wrinkle?

"It's no joke," Dahl said after five minutes of silence by Kresten's estimation. "We have some serious concerns about your loyalty and actions since you arrived home from Cereth. Specifically, as they pertain to Amaryllis Camden."

"You must have more than concerns"—Kresten tried to pull his hands free, but his wrists, slick with sweat, only slipped around inside the metal—"if you've got me in here like this."

"Perhaps." Dahl folded his arms and checked his nails. Clean, of course. Bastard was getting better at this. "It's strange that someone who's vocally and consistently eschewed any involvement with an Eradication Council slave —refuse to have them in his household at all— suddenly changed his mind, don't you think? She's rather lovely, I'll give you that, but you've always had ethical standards I can't begin to understand. It's a strange, strange thing."

Kresten's stomach flipped at how casually he'd spoken about her. "I don't need or want domestic slaves, but I changed my mind with her. Colonel Löfgren specifically told me I could request the Eradication Council grant her to me. That I could use her as part of my rehabilitation if I so desired. I wanted to come back to work—fully. This ban on my telepathic powers has gone on long enough. Why not use her to work toward my goal of coming back?"

Dahl didn't so much as bat an eye at his commander's name. "Well, we'll talk about that later. It's rather frustrating to be legally prevented from reading your mind," he said, in a seeming non sequitur. "It's why I fought against having you assigned to this team in the first place. It bothers me quite a bit that one of my own officers isn't subject to the same measures we're allowed to implement on any other prisoner."

Anxious or not, Kresten suppressed a smirk as Dahl's façade slipped. Very few Vilarians were safe like he was—the emperor's immediate family and personal servants knew too much sensitive information for Shadow Force to access. Even when he'd been subjected to the procedure in training, it had been terminated as soon as the telepath had entered his mind—he'd experienced the pain and initial violation, oh, yes, but the questioner hadn't stuck around after that. The restriction was an advantage he'd never considered until now.

"Yes," he said slowly. "I can see why that would bother you."

"Don't look so smug, Lieutenant. You know it's a shortcut, and I have no problem keeping you here until you tell me what I want to know. I would like to believe that's an embarrassment to the royal family that you'd rather not impose."

Kresten swore to himself. That much was true. He hadn't seen his father in three solar cycles, and the man was no doubt too busy to deal with this kind of situation, but he'd no doubt send Austet in his stead. He'd be dead before he allowed his brother to see him like this. If Austet learned of this, no one would ever hear the end of it. And he'd kill the emperor's heir before he could get involved with finding Ryllis.

"What exactly do you want to know?" Kresten asked.

"You know." Dahl tapped his fingers on the table, like he had all the time in the galaxy. A long, slow anxiety began deep in Kresten's chest. Maybe he did. "Start at the beginning," he went on. "When you first started working with Amaryllis Camden, what her plans on Cereth were, how you became involved with her, what your part in the Cerethian resistance is. Anything and everything."

Kresten's blood ran cold. Their bad information, wherever they'd gotten it, was worse than he'd thought.

"My part in the Cerethian resistance?" he asked. "I won't confess to that, because there's nothing to confess. This is a ridiculous accusation, and I demand to know who's made it."

"You aren't in a position to demand anything, though I don't quite blame you for staying silent," Dahl said. "But this is obviously a delicate situation, and we can't go publicly accusing you without proof. We also can't free you, suspecting the kinds of things you've been involved in." He sighed and tapped his fingers again. "So, until we have a full confession, I suppose you'll simply have to disappear."

He didn't have to explain further. The most significant Shadow Force prisoners disappeared all the time, deprived of any trial or even an official Eradication Council sentence. Not that a member of the royal family ever stood in front of the Council anyway—in the past, they'd been executed. That was harder to explain to the public now, and his father would never authorize it without proof, but the implied threat was enough to make him sicker.

"Ostensibly send me to Dannerth for a few solar cycles, will you?" Dannerth, on the other side of the galaxy, was known for its lack of communication. No one would question his disappearance, even his family. He'd vanished for two solar cycles before, hadn't he? "While I pass the time in a cell?"

"With orders to be renewed upon their expiration, naturally." Dahl stood, and the scent of soap and aftershave went with him. "You'll have plenty of time to think over your situation for the next few lunar cycles, Lieutenant. I suggest you use it."

They processed him in a separate part of the building, through a door marked Research, then another three unmarked doors with plainclothes guards outside. The kind that carried rifles and didn't wear name strips like the rest of the Fleet.

He knew about the clandestine Fleet prison in Arvika, of course, had questioned the occasional prisoner incarcerated here, but as he stood in front of a blank wall for a series of photographs, the magnitude of his circumstances hit him. Dahl hadn't been joking about his future, and since he'd disappeared after passing Kresten off to a group of stone-faced guards, he hadn't been making an idle threat, either. They truly intended to lock him up and forget about him for a long, long time.

But this was salvageable. They'd release him almost immediately if he did what they wanted. He could tell them everything. That he'd given Ryllis little gifts in that prison in Cereth because the look in her eyes had killed him, and just seeing the slightest hint of her quiet smile had made his heart do funny things. That he'd been sure enough of her innocence to only go through the most cursory of questioning and investigations once he'd brought her to Vilaria. That she'd tried to kill him and because of the communication issues on the mountain, he hadn't said anything at first, but the situation was now under control. That he still believed she wasn't guilty of the things her father had accused her of, and as a Shadow Force officer, he had every right to declare her innocence as well as her guilt.

But would it be enough?

He debated that as they pulled him into a small room with gray walls. In the end, as they stood him in the center under a set of hanging irons and sweat began to bead on his forehead, he decided he didn't care if it was enough or not.

He'd never say anything. They'd never find out anything she'd told him or the things he'd said and done to her or how he felt about her.

No matter what they did to him.

"Strip."

The order roused him from his thoughts. The guard who'd issued it glared at his hesitation and repeated it. Kresten dropped his pants and shirt in a pile on the floor, then hesitated before he stripped off his underwear, acutely aware of how Ryllis must have felt when she'd been processed on Cereth. That dawdling only earned him a slap over his kidneys with a shock stick, but he scarcely felt the pain, such was his grief. If this was meant to be humiliation by Dahl's order, it had failed—by living even the briefest and most ephemeral of her experiences, he'd become more determined to protect her. Dahl could read a subject's mind like no one's business, but he could stand to learn a thing or two about love.

He became even more convinced of that fact as the guards searched him, and with an eventual detachment he welcomed more than freedom itself, he did everything they asked. Without protest, he opened his mouth and moved his tongue around, squatted and coughed, put on the dark gray uniform he was so used to seeing from the other side. What did it matter now? They could degrade him as much as they wanted, as long as they were doing it to him and not her. But when they sat him at a console and told him to sign, he finally objected.

"What is this?" he asked. His voice was still firm, still Fleet officer, and for that he was grateful. It took away from the bruise that was forming over his lower back.

"Your orders to Dannerth. Sign your receipt and acknowledgment, Lieutenant." The use of his rank was a mockery.

"You've got to be kidding." Dahl had said as much, but Kresten hadn't honestly believed it. They'd gone so far as to falsify orders? Of course they had. He looked up at the chief who stood above him, wearing a smirk he would have never chanced in front of an officer three solar cycles ago. "I won't do that."

A punishing agony shot up his left arm from his elbow, red-hot fire through his muscles. Kresten fell against the console, gasping for air that didn't exist anymore, clutching for any kind of sanity that remained as his nerves misfired. The cool glass of the screen cut through the fire, and he focused on that. *Cool, like water.* The wave of pain finally retreated, and he sagged forward, his face against the screen, limp. Everything hurt. His muscles, his skin, his eyes, his heart.

Dakk.

"You will sign them. Or you'll find out what that feels like on a place a lot more sensitive than your elbow." Kresten flinched as the guard tapped the stick between his legs, then returned it to its holder. "Sign the orders, *Lieutenant.*"

Kresten reached out, his right hand wavering, and managed to sketch out a semblance of his signature. He had to wipe his own drool away first, and it looked like he'd been writing after a three-day bender, but Shadow Force would claim that he had been. It was the reaction of most Fleet personnel sent to Dannerth. He stared at his signature, the death of all his hope of escape, as they yanked him up. After the near-electrocution, he could barely walk, but that didn't stop them from jerking him down a hallway and past a row of doors.

A few guards stared at him, recognition on their faces, then walked off as indifference replaced it. Kresten knew what they were thinking. It was only an exercise, like the Fleet liked to do every so often, and Lieutenant Westermark, His Imperial Highness, had finally had his number drawn. They'd all forget about him in another day or so, would never realize he was still locked behind one of those doors. And if they found out? They'd wonder, but they wouldn't do anything to stop it.

He knew the procedure his guards were about to subject him to, knew what was coming, and held his breath as the guards shoved him to the floor and restrained his hands behind his back. They injected the control chip in the skin at the base of his skull as he gritted his teeth, and before the wound had stopped stinging, they pulled a hood over his head and cinched it tight around his neck. Trained or not, Kresten struggled to control his panic. Sometimes knowledge was misery. Ignorance would be more pleasant in this place.

After a few deep breaths, the darkness—and the knowledge of what was to come—became his friend. It would get worse when they removed the hood, that he knew. The denial of sight was only until the chip read and stored his biological operations—once it aligned itself to his pulse, respiratory rate, and brain waves, the guards could use it to do any number of things: paralyze him, blind him, create hallucinations, cause him pain. It wasn't something anyone in the Fleet had a problem with until it was under their skin. He hadn't thought anything of it before now, just like he hadn't thought anything of most of his life.

He had to think of something else, anything but what was coming, anything but how the rough fabric of his new uniform rubbed his overly sensitive skin.

The mountains.

Lina's raspberry tarts.

Fresh snow.

The way Mother looked at him on those rare mornings she still knew who he was.

Anything to keep his mind of what was coming. But as the burning of the injection faded into a minor annoyance, he couldn't focus on any of those. He rolled to his side, the metal cutting into his wrists as he did, and thought of how much he wanted to run his fingers through Ryllis's hair.

CHAPTER SIXTEEN

*D*im light flickered down the passageway, and Ryllis pressed herself against the cave wall, behind the large boulder. If it wasn't Lina with the prince, there probably wasn't any way to hide herself, but it was the only thing that made her feel safe, even if her back was now covered in dirt. She shivered again, trying to keep her teeth from chattering. She'd meant what she'd told Kresten —she couldn't handle the cold anymore.

"Ryllis?"

Lina's voice echoed through the chamber, but Ryllis didn't move from the wall. She was earlier than they'd agreed, wasn't she? It was so hard to tell without the sun and moon, and idly, Ryllis realized she should have brought a clock. It could be a trap. Those Fleet officers that had taken Kresten away could have forced Lina to lead them to her.

"She said she'd be here, Your Highness," came Lina's voice. The light flickered around the chamber, casting eerie shadows on the rock. "Ryllis?"

"For pity's sake, Kresten," the prince hollered, "This isn't funny. You're supposed to be headed to Dannerth, and I'm supposed to be on my way to Carilles for some much overdue relaxation. If you've had me dragged me back to this cave as some sort of prank, so help me—"

Ryllis stood and blinked in the light. The prince was cleaner than he should have been after his crawl through the tunnel, but a smear of dirt marked his cheek. His face went pale, then red with rage when he saw her.

"You. What's going on here? What have you done?" He twisted toward Lina. "If you've brought me here to to—well, I can't even imagine why you've brought me here. An escaped slave? Where's my brother? Dead?"

"No! Your Highness." Ignoring all sense of reason, Ryllis darted from behind the rock and stood in front of him. "I didn't know who else to turn to. I need your help. Your brother needs your help. They've taken him, and . . . it's my fault."

"Well yes, they've taken him. He's headed to Dannerth for two solar cycles—and you were supposed to be with him." He whirled toward Lina again, like she was responsible. "You knew about this? That she escaped—or whatever she's doing here?"

Lina put her hands in front of her, trying to placate him. "Your Highness, my lord, that's not where he is. Ryllis saw them take him away. I can't begin to guess where he is right now, but it's not Dannerth."

"You're crazy," he said, pointing at Lina. "And you—" This to Ryllis. "I'll be notifying the Eradication Council of your whereabouts. Whether they decide to send you to Dannerth with him or execute you isn't my business."

He turned to go, leaving Ryllis wondering which version of him was worse—the prince who'd grabbed her or the one who was ignoring her plea and his brother's predicament.

"Wait. Your Highness, please." She ground her feet into the cave floor. "Do you love your brother?"

The prince froze, his back to her. Ah, there was the mud. He'd slid through the passageway on his back for some reason.

"Because I do, too. And he's in this position because he loves me. You may not believe me, and I wouldn't blame, but you even if you don't —I have information the Fleet would be interested in. Consider this a chance to return an escaped Fleet prisoner to where she belongs. That's all I'm asking. You won't be involved in anything untoward. Just leave the Eradication

Council out of it for now, please. The Fleet is who took him, and that's who's looking for me. You have nothing to lose by turning me in to them."

She held her breath as he stood there in the dim of the cavern. If only she'd decided on this course of action while the Fleet had still been roaming the hills searching for her. If only Kresten would do the right thing and tell them where to find her—for surely, he had must have some idea. If only his brother would listen.

"You're serious about this."

"If I turn myself in, they'll let him go—but they're gone from these hills as far as we can see. Short of walking to Arvika, I have no way to do that. And even then, they'd be wary. I need a way to get to them without arousing suspicion."

"Whereas if his brother happened to come across you while he was helping to secure the lodge after his departure, no one would be wiser," he said to the low ceiling of the passageway.

"No, Your Highness." Her voice cracked. The prince was going to agree, and the Fleet would . . . she couldn't think of what they would do to her. "They would not."

The prince turned around and looked at the cavern floor as she held her breath. "I will do this for you."

Her heart leapt.

"But not out of the goodness of my heart."

"I—" Her legs began to shake. "I don't understand."

The prince closed the distance between them in two breaths, and she looked away, toward the blossoms.

"You say you love my brother," he said, "and I believe that. I also have no reason to contend what you've said about him. So even though I'm unaccustomed to being told I can't do something to a slave, even though I'd love to sample what he hasn't"—his eyes roamed over her breasts, and she braced herself for his touch —"I'll respect whatever relationship you have.

The Realm know he needs to get some eventually."

She wanted to back away, but she wouldn't show fear in front of him.

"But I can still look and admire. While you work in my garden, perhaps. I've noticed how much better Kresten's are looking since you arrived."

Her heart fluttered. Prince Vidar didn't know what he'd just suggested. It was the easiest thing he could have asked of her—and how fitting that the secret that would kill her would be responsible for Kresten's salvation?

"I'll do it," she said quietly. "But for how long? There can't be much time before—"

"You let me worry about time." The prince's eyes lit up in the dim of the cavern. "You just worry about how you're going to turn my garden into a paradise—and only then will I hand you over to the Fleet."

If Kresten's lodge in the mountains had been warm and comfortable, the estate the prince had brought her to was cold and hard. Ryllis shivered under the thin blanket as the auto-lights grew brighter. They gradually illuminated her new room: the small bed in the corner on which she lay and the empty table next to it. Those two pieces of furniture and a few servant's uniforms hanging on a hook by the door were the sum of the contents. It wasn't a cell—there wasn't even a lock on the door—but the lack of windows and plain concrete floor made it feel the same.

I'll come for you in the morning, the servant who'd deposited her here the night before had said. Ryllis had gone to sleep almost immediately afterward, bone-weary yet missing the cavern floor, only to awake already missing Kresten's lodge and the fireplace in his bedroom—not to mention his arms.

The clothes she'd been wearing when she'd fled the lodge were dirty and reeking of cave mud, and that was the only reason she deigned to change into the uniform. They were scratchy compared to the luxurious fabrics she'd worn in the mountains, but Kresten was likely dealing with worse. She couldn't let herself forget that.

While she perched on the edge of the bed and waited for the servant to return for her, more sleep was out of the question. The woman finally did, a few biscuits and a cup of tea in hand, but eating was out of the question as well. Ryllis declined the food and followed her to the main house, all white marble and bright lights and crystal fixtures. It was colder than the servants' quarters, and she was shivering in the corridor behind the kitchen when the prince appeared.

He looked her up and down and smiled. "Kresten was right to allow you to dress as he did. The brown does absolutely nothing for your complexion."

"It also has no bearing on my ability to fix your gardens. Show me, please, Your Highness."

The prince's smile only grew more brilliant. "This way."

He led her to a cavernous kitchen, not the gardens like she'd expected. Like the rest of the building, it was cold white, so different from the rustic charm of Kresten's mountain hideout. It was everything she'd expected when Kresten had told her of his identity, and seeing her fear in real life sent a shiver of dread through her.

"This isn't the garden."

"To think he managed to find himself a smart one, too." He pointed toward a row of brown herbs in matching white planters. "Fix them first. Then the gardens."

Ryllis couldn't hide a soft snort. "Your Highness —they're dead."

"So?"

The dread grew thicker, like a vine wrapping around her middle. The prince had done this on purpose. He didn't appear to hate his brother, but he clearly didn't understand how much was at stake. A playboy, then, who cared about nothing but his own pleasure and amusement —and unfortunately, she seemed to be the moment's entertainment.

"I can't make them come back to life!"

"Pity." He pulled up a chair upholstered in ivory velvet and flopped into it, arms crossed. "Try."

Her shoulders sank. How long would she have to play his game? She should have negotiated his terms more carefully, but she'd been desperate back in the cave. Cautiously, she carried each of the planters to the deep—and unused, of course—sink. The prince would be ignorant enough to think a bit of water would revive the plants, wouldn't he? It was worth a try.

She hated searching his kitchen for supplies, but he didn't say anything as she rifled through several cabinets for a pair of scissors. Trimming back the plants would be a start, and hopefully her presence would be enough to change their mind about dying.

The scissors refused to show themselves, so Ryllis returned to plants and broke off the worst of the dried branches. The aromatic scent of rosemary and basil filled the air, so perhaps the herbs weren't as far gone as they appeared. They certainly looked better, even though as she worked, she reduced the size of the plants by half. She prayed they wouldn't spring immediately to life right in front of the prince who was watching her intently—perhaps her mother had been right about staying away from the flowers.

Satisfied at last, she waved him over. "They'll need regular watering and a little more light than they're getting now. But I think they'll make it."

"Brilliant." The prince gave the slightest glance before turning his attention back to her. "I suppose time will tell, won't it?"

"How much time?"

He shrugged and gestured down a corridor. Ryllis followed him through a high-ceiling gallery toward a set of glass doors. The morning sun shone brilliantly through it, making her squint and long for the early morning fog of the mountains. Though she'd told Kresten over and over how much she despised the cold, the truth was, she'd begun to love it because it reminded her of him.

The prince pulled over the doors with a flourish. "Here we are!"

Ryllis froze next to him at the sight.

The rear garden was a disaster, even for spring, later here than in the mountains. A large conservatory, half its glass panels broken out, filled the left side of a wide-open space. A few spikes of green shone through the glass, but those robust plants were in the minority—most others were brown, and even from this distance, dried and dead. She averted her gaze from it. The greenhouse would take a lunar cycle itself.

The rest of the garden wasn't any better. What should have been a riot of color this time of the solar cycle was a wasteland of weeds and stunted shrubs. A trellis at the far end of the stone path was overgrown with a vine she couldn't identify, and the gazing pond to its side was filled with green muck. A few stubborn roses showed off some green leaves, but they were spindly and sick at the same.

Ryllis put her hand to her mouth. She'd agreed to an impossible task.

"You look surprised."

"It's—but Your Highness, you must have a gardener! Or several!" She couldn't hide her shock.

"Quit. Four of them now. Something about me being difficult to work for." The prince winked at her.

"You knew it was this bad. You knew there was no way I could fix it."

"Indeed. But you never asked."

Ryllis clenched her fists until her knuckles were sore. "This was not a fair agreement."

"Again, you never asked about the state of the garden. Just stated you would do anything for my help."

"But he doesn't have this much time!" The stillness and unnatural silence of the place seemed to agree with her.

"Then I suggest you work fast." The prince pushed by her and settled onto a stone bench next to the path. "Might I suggest the weeds first?" he called. "I'd love to see you bent over."

Ryllis marched to the conservatory instead. The front door nearly came off the hinges when she yanked it open, and she left it lying against the front. She'd regret her choice of starting place when it rained and she was outside trimming shrubs, but the prince wouldn't follow her inside here. It was simply too hot. She stood in the center, hands on her hips, and stared. Where to even begin?

It matters less where you start, than that you start.

A little more hope sprang into her heart at the idea. Her eyes landed on the packages of seeds in a far corner, and she hurried over to them. Seeds would sprout in a few days if she paid attention to them, and the prince didn't seem like he'd realize if they did it a bit *too* quickly. The color would go a long way toward making the greenhouse seem clean, even if it wasn't something she'd be proud of anywhere else.

She ignored the dirty gloves on the potting table, relishing the feel of cool dirt. Vidar might have been watching her from his bench outside, but she didn't care as she filled four seedling trays with soil. It smelled the same on any planet, and she took deep breaths each time she packed another section with seeds of herbs and wildflowers.

That completed, she stepped back and examined her handiwork. The wire racks looked a little more cared-for at least, and she ran her fingers as lightly as she could over the dirt, pretending to smooth it. She'd never dared do such a thing at Kresten's estate, and the guilt over doing it now took away some of the joy she'd felt in planting the seeds. Necessary, yet frightening and unwanted at the same time. What had Kresten said, so long ago?

. . . *if his gift was that uncontrolled, he had to die.*

Hers wasn't controlled. It barely existed in the first place—just enough for the Star Realm to fear and forbid it. She'd never even considered it a *power* until her mother had watched a cut rose grow roots as Ryllis had adjusted it in a vase.

That had led to all sorts of lectures and warnings, and though her mother had never told her father what she'd witnessed, she'd prohibited Ryllis from being anywhere near the garden. When she'd died, Ryllis had taken the opportunity, and her father, in his ignorance, hadn't fought her choices of studies. She was cautious, oh, yes, but being able to be near her beloved plants had been like another chance at life.

Ryllis ignored the memory and brushed the dirt from her hands on to the horrid brown pants. It was an improvement of a sort. She could trim the thick vines off the trees later, and then, perhaps, it would be clear the trees weren't dead but merely slumbering. The building itself . . . well, nothing could be done about the broken glass this morning. Vidar would have to order his own replacement and find someone to install it. She could clean the remaining glass, though, as much as she could reach.

With a sigh, she picked up a rag and began to fill a bucket.

It was hours before the prince entered, his eyebrows raised and no smirk on his face at last.

"Kresten never mentioned you were such a hard worker."

Ryllis wiped away the sweat from her brow. The broken glass made for a bit of a breeze, but not enough. The prince was wasting this space —he could be growing all sorts of exotic tropical plants in here.

"Perhaps he's not fond of working me to death," she replied.

"You're a slave." The prince's brown furrowed. "You're not warming his bed, so what else would he do with you?"

Ryllis almost snapped at him, then stopped. Prince Vidar's confusion was real, and she found she didn't know what to do with a reality she'd never understand. She shrugged and pointed toward the holes in the ceiling and walls.

"Sixteen panes missing. I wrote the measurements down. You can have someone order them."

He frowned, then looked up. "It looks good in here otherwise. I thought it would all be dead, but it's quite a bit greener that I'd expected."

"It's not difficult, nor is everything dead. It was just desperate for a bit of care."

"Yes." He cleared his throat. "Now what?"

She edged by him toward the door, trying to work a thorn out of her thumb. Her muscles were screaming for a hot bath and she was desperate for a drink of water, but asking the prince for anything was out of the question.

"I start weeding, I suppose," she said.

The prince grinned. "I was hoping you'd say that. Let's, shall we?"

CHAPTER SEVENTEEN

*N*o one had ever told him the hallucinations precipitated by the thing in his brain were so real. Blind yet again, Kresten writhed on the floor, trying to recover from the latest chip-induced seizure, but the vision in his mind didn't go away like his tremors were beginning to. Right there, just in front of him, stood a graceful yet soft figure. He reached for her with shaking arms; she laughed and took a step backward.

I need you, he called out.

I need you, too, Ryllis's figure mouthed at him. Her laugh stopped, and she stood there, gazing down at him, thoughtful. *But you know it's not going to happen.*

"Ryl—" He slammed his mouth shut before he could call out her name. This could be a test for all he knew. They could be trying to find out how he felt about her.

Ryllis, he said in his mind instead. Speaking to her like this was so comfortable, so natural, so sensual. The seductiveness of speaking to her telepathically like this coursed through his veins, and for a moment, he forgot where he was and what he meant to say. It took feeling around the wound at the back of his neck to remind himself, ground himself in reality again. *Why isn't it going to happen?*

You know. You've always known, since you brought me here. Her expression grew sad, and he swore in his mind. It was so real. So real. *They're going to kill me. I'm sorry, Kresten. I know you wanted more, and I did, too. But you'll get over me. You'll be happy again. I promise.*

Kresten was beginning to formulate an argument in his head when the black figures approached behind her. He wanted to scream at her to turn around and defend herself, but something told him she already knew what was about to happen—and was going to allow it.

Arms, dozens of them, grabbed hold of her, at her arms, at waist, at her neck, at her legs. Ryllis flinched as they pulled her toward the shadows, then began to struggle and scream, but it was too late. The hands multiplied, clutching at her, until he could scarcely see her devastated eyes any longer.

I love you. Ryllis—I love you.

She couldn't hear him, even though he screamed the words inside his head. Something deep in his soul told him she couldn't hear him anymore. Still, if he said it over and over, maybe he could stop them.

Don't go. Don't do this. Don't let them take you. They'll do things—listen in—get off her!

As if in reply to his order, the hands vanished. Ryllis collapsed on her side, her bare skin wraithlike in the dark of his cell. He watched her chest move up and down, rapidly at first, and then too slowly. She didn't speak to him as she lay there, even though he repeated her name over and over in his head.

The gurney appeared in the corner of his vision as he called to her, and he vomited, though it didn't make a noticeable difference in the already rank and filthy cell. Was it still a hallucination or was it a memory? He knew, intellectually, that it was nothing more than a vision, but it felt like both, because he'd done this very thing to others. He'd sat next to prisoners strapped to a gurney just like this, sometimes listening to them scream for mercy, sometimes simply watching as they stared at the ceiling with eyes that had given up.

And now the same hands were reaching for Ryllis again. They lifted her up, stretched her on to the gurney, then attached leads to her head. Kresten pushed himself up from the ground, but something clicked audibly in his head, and his legs went immobile. He crashed to the ground, landing on his shoulder, and screamed —not from the pain, because this was mild, but out of rage and frustration. The guards were controlling him from somewhere close by, with the knowledge that they were keeping him from someone he loved.

He bit his tongue enough to draw blood and dragged himself toward the gurney with shaking arms. Another click. He almost vomited at the sound, but his head fell straight down before he could, landing on his nose that time. Metallic-tasting fluid filled his mouth, and as it pooled under his face, warm and sticky, he idly realized that he'd broken his own nose with his weight.

Idiot. It's not real. It's not real. She's safe, somewhere out in the mountains, trying to find her way back to Cereth.

He lifted his head off the concrete just enough. Hallucination or not, he would watch. If he didn't, they'd do much worse, and there wasn't much point in entertaining them with his pain for no reason. As if she was truly there, Ryllis turned toward him as the tattoo needles began to dance across her skin. The smell of burning flesh, acrid and strong, filled his nose.

I love you, too, she said. *And when I'm gone, you need to remember that. I need you to remember me.*

Stay with me. Just stay with me. I can talk you through it. I can help you keep them out.

It was a lie. He knew it, and she knew it. Her mouth opened in a grotesque reproduction of a shriek, then her eyes rolled back in her head. Frozen from head to toe, he could do nothing but stare while she convulsed from the nanobiotes that began to flow through her bloodstream. He called her name over and over again, silently and then out loud, but she never responded again.

The black circle, when it finally bloomed across her side, made him scream.

They hauled him, stiff and shaking, from the cell. Kresten didn't think he'd been able to see for over a lunar quarter, but in this place, who could tell? The hallucinations of Ryllis's treatment had been the worst by far, but the rest wasn't pleasant—physically, if not emotionally. They shocked him from a distance through the chip in his neck whenever he closed his eyes for longer than they felt appropriate, and when they weren't doing that or trying to convince him of his own insanity, he was blind. It made eating difficult and finding the hole that passed for his toilet almost impossible. No, they hadn't forced him to piss all over himself yet, but that was about all he could say for them.

He wondered about his temporary release from the cage as they dumped him in a chair and restrained his hands. It couldn't be anything good—or it could just be a break. Dahl not wanting to see the outcome of his work. There was no room for squeamishness within Shadow Force, but even so, some handled the work better than others. Sure enough, his ears picked up the unmistakable sound of Dahl's footsteps and annoyed breathing outside. When the door hissed shut, Kresten forced the stress from his shoulders. It didn't work.

"This would be a lot more comfortable if you'd let me see," he said, as Dahl's chair screeched across the floor.

There was a long pause, like Dahl didn't know what to do with him speaking first. A small click echoed in his brain, and the blackness became gray, then the interview room appeared in his vision, hazy and dark. Kresten tried to blink the rest of the fog away, but it hung around him like mountain fog on an autumn morning.

"What do you say?" Dahl asked.

Ass. "Thank you, sir."

"You're welcome. I can't promise how long it'll last, but watching you stare at nothing gets to me. It's unnatural."

"Yeah. I bet it really bothers you. My heart is breaking for you and the discomfort seeing me like this must cause you." The very last shred of politeness he'd been holding onto had gone out the window when they'd stimulated the chip and sent painful spasms up his calves a few days ago. The treatment had lasted longer than he'd thought he could survive; it was surprising he could still walk.

"You can believe me or not, but I don't relish this, Lieutenant. It guilts me, to be honest. Not that you're going through a punishment that's so richly deserved, naturally, but that I have to do it to one of my own people. Without His Majesty knowing, as well. Keeping that kind of secret makes everyone here anxious."

"And you can believe it or not," Kresten said, as the room finally sharpened, "I don't much care how anxious you are."

Dahl chuckled. "No, I wouldn't think you would."

"Then why am I here?"

Expected me to change my mind so soon?

"I'd like to go through all the information from Governor Camden with you. I understand that you'd rather believe his daughter is innocent, and I can't say I blame you for that. But regardless"—Dahl put his hand on a stack of paper and pushed it slightly toward him—"she's not, and his hours of voluntary interviews and the documentation he provided will prove it. Just take a look."

Kresten glared.

"Oh," Dahl said lightly. "That's right. Perhaps I'll need to read some of the more interesting bits to you. Here's a good one. Interviewer: When your daughter didn't arrive in the office that morning as scheduled, did you try to contact her? Camden: Yes. Interviewer: Were you able to reach her? Camden: No. Her comm was off. Interviewer: Did she often leave her comm off? Camden: Never."

"That's your proof? You're reaching."

"It's proof she didn't want to be tracked."

"Or that she didn't want to be bothered."

"Know her that well, do you? I suppose that's no surprise." Dahl smiled. "Interviewer: When you came home that evening, what was she doing? Camden: Throwing a bunch of herbs in the garbage disposal. When she saw me, she tossed a few data drives in behind them. Interviewer: Did you recognize the drives? Camden: No. Everything I use at home is in the network. Ryllis as well. Interviewer: You don't even own any? Camden: They're a security risk. I don't allow them in the house."

Kresten closed his mind against the memory of the most recent hallucination. "So she trashed some disks and plants. So what?" The answer was building in his head, but the chip must have slowed down his thought process.

"Disks her father said weren't allowed in the house. Why would she have any portable data, unless she meant to hide it from him—and by extension, us?"

"Possibly because she's an attractive young woman? They have secrets."

"The governor says their relationship was fine."

Dahl couldn't possibly be this dense. "She's an adult, forced to live with her father and stepmother because we denied her a work permit. I would assume that drove a wedge in between them."

"Sure," Dahl said. "Maybe enough of one that she decided to take out her frustrations on the people who put her in that position."

"None of this proves a thing." He was shaking now, but it *was* cold. Dahl wouldn't think anything of it.

Kresten was thinking, though. The answer spun around and around in his head, the ban on reading the minds of members of the imperial family took on a new importance. His thoughts were safe, and now that was crucial. Because this one, right on the surface, bubbling like seafoam, the first thing any telepath would see if they cared to take a look—there it was.

Ryllis had a secret, yes. He hadn't been entirely sure of the extent of her secret, not before, but he knew now.

Those beady-eyed, hostile chickens that had *listened* to her.

His garden. It'd been a late spring, but you'd never know by looking at the flowers.

The way she'd panicked when he'd told the story of Carl Hellquist. When he'd told her Hellquist deserved to die for using his powers.

How she'd refused to let Shadow Force into her mind, even to clear herself.

The flower in her cell back on Cereth. It hadn't died.

Ever.

Even pruned and without light.

Ryllis had an innate power.

What it was, he didn't know. There were so many gifts in the history books and the Vilarian aristocracy now, and most couldn't be identified by any kind of name or even skill: some could cure disease by the laying of hands, some like himself received telepathy, others 'saw' through wormholes, allowing the Star

Realm to conquer new worlds. Ryllis, it appeared, talked to nature.

Harmless, and yet, the Star Realm didn't care anything about that. They only cared that through some genetic accident—for Governor Camden wouldn't have been able to hide anything like this—she'd been gifted with a power rare yet feared.

And Dahl couldn't know. Kresten would die here before he let anyone know. No one would touch her, no one would harm her.

"It proves enough." Dahl arranged the paper in a clean stack and folded his hands on top of it. "But just for you, when we find her and bring her here, we'll read her mind. Just to make sure."

Like the hallucinations the chip prompted over and over. But they couldn't. Ryllis wouldn't be able to hide it. She'd been hiding it from him, and that meant it was right on the top of her mind. It wouldn't take thirty seconds for them to find out, and then they would kill her, just like she'd told him in his hallucination. She had known, from the very first day, that it would end like this. Even when he'd brought her to the lodge, even when he'd carried her and healed her ankle, even when he'd kissed her and she'd cried afterwards.

She'd known.

And beyond protecting herself, she'd been protecting him.

A blast of pain shot through his head, but it wasn't from the chip this time. Love hurt. Fear was physically painful. No one had ever told him that. Not until Elise had died, anyway, and he'd hated everyone for a very long time for not warning him how much he would mourn her.

But he'd survived, as most who suffered such a loss did. What else had there been to do but push forward and let each morning arrive like its own gift? The pain waned after a time, and he'd forgotten—they said women forget their labor pains, and maybe the same was true of the death of a spouse. He doubted it, but perhaps.

Then he'd met Ryllis. Heedless of the hurt she might one day cause him, he'd gone after her,

349

certain he'd never experienced pain like Elise's loss ever again.

And now it was happening. The worst thing he could imagine.

Kresten opened his mouth to argue, and his vision went black.

CHAPTER EIGHTEEN

*R*yllis woke sore and sunburned. The small room was hot, and she dreaded heading out to the garden for another sweltering afternoon. Spring here was nothing like the cool spring of the mountains. No servants escorted her anymore, and even the prince had taken to watching her from a distance—though he did still watch. Her skin had stopped crawling though, almost as if it realized there was nothing to be done about his lecherous stare.

She downed the cup of tea she'd made the evening before and gave the biscuit a short look before stashing it under her mattress. It was an automatic movement learned in her last days on Cereth, and she hated herself for reverting to such idiosyncrasies of scarcity, but even if she wasn't hungry now, she might be later. Bothering the estate's few servants for food when they didn't provide enough was uncomfortable, so she avoided it.

Prince Vidar wasn't around as she crept through the silent house toward the garden. One thing she'd learned over the past few days was the prince slept in late most mornings, and if she woke early, she would have a few hours to just sit. It was still work, after all. The plants responded to the quiet time in a way they didn't when she was bustling about, pulling weeds, moving pavers, and feeding the younger plants.

This morning dew still glistened on the greening lawn, and she sat cross-legged on it just off the brick path, ignoring how the dewdrops turned her uniform damp. Nothing but the singing of early rising birds disturbed her solitude; streaks of emerald appeared in the grass as she ran her fingers through it. There was a certain peace about it—tinged with anticipation and dread, naturally, but the tranquility almost overwhelmed those.

"And who are you?"

Ryllis started and jumped to her feet at the feminine voice.

The woman who'd surprised her was elderly, almost as much as the prince's half-blind housekeeper. But unlike the housekeeper, she was dressed in finery that put the clothes Ryllis had worn on the mountain to shame. Gauzy fabric draped her body, the bodice embroidered in vines and flowers. It wasn't a design Ryllis could have ever imagined on anyone over ten, but the woman wore it well —the only concession to her age was the color, a deep wine edged in gold that matched the locket around her neck. Fine lines traversed her face, though the delicate scarf she'd wrapped over her shoulders shielded the rest of her exposed skin from the sun.

And—Ryllis's breath caught—and it was Kresten's brilliant and intelligent eyes that peered out from her face.

"Your Majesty." Ryllis sunk to one knee into the damp grass, though it was more from the fear of the prince seeing her do anything else than what this woman could do to her. "I—"

"Vidar's servants aren't allowed to sit." Her gaze grew sharper.

"No, my lady. I apologize. I was only—"

The empress laughed out loud, then raised her hand. "Stand up. And don't look so frightened. I was merely surprised you were brave enough to do it. My son is still lazing about in bed on this beautiful morning, then?"

"I'm sorry—I don't know the prince's whereabouts. I only work in the garden, my lady."

"The garden. Yes. But Vidar hasn't had a gardener in . . ." Her forehead scrunched together. "At least five solar cycles, I believe."

Five? By the state of the place, Ryllis believed it. "He has one now, my lady."

For a time.

"However did he convince you to do it?" Her eyes narrowed at Ryllis's hair. "Are you a slave?"

Ryllis grasped her hands in front of her to keep from picking at her nails. "I volunteered."

Those eyes of Kresten's narrowed. "No one volunteers to work at Vidar's estate."

Ryllis pinched the palm of her hand. With that, the empress was getting too close to the truth. "I did. It was better than the alternative. My lady, I really must be getting to work."

"I would like to help. It's been a long while since I felt the earth between my hands." Her gaze grew distant.

"No!" The empress took a step back at her tone, and Ryllis swore to herself. "Your Majesty, please. There's no need for that. Your hands, your dress—the prince will be here soon and—"

"My hands are old enough already, and fabric can be washed. And my son is loyal enough to not deny his mother whatever she wants, isn't he?"

Ryllis opened her mouth, then closed it. The garden was her sanctuary, hers alone, and the empress was hardly benign, but there was no graceful way out of this situation. Not after the woman had delicately questioned her allegiance, which was tenuous to begin with. Either she yielded to imperial desire this very second or . . .

It wasn't worth thinking about. Only Kresten's life mattered now.

She dipped her head. "I am sure he will not, Your Majesty."

"Good. Then show me where you planned to work."

Her feet were half frozen to the damp ground in anxiety, but Ryllis motioned toward the greenhouse. "Inside, I suppose." She trailed the empress by a pace. If further back was more appropriate, she had no way of knowing. "I need to water the seedlings I have set up."

"I'll do that." The woman bypassed the automated watering system and reached for a large metal can. "No, don't look at that spraying system. If only Vidar had any idea how peaceful it was to do things the old-fashioned way, he might spend more time out here. Realm knows the place needs it."

She busied herself with the can, and Ryllis moved a few rows away, toward the trays of seedlings. They had already sprouted, and she ran her fingers down the edges of the trays, letting them linger on the sections where no green was yet visible. It was an ordinary enough gesture, even though her heart began to pound as she touched the plastic. But empress in sight or not, she needed to do the prince's bidding, and there was no time to waste. Kresten would risk everything for her life, wouldn't he?

"You are not here of your own free will," the empress interrupted, refilling the watering can. She was getting closer and closer to the small nest of mice Ryllis had noticed before, but she didn't dare a word. Royalty didn't like pests.

"No, my lady," she said. "I was brought here from Cereth. Against my will."

"Well, that much is obvious." The empress lay down the can and peered at her. "But I meant here, at Vidar's estate. You were not brought to this place directly from Cereth, and you were happy for a time on Vilaria. You didn't volunteer to serve to Vidar as you claim, so why are you here, at my son's estate? And why are you so unhappy now?"

The woman's uncannily accurate recounting of her experiences was bad enough, but the idea that someone could tell how miserable she was filled Ryllis's eyes with tears until the greenhouse wall blurred in front of her. Vidar would be furious if he found out.

"I have never been happy on Vilaria," she said.

"You dare lie to me, girl? You were happy once —more than that, you were in love. I can sense your loss and guilt. Almost anyone could, and there is only one reason you'd feel that guilty, I would think." She twisted toward a full planter and spoke to the bulbs there. "You fell in love with the wrong person. A Vilarian man, and you would do anything to make the memories go away."

Ryllis took a step backward. Her foot hit the stack of pots behind her, and they crashed the ground, echoing through the greenhouse. The empress was—*oh, stars above, what a mess.* How could she have walked into it? Well, it made sense. Kresten's gift was genetic. She crouched down to gather the pots and looked up, wishing she was anywhere else. Or that the prince would barge in. Or that she was wrong about the empress.

"You're a telepath, Your Majesty?"

The old woman set down the can with a soft chuckle. "I prefer to call it thought transference, but yes. It runs through my father's distant branch of the imperial family, though only one of my children ended up with the gift. I had hoped for more, but it is for the best that it's limited. Being feared like we are is no way to live." Her eyes grew distant, then focused on Ryllis again. "Do not look so afraid of me. I cannot read your thoughts—I can only feel your emotions right now because they are so strong."

"I know how it works," Ryllis said quietly, the mice temporarily forgotten.

"Oh? A Cerethian is familiar with the process? That's odd." Her gaze fell to Ryllis's forearm. "But you don't wear the mark, which means you must have met Kresten. He visits here every so often, but it's been a long while now." She smiled fondly, an expression full of the past and love. "He's at the academy now, you know. He'll make a fine officer one day."

"One day?" The woman's out-of-sequence ramblings made no sense. Kresten had to be a dozen solar cycles out of the academy, if not more.

The empress chuckled. "Well, he's practically a child, after all. I feel it was only last lunar cycle that I rocked him to sleep as he cried."

Ryllis stared at her longer than appropriate. *She's rather ill*, Kresten had said. *She scarcely knows me anymore, and visiting usually makes things worse for her. Kresten is her baby, not a man.*

Vilarian royalty or not, the situation made her heart hurt.

The empress wandered off like their conversation had ended more politely, then glanced at the nest of mice in the empty pot in the corner. Her eyes narrowed, and she bent down toward them. "What's this?"

"My lady—" Ryllis wanted to snatch the pot away.

"Don't look so fearful. Babies are babies, no matter the species, and I do miss them. Ten days or so?"

"I'm not sure. They were here when I arrived."

Blind and hairless they had been, and no matter what she'd promised the prince, Ryllis hadn't been able to bring herself to dispose of them. Their eyes had opened just recently, and they had stared at her every time she'd checked on them, only breaking their gaze to nurse. The mother was little herself, and there was no doubt the babies were borrowing her power to make up for what their mother couldn't provide.

She set the pot down and eyed Ryllis. "You may be worried about them, but you needn't be. They will be healthy and have enough descendants to fairly torment my son. And you . . . you will be happy again."

Ryllis could have laughed, but the seriousness in the empress's tone. "You prophesy as well as read minds, Your Majesty?"

The empress smiled. "No. I just have faith."

"I don't believe in faith anymore." Ryllis looked away, then gritted her teeth. "Your locket is lovely, my lady."

And it was—where Ryllis would have expected that dreaded imperial crest that was stamped inside her servant's uniform and woven into the iron that made up the prince's garden gate, the locket was etched in an organic vine pattern.

The empress pried it open it with gnarled fingers and handed over a dried flower with the faintest reminder of a stem. "Meadow sweetvine," she said. "It fairly covered the imperial gardens until a virus swept through ten solar cycles ago. They never figured out what it was, and within two solar cycles, they were gone. We tried cloning what remained, but it was too late—none are left on Vilaria."

Ryllis brushed a light fingertip over the crisp petals. To think she was holding the last of its kind. "And you miss them."

The empress nodded. "They were a part of my past. I brought them to Carilles from my hometown when I married. They were a reminder, even at my loneliest, that the things I loved weren't truly gone." She picked up the watering can again. "But sometimes even flowers die," she said over her shoulder.

Ryllis's heart skipped. Dare she? There probably wasn't any essence left in the dried bloom, but as easy as cloning was for the average gardener, it was as easy as breathing for her. Even easier, sometimes. And the empress's mental state was too deteriorated for her to realize where any new flower would come from, wasn't it? Without thinking, she snipped off the small stem with her fingernail and stuck it in one of the seedling trays. By tomorrow, she would know.

The empress turned back toward her. "I'm tired," she announced, sticking paper-like petals in the locket once more. "I think it's time for a rest."

Ryllis nodded and handed the flower over before placing her hand over the stem. Her breath caught in her chest at the familiar sensation. It already felt warm. Alive. Everyone on Cereth might think it wrong, but Kresten's mother deserved a little of her happiness back—some of her memories, too.

"Mother!" Prince Vidar strode inside the greenhouse, dressed in finery, like he was about to have a formal audience with the emperor, and Ryllis yanked her hand away from the seed tray. "I didn't expect you here today. What in the Realm—"

His gaze landed on Ryllis, and she pressed herself against the greenhouse glass, as though she could disappear into it. She wanted to reach out to the little stem again, but the way the prince was looking at her . . .

"And you, slave. There are some Fleet officers here to ask you some questions. Your work in the garden is done. You'll go with them, and I don't want to see you back here again."

Suddenly, with her future staring her right in the face, handing herself over to torture and execution—even to save Kresten—didn't seem as appealing. Ryllis leaned her cheek against the glass, heat and ice and terror fighting to outdo each other. She couldn't stare at his hard face and embroidered jacket. She peered into the garden, squinted into the sunrise. On the other side of the thick glass, three silhouettes paced about in dark blue, angular weapons at their sides.

She looked inside, back at the prince, begging him for help with her eyes, but his expression was inscrutable. There was no aid here, for her or Kresten. The prince had fulfilled his bargain, all that she'd asked and nothing more.

This was it, then. She wouldn't fight; she wouldn't run.

With a short curtsey to the wide-eyed empress, Ryllis raised her hands to her sides and walked on to the dew-covered lawn to meet her death.

CHAPTER NINETEEN

They walked her through the heavy steel doors without a word, and her knees refused to stop shaking. Only the thought of Kresten suffering in this place kept her moving forward. Not even the shock sticks they nudged her with when she slowed frightened her from her goal.

She would tell them everything. That she wasn't a traitor, but she'd been hiding her gift for almost her entire life. That Kresten hadn't known. That he hadn't done anything wrong. That he'd questioned her, yes, and she'd denied everything, because he'd never hit on her real secret. That they needed to release him, because he was innocent of whatever they had accused him of.

They would question her the regular way at first, yes, even though she doubted her hand was capable of holding a stylus. And then, when she signed her confession and read it back to them, they would insist on doing just what Kresten had asked of her.

They would read her mind.

She stumbled that time, and the stick hit her in the ribs, right over where they'd hit her before. How far were they going to walk?

Too soon they yanked her to a halt and pushed her into the center of a bland, empty room. There was a man there already, tall and blond with watery blue eyes and a Fleet uniform like Kresten had once worn. Ryllis wanted to lunge at him and wipe the self-satisfied smirk off his face, but she stood there, silent, as he waved off the guards.

"Why did you turn yourself in?" he asked as the door closed.

"I didn't."

The blond man folded his arms. "Don't lie to me. I'm not stupid."

"Because I can't run forever, and I can't hide, not on Vilaria." It wasn't the entire truth, but protecting Kresten meant protecting his brother, to an extent.

He focused in on her. "That's true. Most take a little longer to figure that out."

Ryllis stiffened. "And because he's innocent of whatever you've accused him of."

The man chuckled. "How would you know?"

"Tell me what it is, and I'll tell you." The air vent turned on, and she almost jumped at the sound and sudden breeze.

"Concealing you, for one thing. Learning of your crimes and not informing us makes his crimes as bad as what you've done."

"And what if I told you he didn't know what I was hiding? That I have nothing to do with any resistance on Cereth, but still have a secret you'd be interested in. That Lieutenant Westermark was still questioning me, still trying to learn what I knew, even as you dragged him out there? He was close, too."

He flinched just enough at that, and Ryllis almost wanted to smile. She'd turned his investigation on its head and criticized his competence at the same time.

"I wouldn't believe you."

"Then it's a good thing," she said, her heart threatening to race out of her chest at what she was about to suggest, "that you don't need to."

"You're right." He moved by her and rapped on the door. "But tell me one thing first—because I need to know, out of nothing more than desperate personal curiosity. Why are you really here?"

"I told you. I was tired of running."

"After only a lunar cycle? You seem to tire rather easily. Were you tired of running or trying to protect him?"

"Why would I protect him?" she snapped.

"Why do people do half the things they do? Because of emotion. Misplaced devotion and some ill-conceived notion of a future together. I won't pretend to understand it, but I know it happens."

"You're reaching."

"Am I? He's spent half his time here calling your name."

The door opened—she'd been waiting for her fate. They were coming for her now, and she wanted to run, but there was nowhere to hide, and her feet seemed to be glued to the floor. But the guards who entered were dragging something between them—a figure, broken, and defeated, its feet scarcely reaching the floor. It looked like Kresten, but it wasn't. This thin, fragile, haggard man with unkempt hair couldn't be Kresten.

Tears that hadn't been possible at the prince's estate sprang into her eyes. "What have you done to him?"

At her voice, the figure looked up.

"Ryllis?" He struggled against the guards' hold, and his voice broke when they dropped him to the floor. "You bastards. Again, with her? Anything but this. Can't you come up with something more creative, Dahl?"

The man shrugged at her. "He thinks he's seeing things." He leaned down and gripped Kresten's chin. "Not a hallucination this time, Lieutenant. She's turned herself in. At least one of you has some sense of honor."

"She's here? Really here?" he whispered. "Ryllis —run. Don't let them do this. Not for me."

"Give it a rest, would you? She's not getting out of here, and neither are you. We're about to head to the telepathy clinic, in fact. Would you care to join us?" It was a needling question, delivered in the same tone as a dinner engagement request.

Kresten took a swing at the nearest guard, catching only the tips of his fingers against his ankle. The guard kicked a boot at his neck, and that time Ryllis couldn't stop herself. She fell to her knees next to him and cradled his head in her hands, shocked at how cold he felt. He looked up at her, unseeing, and she brushed her fingers lightly over his eyes.

"He can't see," Dahl said.

"Why not?" The chill of Kresten's body was beginning to spread into hers.

"They put a chip in my brain," Kresten interrupted. "They can do all sorts of things with it. Don't you understand? Once you confess, they're going to do it to you, if they don't execute you outright. Keep you from—" He sounded like he was struggling to catch his breath. "I tried—I tried to keep you safe. Why did you come here? Why did you—"

The horror of what he'd experienced—what he'd said they would do to her—smashed into her. But she'd known, hadn't she? From the very second they'd arrived to take her away from home, she'd known her life was over. Wasn't it worth saving someone else at the same time?

"I had to," she said to Kresten. "Because I love you, and I couldn't leave you to this. I can't save myself, but I can save you—and I won't regret that, for as long as they let me live. But if you feel like you need to repay me, then stay with me until the end. And then you can let me go."

They didn't let go of her arms as they walked her to the telepathy clinic, and Ryllis wanted to scream at them that she'd surrendered of her own free will. That she'd do anything for Kresten, even this. But her escorts were cold and silent, and it matched the landscape. The gray jumpsuit they'd made her change into, and the blue uniforms of the guards were the only color in the brilliant white hallway, and the room they ushered her into was similarly blank. She could only guess that having nothing to focus on limited the subject's mental resistance.

Kresten, his vision temporarily restored, paced in shaky circles as she sat on the gurney. Ryllis ignored him, his feral anxiety and pain too disconcerting to manage.

"Lie back."

The ceiling was just as white as the rest of her surroundings. She began to shake in panic as they attached the electrodes to her head and cut the seam of her shirt just enough to access her collarbone. Dahl looked down at her, detached. His gaze held her, even though she wanted to fling her head around and find Kresten again.

"Regardless of his present situation, the Fleet has concurred with Lieutenant Westermark's argument that you are the property of the imperial family and should be returned to His Majesty's ownership if there is insufficient evidence of further crimes committed after your eradication from Cereth. Do you understand?"

She took a breath and nodded. That was something, at least. It meant this would happen just as Kresten had said. They'd mark her with the imperial crest. To not be tarnished over and over with the dreaded circles that would declare her a Shadow Force prisoner—that meant something. If they decided against executing her, they would never allow Kresten to keep her now, but perhaps the emperor would send her back to Prince Vidar. It had been a personal hell just a few days before, but now it was something to pray for.

"Good. Then we'll begin."

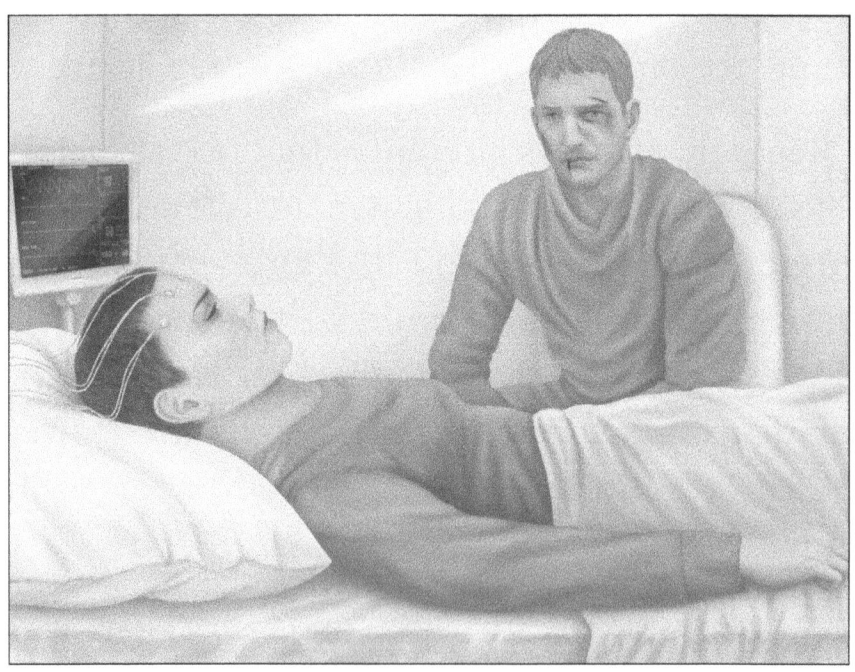

Ryllis closed her eyes. The antiseptic was cold. The whirr of a machine began somewhere behind her head, and she jerked her head up.

"Strap her down if she won't stay still," a new voice said with more irritation than she thought was warranted. "You should have known better, Ivar."

"Don't. I said I wouldn't fight this," she whispered. "I have no reason to."

"Ryllis." It was Kresten's voice this time, but as desperate as she was to see him, to indulge in his reassurance, she was afraid to move. If she laid there and did nothing but breathe and think, they wouldn't restrain her. "Let them do it. It's going to hurt, and you're going to—" His voice cracked. "It will help. I swear."

Some panicked part of her remembered he'd been through the same thing. That was, perhaps, more frightening than anything else. He knew. He knew and was afraid for her. What she'd go through and what she'd say.

Hands held her down as she struggled to breathe, and they didn't feel anything like Kresten's gentle ones. She closed her eyes, desperate for escape.

"Time?" Dahl asked someone she couldn't see. "Beginning now."

The needle hit her skin, and she flinched into the bed. It dragged across her collarbone, and she had the immediate thought this wouldn't be so bad. Not like Kresten had told her. It burned, yes, as anyone would expect, but it wasn't so bad. She could handle this.

"Do not touch her, or you'll be removed," Dahl said sharply. She was afraid to look at who he was talking to. "You know that will cause unwanted interference."

Fingers stopped just short of hers, close enough she could feel a breeze. Ryllis wanted to reach out and grab them, but Kresten needed to stay. It was the only thing that would make this better. She just didn't know if she wanted him to stay for her or for himself.

"Injecting nanobiotes."

Her heart began to flutter, a commotion echoed in beeping of the leads attached to her chest. That was why it hadn't hurt before. They'd only now started. She tried to swivel toward Dahl, even though he'd ordered her to be still. She found she couldn't move her head, but with one last moment of conscious thought, she met his eyes. They were still the same watery blue she'd noticed earlier, but the water was turning to ice. She should have tried to find Kresten one last time instead, should have—

The sudden pain took her breath away.

Only it wasn't pain like she'd ever experienced. This was agony that twisted inside her every cell, starting from a point on her shoulder and radiating throughout her entire body. She couldn't breathe. She wasn't sure her heart was still beating, either, and she couldn't hear the machine any longer.

She was dead. No one could live through this. No one—

A strange jerking feeling crept through her legs, and she felt her entire body begin to convulse.

"Stop!" Ryllis screamed the word over and over as she shook. No one listened. Maybe they couldn't hear her. She screamed louder, and an incessant beep in the background drilled into her skull. "Kresten." She barely heard herself that time. "Stop them."

He didn't rescue her that time, either, and the pain took on a new quality. Where it had been a sharp dagger to start, now it was an inferno scorching her from the inside out. She tried to pull away, only to be stopped by something that might as well have been steel.

After what had to have been a year, the pain settled to a dull ache. Her vision was still blurry, and the room was a haze of brilliant white, but she could breathe again. She couldn't feel her heartbeat, but a rhythmic beep from some machine or another on her right reassured her.

Someone moved beside her.

"She's ready. It's time."

Dahl.

His hand fell against her new mark, and though she was sure he hadn't struck her, it felt like his entire weight had landed on one tiny part of her body.

And then—

She lunged against the restraints once more. A scream echoed, and the smallest part of her brain that she still controlled told her it was hers.

Dahl's hand was reaching inside of her, like he had entered through the tattoo and was hunting and searching through her nerves, squeezing through the tiniest of spaces, stalking his way through her body to her mind. Almost like she'd felt crawling through the passageway to hide in the cavern.

The memory was calming. Any second now, he'd locate her mind, and the pressure would cease, just like the cave had opened around her, allowing her to breathe again. It couldn't hurt this badly forever, or the telepath wouldn't be able to discern any thoughts outside of pain. In a flash, the uncomfortable feeling disappeared like she'd predicted, and an immense pressure filled her head—then was gone. Emptiness, tinged with a presence she couldn't identify, flowed all around her.

Does it still hurt?

She gasped out loud at Dahl's voice.

I'm sorry. That's usually a shock. There was a pause, like he was thinking. *Everything you're feeling will settle down soon. When I'm done, if you've been telling me the truth, you'll be allowed anesthesia.*

Pain meds sounded wonderful. Like a dream.

A faint chuckle echoed through her head. *They do, don't they? Just focus on that, and you'll get through this.*

She'd already forgotten he could hear everything she called to mind. *Just get this over with and let him go. Quickly. What do I need to do?*

Relax. Don't fight. Try not to think about anything specific. Right now, I don't care what your deliberate thoughts are.

Right now? Will you want to know them later?

Perhaps. Eventually.

The white ceiling blurred again. Tired. She was so tired.

That's perfect. Just like that.

She felt herself jerk from the easy slumber. *I can't relax if you keep talking. Just do what you need to do and get out of my brain.*

Another soft chuckle. It wasn't an unpleasant sound. Dahl was infinitely more pleasant as a disembodied telepath than a man.

That's unkind. Not all of us like people. Stare at the ceiling again.

And she did. Her eyes, just like the rest of her body, grew heavy. She could picture herself lying on the gurney, limp and unresponsive, eyes open but unfocused. Closing them would be better. The way she looked must be upsetting to Kresten, and—

I already know about him. You don't need to hide what you feel for him. But you're making this difficult. I don't care to know details.

The softness of Kresten's lips flew into the forefront of her consciousness, and a loud sigh filled her head.

I'm sorry.

She wasn't, but she tried to force blankness into her mind again. Dahl's presence fluttered against it, like butterflies in a spring garden, and the feeling was somehow calming, the trickle of a creek over her feet. Her muscles became weighted; her already dulled senses became as featureless as the room, unable to determine cold from hot, pain from contentment, horror from delight.

You really didn't have anything to do with the attack on the transport building in Therus, did you?

She jerked from the unnatural relaxation at Dahl's surprise.

I told them that on Cereth. For almost a dozen lunar cycles. It's not my problem if they didn't believe me.

He was quiet for a moment. *Your father was convinced of it.*

He was convinced of nothing. The painful answer she'd been ignoring for so long wasn't worth hiding anymore. *He and his new wife were tired of me being around, and who ignores the accusations of a regional governor?*

No one, I suppose. The feathery feeling returned as Dahl probed around her memories. *I'm still surprised,* he said, a little kinder this time.

Yes, fine. You're surprised I'm not a terrorist. Can we get on with it?

You're still hiding something. What? What is Lieutenant Westermark involved in?

Before she could stop it, a vision of Kresten's mountain garden flew into her mind. Roses bloomed; bulbs sprouted. She showed Dahl a vision of her walking through the garden, brushing her fingers against the wintered trees, smiling at the pines in the distance. Behind her, in an exaggerated motion that he surely couldn't help but notice, flowers erupted from the path under her feet.

Dahl's presence faded as the vines curled over the garden wall, then seemed to flinch.

You're not as innocent as you led me to believe. He sounded shocked.

I told you I wasn't completely innocent. You chose not to listen. But I swear to you, Kresten didn't know. I hid it from him—from everyone. It was spring when he brought me here. He didn't think anything of this garden coming to life.

You know your power is illegal in the Star Realm.

I know. The weight off her shoulders was immeasurable, nonetheless. It was over, and being over was a relief, no matter what came next. *There was nothing I could do about it. It is what it is.*

You should have turned yourself in when you first became aware of these powers. His earlier gentleness took on a tinge of reprimand. *It was your obligation as a Star Realm subject, regardless of whatever consequences you feared.*

To what? Strange how even a thought could be bitter. *Death? The Star Realm asks too much of us. Eradication is one thing, but no one would voluntarily surrender to that. I was a child when I learned of my gift.*

Not necessarily death. Depending on the extent of your power, a suppression chip and imprisonment is an alternative. The court will decide what punishment your crimes warrant.

That might as well be death.

I'm sorry, Dahl said, and it sounded like he was. *We see it as mercy.* He grew quiet. *But it may be too late for that mercy now. I will have to write up an official report so the court can make their decision on your fate. And no, before you ask, I have no control over what happens. I can only report what you're capable of and what you've done, then wait, same as you. I'll look around one more time to ensure the report is complete, and if you don't fight me, this can be over quickly.*

Then do it.

She didn't mean to struggle, but she couldn't relax any longer. She didn't fight Dahl as he skimmed over her recent memories of the prince's estate and plunged into her thoughts of Kresten's gardens and time on Cereth, but the fear made it nearly impossible to focus on nothing. Over and over, visions of living out her life in a cage assaulted her, but Dahl waited patiently until each wave of dread subsided, only to dive back in every time her heart and thoughts returned to normal. By the time the sensation of fluttering wings departed for the last time, she could have sworn she felt his fatigue.

You have what you need? she asked.

Yes. Enough. Dahl's regret was palpable.

And you'll let Kresten go now? Her life was over; his was the only thing that mattered anymore.

Yes. She could hear his guilt, and she was glad for it. *He'll be released to the infirmary to recover. Is there anything you want me to tell him?*

Tell him? Why can't I?

We don't believe in tormenting people with waiting. Either you wake up in a cell with a chip implanted, or you don't wake up at all. Now sleep. It'll make things easier.

With that, Dahl disappeared the way he'd come, twisting aimlessly through her nerves toward the imperial crest, leaving her alone with her terror. Her eyes grew heavy again, and she wanted to fight, but the blackness Dahl had ordered approached her from all sides, shadowy and cold. When it seized her, thousands of hands clawing and grabbing at her skin, she tried to scream, but even that was effort she couldn't manage. She took one last conscious breath before the cloud carried her away to nothingness.

CHAPTER TWENTY

*T*he back of his neck stung where they'd cut out the chip. Kresten had declined the medic's offer of pain relief, tired of needles and drugs and everything else. It would subside. The wound and other various injuries that plagued him after his time in the prison were mere annoyances compared to the pain in his heart.

They knew about Ryllis.

When he thought of her, his chest threatened to cave in on itself. He didn't know why she'd done it. He'd have done it for her—*had* done it for her—but it wasn't supposed to have happened like this. She was supposed to be free, trying to make her way back to Cereth, and he should be in that cell, suffering, yes, but with the knowledge that she was safe.

Instead she was unconscious a few rooms over, and if the court had their way, she would be dead before she ever graced him with that smile again. Or imprisoned somewhere far away, her gift taken from her against her will, condemned to a fate she dreaded because she'd had the misfortune of inheriting something harmless and yet forbidden by the Star Realm.

It wasn't fair.

But the laws didn't have to be fair. They didn't have to make sense. They simply were, and he'd never given them a second thought before now. His own gift was allowed twofold, both by virtue of his birth and chosen career, and he knew of no one else besides the telepaths in Shadow Force, permitted to live free because of their service to the Star Realm. Didn't Dahl understand how differently his own life could have gone?

Kresten closed his eyes. He just had to make it out of here, back to the mountains, and then he could fall apart, alone. It didn't seem possible that he'd make it. The lodge was so far, and he was in too much pain to push things with Dahl —his release from the infirmary, transport back to his house, whatever other logistics were needed. His heart was too broken to focus on anything but Ryllis, and he couldn't make himself forget about her, he couldn't make things better for her.

He could say goodbye, though. With the greatest effort he could muster, he swung his legs to the floor and tested his balance. The floor began to spin immediately, driven by too many days lying on a floor, having them dakk with his vestibular system. His bruised liver didn't help matters, and the medic would tie him and down sedate him if she saw him up and about like this, but she could dakk herself, too. They all could.

The wall made acceptable support, and he clung to it as he made his way out of his room and towards Ryllis's, finding sore muscles he hadn't known existed. It took forever, and he was half afraid they'd have removed her by the time he made it there, but she lay where he'd left her, ashen and cold. For a moment, he could only stand in the doorway and stare at what they'd done. Perhaps remembering her as she'd been on the mountain, the sun on her face and her hand in his, was best.

No. He'd promised he'd stay with her until the end, and he'd meant it. If they imprisoned her, he would be on the shuttle that took her to a dungeon on some out-of-the-way, quarantined asteroid, and if they decided on death, he'd be holding her hand as she slipped away. Even if she wouldn't know he was there with her. He collapsed on the stool by the bed, gasping for air, and brushed his fingers against hers. They were like ice, and all he wanted to do was warm her.

"You should be in bed," a voice called from the corridor outside.

Kresten couldn't force his body to turn at Dahl's not-quite command. "I should be next to her."

"I can't allow this."

"Can't allow what?" Kresten asked sharply. "I've been exonerated, and I'm doing nothing but holding her hand."

"I understand you're upset. But you'll get over it. We can give you some demanding assignments, let you try telepathic questioning again when you tell me you're up to it. It'll take your mind off things."

Kresten didn't reply, and behind him, Dahl cleared his throat. "You didn't honestly think you had a future with her, did you?" he asked. "A Cerethian, a prisoner, a slave. Your family—"

"You know nothing about my family. They have limited say in my actions, including my father. I would have married her regardless of his opinion on the matter—of which you have no idea of, I might add."

"You're letting your feelings get the best of you, Lieutenant."

Kresten swung around at that, grimacing at the bruise over his ribs. How dare Dahl reduce what he was feeling to mere *feelings?*

"And feelings are something you'll never understand, aren't they?"

Dahl pressed his lips together. Kresten turned back to Ryllis, wanting nothing more than for her to wake up. She looked peaceful, and the medical equipment agreed, but it was a lie. He squeezed her hand, but her eyes were pressed closed, forced into slumber by Dahl's telepathic command and the drugs that kept her unconscious until the court returned their verdict.

"I love you," he said, bringing her soft hand to his mouth. It was cold—the medics didn't believe their doomed patient was worth wasting a blanket on. "I always will. And I will never forget you."

Her eyelashes fluttered, and Kresten shot Dahl a look over his shoulder.

Dahl frowned at a monitor. "Stats normal. She's dreaming."

A flame of hope welled up in Kresten's chest. If she woke up, he'd have a chance to say goodbye before the medics ran in and sedated her further. He gripped her fingers tighter and pressed them against his cheek, but the optimistic feeling died almost as soon as it'd come. He shouldn't have touched her like that. He shouldn't have wished for her to wake up. There was a reason she was unconscious—it was the one kindness the Fleet allowed prisoners like her.

"She shouldn't be dreaming. She shouldn't be thinking or feeling anything." Before he could think better of it, he lashed out. "You couldn't even put her to sleep correctly."

Dahl stiffened. "It was a textbook interview and placation."

"Obviously not, if she's got more brain activity than she's supposed to have." His anger was building now. If Ryllis awoke, she would wake to a misplaced hope. He couldn't allow that, as much as he wanted to talk to her one last time. The devastation in her eyes when she learned it was a mistake would kill him. Unless—

The answer tickled his brain, but the pain in his abdomen was growing by the second. Kresten brushed away his confusion and undid the straps holding her arms down. He had to say goodbye to her with all his senses intact. He couldn't grieve properly if he had to watch in agony, unable to concentrate on anything but his own pain. He would find a medic, wrangle some medication out of them, and once he felt better, he'd come back. Then he'd feel well enough to slug Dahl for what'd he done.

"I love you," he told her, struggling to his feet. "And I'll be back. A promise is a promise, right? I just need to take care of some things first."

With Dahl's protests ringing in his ears just behind him, he let his lips brush hers, then turned away, hand on the wall. It was harder to walk than before, and when he stopped in the doorway to catch his breath, a strange feeling flooded him, almost like someone was trying to force their way into his mind.

"Kresten?"

It took forever to turn around at the sound of the voice he thought he'd never hear again. Ryllis's eyes, gray and sad, stared back at him from the bed, and her expression turned to confusion when she focused on the way he was standing against the wall. Clutching his side, Kresten stumbled toward her while Dahl stood frozen behind him, his mouth open.

"You woke up," he said. His tears dripped onto the edge of her bed, and Ryllis looked at them, frowning. "You weren't supposed to wake up." He glanced up at Dahl, but the entire room was spinning. "What did you do to her?"

"Nothing." Dahl ran his fingers over the machines, at her vital sign printout and the pump that controlled the drug seeping into her arm. "I swear. I went to follow you out because you looked like you were going to collapse, and she said your name. I'm going to call a medic."

"You're not going to call anyone. You've fouled this up enough. The least you could do is let us say goodbye."

"Then they haven't decided yet." Ryllis's soft question that wasn't a question at all interrupted Dahl's response.

"My love." He grabbed her hand again. There was nothing he could say to make this better. "They haven't. I don't know what happened— you weren't supposed to have fought through Major Dahl's suggestion. It just doesn't happen. I'm sorry if that gave you hope. I—"

"I didn't fight it. There was this blackness, and it was so heavy I couldn't do anything about it, even breathe. And then it began to fade away, so I swam through it, and the light began to appear —" She closed her eyes, like she was trying to memorize the feeling of his touch. "He said you would be cleared?"

"Yes. They've taken care of that. But that doesn't matter. I wish you hadn't done this."

"That wasn't your decision, was it? I couldn't leave you to that fate. And it's too late for second-guessing now, I think. They took that awful chip out of you?"

"Yeah." He tried to laugh as he ran a hand over her head. Her hair was growing out, like soft brown velvet. It wasn't an unpleasant feeling, and maybe his touch would calm her, because he couldn't imagine the fear she was feeling right now. "With a scalpel. It hurt more than when they inserted it."

Scalpel.

The word meant something, but thinking was like walking through quicksand.

"I bet it did," she said.

Her sadness was almost tangible; it was clear she was thinking of one being inserted into her. He didn't want to tell her the odds of her being allowed to live were so very slim now, a broken thread beginning to unravel. The Star Realm didn't look fondly on gifted subjects who didn't turn themselves in for a suppression chip as soon as they were aware of their powers.

With reluctance, he released her for a moment and clutched at his head. They hadn't struck him there, so why was a headache coming on so suddenly? Maybe considering his options was just too painful.

Except—except perhaps there was one last chance.

"Wait," he said to himself.

Ryllis looked up. "Are you all right?"

He shook his head. "I don't think so. My head's killing me."

"That's because you shouldn't be up," Dahl said. "Let's get you back to your room."

The shock of how quickly things were falling into place grabbed him. "I don't think I can make it, sir. Can you get a wheelchair for me?"

"I'll find a medic, then," Dahl said. "And a few security guards." He glared at Ryllis, then plodded into the corridor.

Kresten grabbed her hand again. "Listen to me. I have one last idea. I don't know if it'll work, but—"

There it was again, quivering in his belly. *The hope.* Maybe it knew.

"Don't keep pushing, Kresten. My fate's sealed. Don't make it worse. Major Dahl was right—it was easier to wait for my sentence in a cloud of nothingness. This—" She reached up and stroked his cheek just before the tears began. "This is a horrible thing to have to wait for."

"You don't understand." His heart ached for her, but he wouldn't trade the joy in her eyes when he told her for anything. "They can't touch members of the royal family."

"So what? That doesn't include me."

"By birth—" He squeezed her hand. "Or marriage."

"Marriage?" Ryllis's mouth dropped open. "But —what's the catch?"

"The catch is—the catch is that they may not accept it. The only ceremony we can manage in here is an ancient one, and it hasn't been accepted as legal in hundreds of solar cycles. But you know, we outcast royals do things differently in the mountains, and that's always worked to my benefit. And fortunately for me, the one man who can deny the legality of this rite shares my name."

"Your father?" She shook her head. "I lied to you. Why would you do this for me?"

"What did you lie about?" He hated replying to her question with another question, but he couldn't answer hers. If he told her why he was really offering, he might frighten her off, and then he was sure to lose her.

"My powers." Ryllis looked at the floor. "What I've been doing in your gardens. I didn't do it intentionally, I swear it. I was too afraid. But the gardens were the only place I felt safe when I first arrived on Vilaria. Being outside, especially in those mountains—it gave me such a feeling of peace. That's how it works for me, it's mutual. When the snow ended, I knew you wouldn't notice the grounds coming alive, so I let it happen. And Lina's chickens? I told them to leave you alone, and they agreed. They—I don't know how else to say this, but they listen to me. I know that all sounds unbelievable, and I'm so sorry I did everything I did, and I'm so sorry I didn't tell you before now."

Kresten would have laughed at her confession but for the heartbreaking expression on her face. She actually thought that what she'd done —who she *was*—would change how he felt about her?

"My darling star, I'm so sorry for what I said by the waterfall. It's an antiquated law, and I was wrong to say I agreed with it. I was wrong to imply you deserved to die over this. You have to understand, I don't care what you did. It's a part of you, and I only care that I love you and can't live without you. Every part of you. You are kind-hearted and intelligent and loyal and beautiful and so courageous you put me to shame. You never need to be afraid of being yourself around me—ever."

"And you're a smooth talker." Ryllis pushed herself up to a sitting position to face him, let her legs dangle over the bed, and nodded. "All right. How?"

She didn't believe him, and he needed her to believe him more than anything he'd ever needed before, but they were out of time. With the greatest reluctance, he let go of her and dug through the nearest cabinet for a scalpel. "You cut my palm. I cut your palm. And we press them together. Easy."

She eyed the sharp blade in his hand. "I wouldn't call having myself sliced open an easy task. But give it here."

Kresten handed it over and hovered over her, desperate for a swift turn of luck, as she tested it on his skin. With a sharp flick of her wrist, a thin red line appeared on his palm, and she handed the scalpel back, her lips pressed closed. Without hesitation, he ran it across her palm before she could panic further.

The scalpel clattered to the floor as he held out his hand. Her fingers intertwined with his, and a jolt of something enormously pleasurable coursed through him as their palms met. It was nothing more than a latent reaction of his  telepathy to the proximity of her tattoo, but he didn't care why it was happening. Only what it told him.

Ryllis was happy.

No, she was beyond happy. Ecstatic, delighted, at peace—none of those humble words could fully encompass what she was feeling. He'd worried she'd only agreed to the rite out of fear for her life, but her emotions left no doubt.

Well. Not quite no doubt, but very little. Dare he risk it? She'd turned him down before, the last time just a few minutes ago, but she deserved to know the other reason he'd suggested this solution. And his soul needed to know her answer.

"That's it?" she asked. "We don't have to say any words or anything?"

"No words or anything." He kissed her forehead. "But that's not quite it. There's one other thing you need to know, and I need you to hear me out before you say anything. I was serious before when I said how much I need you. I love you, Ryllis. I don't think you quite understand how much. After you turned me down in the cave, I had every intention of asking you to marry me again and again until you said yes, but you were right—in those circumstances, it wasn't fair to you. And perhaps I was a spineless coward as well. I know I'm Vilarian, and that you have every reason to hate me for who I am and for getting you into this situation, but by the stars, if this works, I swear I will spend every waking moment making you happy—and most of my sleeping ones, too."

He let his free hand play about her bare collarbone, avoiding the mark for now. It was an astonishingly difficult undertaking; the draw painful and almost unbearable.

"Because this wasn't an act, and wasn't solely to save you, at least as far as I was concerned. It's because this is exactly what I want, and I've wanted it for so long. I want to be your husband and I want you to be my wife, in every sense of the word, for as long as I live. But if that's not what you desire, I won't force you into it. I can't send you home, but we can live apart— goodness knows half the imperial family does it. I know you'd die in Carilles, away from the mountain, so you can have the lodge and every single crown of mine, if you'd like. I can beg my father for the funds to build another house, and I'll go off somewhere with the Fleet, and you'll never have to see me again."

Ryllis stared at him, her mouth open, and he held his breath.

"Kresten . . ."

She leaned her forehead against his. Tears filled her eyes, and a sickening emptiness like he'd never felt wound its way through him. She was going to agree to his offer. His beloved mountains and the memories he'd made there with her would be hers. He would win her and lose her in the span of ten seconds, and he would never recover from such a loss.

"I wouldn't have the most magnificent palace on Vilaria without you there with me," she whispered.

The unbelievable relief was a punch to his already aching gut. His shoulders sagged, and he all but fell from the stool. It was only her sudden grip on his hands that kept him upright.

"You're—you're sure?" he asked.

The deepest, most fervent kiss he'd ever imagined was her answer. It made him dizzy, but he'd risk falling to the ground for one more second of her lips on hers. Ryllis seemed to sense his pain, because she pulled away just as the floor began to sway beneath him. He leaned toward her, eyes closed, half drunk with pain and desire, and she laughed.

"I'm sure," she said, putting her uninjured hand under his arm. "Which means you have to survive to follow through on all those things you just promised, so let's find you somewhere to lay down. I intend to have you as my husband for more than a day."

"Lieutenant—" Dahl froze in the doorway, a medic at his side, dragging a wheelchair along behind her. His gaze landed on the drops of blood on the floor. "What—"

Their palms came apart. Kresten grabbed a piece of gauze and pressed it against Ryllis's wound, ignoring how he was staining the tile himself.

"It's not polite to interrupt a wedding," he said. "And it's no longer Lieutenant. Consider this my official notice of resignation, Major. You can expect a follow-up letter as soon as I can hold a stylus again."

I should have told her to cut the other hand.

"You—" Dahl stood in the doorway, his mouth opening and closing.

"I think you should go add a postscript to that report. Inform them the princess is now exempt from that law by means of her royal status."

Kresten waved his hand about, mostly to make Dahl go pale as the blood dripped. "Realm's sake, that stings."

Dahl backed into the wheelchair, his eyes wide. The medic had already fled. "You were serious about her. I had no idea."

"Well, now you know. That report, Major. I'd like to see it before you transmit it."

"Yes. Of course. Immediately, Your Highness. And may I say, I'm relieved for . . . the lack of extra paperwork here."

Dahl disappeared, and relief took his place as Kresten collapsed back on the stool by the bed. "Well, that's taken care of, for now."

Ryllis put her hands to her cheeks. "My father and stepmother—"

"Will be"—he couldn't hide his smug expression, despite the pain—"outwardly thrilled. How's the hand?"

"Not bad." She frowned at him as he examined it. The bleeding had mostly stopped, and they could worry about fixing the scar later if it bothered her. "But don't change the subject. I'm worried about you. You look terrible. Lie down, now."

"A fine thing to say to your new husband. I'm going to pass out as soon as I know you're safe, and not a moment before." He allowed her to help him crawl into the bed next to her, anyway. By the stars, but laying on his back felt amazing. Ryllis reclined on her side next to him, and he let his fingers graze the side of her head. "And the rest? How are you feeling? I know how awful that must have been."

"Nothing besides my hand hurts," she said. "I can remember what happened, but it's like a dream. It's odd, though. I hated him being in my head, but now I feel so alone I can barely stand it."

His breath caught. "I can do something about that."

"You?" Ryllis paled again, then seemed to harden herself. "Will it—will it hurt like before?"

Kresten shook his head. "I will never hurt you. I swear it." Her fear broke his heart in two, even if she'd pretend until the day she died that she wasn't afraid.

She nodded, and the trust in her eyes shattered the rest of his heart into tiny pieces. "Then, yes."

A strange warmth rushed over him. Without letting go of her hand, he sat up as much as he could manage and kissed the mark. *His mark.* Her mind opened to the intrusion, but he stayed light, on top of her skin, letting only his emotions fall into her. Ryllis made a soft noise he couldn't identify, and her happiness, when it washed over him, was almost unbearable. He pulled back, enough to regain his senses. Exonerated or not, Dahl would throw him back in that cell to cool off if he did what he really wanted.

"You don't know how long I've wanted to do that for you," he said. "But without the mark, it wasn't possible, and even with it, it can be misused so very badly . . ."

Shadow Force used the same technique for controlling prisoners, after all. He could and had flooded even the most defiant ones with an involuntary tranquility, relaxing them enough to accept whatever came next. It was something he would never do to Ryllis. *He would never do it to anyone, ever again.*

The idea was so freeing it was almost impossible to comprehend.

Ryllis shuddered. "I believe it."

"I won't ever shower you with my own emotions unless you need it," he promised. "And you ask. I won't control you like that."

Those beautiful gray eyes narrowed in confusion. "But I thought you could only read minds. Not control."

"True, for the most part. You were reading my thoughts in return just now, and there's not a soul out there who can resist focused emotions like I just allowed you to feel. When we can finally be together in private—well, you'll see."

He couldn't wait. Could barely keep his hands off her as it was. When he could touch her—speak to her without saying a word—it would be an adjustment for both of them, but they would make it.

Ryllis traced his jawbone with her finger, then settled her head under his chin. His skin hurt where she touched him—everything was painful, including the sheet underneath them—but the feeling was so, so worth it. He'd never leave her again, no matter what.

"Do it again?" she asked.

"Now? I think you can wait a bit, Amaryllis." She made a face at the name, so Kresten laughed and pulled her closer. "We have all the time in the Realm."

EPILOGUE

*S*ummer had come to the capital as Ryllis waited in Kresten's flat during his long convalescence, and the flowers she'd potted in the promised planters were done blooming by the time he was officially able to appear in front of his father to appeal the validity of their marriage. There had been no timeline attached to the emperor's formal invitation, which Kresten informed her was a good sign, but she wasn't so sure. She told him as much one more time as the shuttle landed at the main palace.

"We'll be just fine," he said, helping her out. "I'm certain of it."

It sounded like he was convincing himself of that as much as her, and she clutched at his arm as they walked down the breezeway, surrounded on both sides by a rock garden that reminded her of the granite by Kresten's waterfall. She was ready now, to hike up there and sit and watch the water trickle down the rock without thinking of how she'd almost tried to murder him—and almost lost her own life.

If only the emperor agreed to their marriage.

Darling star, take a breath.

She jumped at Kresten's voice. It had been a lunar cycle and a half since the telepathic bond had been created, and she still wasn't used to figuring out when she was in his mind and he in hers. She would get used to that, too, he'd said, would have secrets again once she learned how to keep her thoughts to herself. Eventually.

I'm breathing. It was hard not to laugh at the imperial sentries who trailed them, oblivious to their conversation.

Not well. I can hear you doing it. I'm betting on the fact that it's rather hard to condemn someone to death when you're looking them in the face. Dahl just has a particular talent for it. And the sentries know we're talking right now. They've always hated it, but they know.

His assurance didn't seem certain. *You're frightened, too. Don't lie to me.*

I'm concerned.

Kresten . . .

All right. I'm terrified. He glanced at her and tried to smile. *But we're almost there, and then we won't need to worry any longer. Either way.*

She looked around, toward the end of the breezeway that opened into a walled garden. *A garden?*

I thought it would be easier on you than the throne room. Kresten sounded sheepish, even in her mind.

And he agreed? The faintest hope sprang up in her heart.

He's my father. He's not a monster.

There wasn't anything to say to that. It was almost impossible to undo an entire lifetime of fear and hate in just a few lunar cycles. Kresten couldn't ask that of her. He just couldn't. Respect, yes, that she could do. Trust someone like the emperor of the Vilarian Star Realm? No, that would have to come much later.

Too late, she remembered her mind was still open.

All's forgiven, Ryllis. I understand. A telepathic chuckle echoed throughout her body. *But try to act like you don't hate him. Just for now.*

I'll—I'll try.

Good. "Are you ready?" he asked out loud, as they approached an iron gate decorated in the same swirls as the one in the garden behind the mountain lodge.

She nodded, unable to verbalize anything. Switching from telepathic language to speaking was becoming easier with each day, but only when she wasn't terrified. Kresten caressed her mind one more time, then backed away, leaving her alone with her thoughts. Severing the bond temporarily was only proper in front of his emperor and father, but the sudden isolation made her shiver. The sentries disappeared behind them like they'd never existed at all, and before she knew what was happening, she was standing in the garden and Kresten was touching her hand, the agreed-upon cue.

She knelt next to him without looking up, even though the breeze that sang through the shrubberies called to her. Strange how little the gesture bothered her this time, even as the shadow of the man she'd been raised to fear fell across her vision. But with Kresten next to her, that didn't matter. The sun on her face mattered, the scent of the roses did, the wind tousling her growing hair did.

But there was no fear.

"Your Majesty"—there was an odd fondness she hadn't expected in Kresten's voice—"may I present my wife."

Soft footsteps sounded, all but overpowered by the singing of a bird somewhere above. The shadow shifted, then stabilized.

"You may. Though I'm disappointed in you, Kresten."

Kresten shifted, his left knee still stiff and aching, Ryllis knew, but she remained frozen. *They'd been wrong.* The hope she'd been clinging to washed away in the summer breeze, and it was all she could do to keep from grabbing him and running. The same hands she'd felt grabbing her in that room at the base in Arvika reached for her again in her mind, and she threw off the memory before she could panic. Kresten would make this right. Wouldn't he?

"Sir?" Kresten sounded more confused than anxious, like he couldn't believe what he was hearing either.

"You made me wait this long to meet her?"

Her breath escaped in one long exhale, and Kresten pulled her to her feet. Ryllis stood there, eyes downward, a deferential distance from him, as he leaned forward to kiss the back of his father's outstretched hand. The emperor was supposed to extend the same to her, but before he did, Kresten wrapped his arm around her waist and pulled her close.

"I love her, Father. And I would do anything to protect her." His grip on her tightened. "Even from you."

"You could lose your title for this decision you've made. Even your life. Is she worth it?"

"I would make the same one a thousand times over."

Kresten's words sounded like a challenge, but when Ryllis looked up, the man standing across from them wore a smile. His rotund physique and cheery facade weren't what she'd expected. Neither was his white, shoulder-length hair, more like Prince Vidar's than Kresten's, or his casual yet elegant tunic. He wore no crown, just a simple gold ring with the imperial crest on his right hand. She tried to avert her eyes, but the sight of her final nightmare was too mesmerizing. The emperor was nothing more than a man.

"Then I am proud of you," the emperor said. "And thrilled to welcome a new member of the family. Hold out your hands, both of you."

Kresten seemed to deflate in relief, right there next to her. Ryllis looked up at him, and he nodded, as pale as he'd been when they'd left Arvika, but with a smile like she'd never seen before.

Everything was going to be all right.

Kresten's fingers through hers, she reached out toward the emperor as he removed something from his pocket. He took a step toward them, and it was only Kresten's presence next to her that kept her from fleeing. With him next to her, she could stand whatever came next.

"Since you decided to circumvent the official ceremony, I've brought it to you." The emperor let a familiar amethyst ribbon dangle from his hand, and her heart almost stopped. "It's not the traditional silk cord, and I'm hardly a priest, but given the circumstances . . ." He chuckled. "I swear, no one can figure out a run-around the law like a Westermark."

She didn't know where he'd gotten the ribbon—Kresten had likely sent for it and Lina would have been more than happy to comply—but as she wiped away tears with her free hand, how it had ended up in this lush palace in a faraway city didn't matter. A token like this . . . could the emperor of the Vilarian Star Realm possibly know how much it meant to her?

Somehow, as Kresten's hand squeezed hers, she found her voice. "It's a lovely gesture, Your Majesty."

He smiled and wound it around Kresten's left and her right wrist, then removed a vial of oil from his pocket. Heavy perfume mixed with the fragrant blooms around them as he poured it on their skin, and Ryllis watched in fascination as swirls and loops of oil appeared in a more precise fashion than she thought possible. When she was finally able to recognize the vague impression of the imperial crest pattern he'd drawn, it glittered in the sunlight, and she batted Kresten's finger away from it. Such a beautiful thing didn't need to be destroyed immediately.

"Joined together with the ribbon, blessed with the oil," the emperor said. "Be happy, you two."

How easy hope was in hindsight. But how could she have ever thought this would end any other way? Kresten caught her eye and she could tell he was wondering the same thing. He squeezed her fingers, and the rest of her fear drifted away into the brilliant blue sky, leaving her weak.

"And now I have something to show your lovely bride." The emperor gestured them toward the edge of the stone, toward a small heap of a plant alight with hundreds of brilliant white flowers. A table sat next to it, and on it, a wreath of them, intertwined with the same amethyst ribbon she and Kresten wore about their wrists. Longer ribbons trailed from it, and she couldn't help her questioning gaze.

"I was amazed to find meadow sweetvine growing in my son's greenhouse, of all places," he said. "And after ten days of extinction, no less. Strangely enough, Vidar claims to know nothing about it."

"I would imagine the prince does not, Your Majesty," she murmured, staring at the tiny shrub and the wreath next to it. It was a miracle they'd survived in Vidar's greenhouse for so long without her presence, but she could smell the blooms from where she stood, redolent and rich, with a heavy undertone of pine. It was no wonder the empress loved them so.

The emperor's smile split his face, then he began to laugh. "I thought not. Ah, well. The empress is thrilled, regardless. She made this for you—call it your first Westermark coronet, until I can talk my son into accepting a finer one for you," he said as he placed it on her head.

"Though it does seem this fits you more than gold or diamonds."

He backed away, toward a gate at the opposite end of the garden. "I would love to speak with you both more," he went on, "but I have some prior and urgent appointments. And you must have better things to do than entertain an old man."

"We'll make a casual visit soon. I promise." Kresten tore his stare from the wreath she wore and took a step forward. "But Father, before you go, one thing. She's not the only one with this gift, you know. This law—"

His father held up his hand. "Thought you'd get in all your favors at once, did you?" His expression grew soft again. "I don't blame you, but now is not the time to discuss such things. Go. Take your wife and celebrate."

Kresten didn't flinch that time. "Yes, sir. We will."

He inclined his head and drew her around toward the back of the garden. *He's thinking.*

The words flew into her mind as he escorted her through the gate. *You don't know the look yet, but I do. Gears are grinding. Even if he never makes a single change, Austet might. Or his children. Or even ours, if it comes to it.*

I'm glad. It's a step, isn't it?

It's a step. A huge one—and you started the change. Do you realize our marriage would have been unheard of a few solar cycles ago?

He went silent as they walked back down the breezeway, and Ryllis tapped on his elbow. "What's wrong?"

Kresten jerked his chin up. *That.*

She followed his gaze, afraid to look. Prince Vidar was approaching from the opposite end of the breezeway, a formal, ornamented jacket slung over his shoulder and an expression of conflicted amusement on his face. Kresten's presence poked at her mind again, and she let him in, greeting him with the mental equivalent of an eye roll.

You can curtsey—slightly—if you feel so compelled, he said. *Or slug him. Either one. I don't care.*

Kresten!

What?

She put pressure on his fingers to silence him and settled for a short nod in Prince Vidar's direction. Vidar stopped, yanked on his jacket, and sighed to the heavens as he buttoned it.

"That's truly unnatural, you know," he said. "I'm not sure you realize how much speaking to each other like that unsettles everyone around you— yes, yes, you're not at all subtle. We all know you're doing it. Don't you remember how eerie it was to see Mother and Father doing it when we were children?" His lip curled when he noticed the ribbon. "And nothing says you have to parade around still wearing that thing."

"What, this thing?" Kresten asked, holding their hands up between them. "I happen to look good in amethyst, in case you hadn't noticed."

He's just jealous. Of course, It's a bit annoying, I must admit, he added silently to her, *but I might not be able to control my hands otherwise.*

Her cheeks flushed, and she bit her tongue before she could laugh out loud. *Behave yourself.*

A low telepathic chuckle echoed throughout her entire body. *Behaving is no fun, and you know it.*

Later. She sent a visual into his mind, and it was Kresten's face that turned bright red that time.

That better be a promise. His voice was rough that time.

Oh, it is.

Vidar huffed again as she tried to catch her breath. "I'm on my way to see Mother. There's an infestation at the estate, and I suspect she has something to do with it. If you can take your telepathic hands off each other for more than five minutes and promise to use your voices, you're welcome to join us for tea." He glanced at the ribbon still dangling from their hands, shook his head, and stalked off.

Kresten spun Ryllis around and against him. "He won't stay long with her. Never does. Once he's gone, if she's up to it, we'll go tell her our news."

"I think—" How was she supposed to explain her conversation with his mother? "I think the empress already knows."

His eyebrows scrunched together. "How?"

"It's a long story. I'll tell you when we have more time." Ryllis laughed. "And then what?"

"And then what? We can stay in my flat as long as you are willing to. Or travel. Or spend some time in the grand palace. We can go wherever and do whatever you want."

So many options. It made her head spin to contemplate them all. "I don't know," she admitted. "I still don't want to travel, especially to another planet. Eventually you'll be able to talk me into it, but I suppose I'm too Cerethian to do it for enjoyment. And I miss your mountains—I miss the flowers."

"You missing the mountains I can handle just fine, but you'll have to wait until the next solar cycle for the flowers. You'll live without working for a while, anyway," he replied. "This season you belong to me, and the garden can have you back in the spring. You've done enough for my sorry excuse of a brother, anyway."

"I suppose that's true enough. Right now, I only want to look at you, anyway." Her fingers touched his jaw. "Husband."

"Only look?" Kresten winked in admonishment. *I think we've already established we can do better than that.*

Kresten . . . She hated saying no, but one of them needed to be responsible. *Don't think I didn't see you struggle to get off the ground earlier. I don't want to hurt you.*

Nonsense. You can't possibly hurt me. He pulled her against his chest, and she nuzzled her head under his chin. *And if you somehow manage it, it'll be worth it.*

Her knees trembled, and the breezeway grew hotter as his lips ran down her neck. The sentries couldn't have disappeared entirely, not with the emperor somewhere close by, but she couldn't see their shadows, couldn't hear their breathing. She could only focus on staying upright.

"You said this exile was supposed to be distasteful," she managed to say out loud. "I'm not sure you know the meaning of the word. If this is suffering, I'm afraid to find out what bliss is." She shivered as he traced the mark on her collarbone with his lips, sending waves of pleasure through her. They would remove it eventually, but for now she would enjoy its power. "Can you die of happiness?"

"You know, I never thought about it. Let's find out, shall we?"

Ryllis glanced around. "Now?"

"Now." He lifted her into his arms. "I'm not waiting any longer."

ACKNOWLEDGMENTS

A new series is an intimidating thing, and I'm forever grateful for the betas who took a chance on it. Thanks also to Megan for the amazing cover, Meghan, who read the unfinished manuscript a dozen times, and Meaghan, for the gorgeous illustrations—as well as Cathy for the editing.

ABOUT THE AUTHOR

Anne Wheeler grew up with her nose in a book but earned two degrees in aviation before it occurred to her that she was allowed to write her own. When not working, moving, or writing her next novel, she can be found planning her next escape to the desert—camera gear included. She currently lives in Georgia with her husband, son, and herd of cats.

Lightning Source UK Ltd.
Milton Keynes UK
UKHW010637280521
384539UK00001B/138